I0551636

A Series of Moments

Unguarded Moments

M.L. Broome

TerraCotta Dragon Arts

A Series of Moments
Unguarded Moments
Copyright © J. E. Soper 2019
All rights reserved.

This book is a work of fiction. References to real people, events, establishments, organizations, or locales are intended only to provide a sense of authenticity and are used fictitiously. Names, characters, dialogue and incidents depicted in this book are products of the author's imagination and are not to be construed as real.

No part of this publication may be reproduced, downloaded, transmitted, decompiled, reverse-engineered, or stored into any information storage and retrieval system, in any form or by any means, whether electronic or mechanical, now known or hereafter invented, without the express written permission of J.E. Soper and TerraCotta Dragon Arts.

Digital Edition MARCH 2019 ISBN: 978-1-7338964-2-9
Print Edition ISBN: 978-1-7338964-3-6

Publishing by:
TerraCotta Dragon Arts
Cover Art by:
Suzana Stankovic, LSDdesign
Editing by:
Emily Tamayo Maher
Interior Design & Formatting by:
Suzana Stankovic, LSDdesign

"Lovers don't finally meet somewhere.
They're in each other all along."

~ Rumi

Dedicated to my beloved friend, Sheryl, who has endured more in the last year than most will in their lifetimes. Through it all, she remained a constant bastion of support and love. She taught me the courage of a smile through tears and the willpower to continue getting up when the world keeps knocking you down.

You are loved, dear friend.

CONTENTS

ACKNOWLEDGEMENTS

To all my friends and family who have supported me, loved me, and continued to speak to me throughout my writing journey and all the ensuing peaks and valleys.

I am blessed that you are part of my life. All my love.

CHAPTER ONE

Jacob

Santorini was breathtaking, but Jacob scarcely noticed the scenery. Filming had moved at a frenzied pace since his arrival three weeks ago and the shoot was running ahead of schedule, an unheard-of achievement on location.

The movie consumed his days, beginning before sunrise and continuing late into the night, but Jacob welcomed for the distraction. It was the only thing maintaining his sanity after Lilly walked away from him three weeks earlier. He understood why she ended their fledgling romance, but it didn't ease the pain. He longed for her, his thoughts and dreams filled with visions of the petite brunette who captured his heart.

Usually, Jacob enjoyed being on location, whetting his appetite on local gourmet foods, exotic alcohol, and breathtaking women. But this time, his mind and heart were preoccupied. He hadn't even contacted any friends or family in England, terrified to discover Lilly had moved on and was forever out of his reach.

"Thinking deep thoughts or just looking like you are?" Miriam inquired as she joined him at the deck railing. She was new to directing, but her acting experience extended for decades. She was a striking woman in her late forties, and she carried herself with effortless grace.

Jacob shot her a wistful smile, remaining silent. He and Miriam were co-stars in two previous movies, and the time together cemented their friendship.

Miriam pushed herself off the railing. "It's a beautiful night, and there are bars overflowing with Ouzo. I say we take full advantage."

"What's Ouzo?" he asked, shooting her a questioning glance.

"Only the most delicious and potent alcohol known to man. It will make you forget all your problems. Hell, it might make you forget your own name. Come on, you look like you could use a drink."

"Victoria arrived this afternoon. She's waiting at the hotel."

Miriam chuckled. "Is that why you're lounging here and not hurrying back to your suite?"

"Something along those lines." Jacob maintained his focus on the undulating ocean waves, wishing they could soothe the gnawing pain in his heart since he lost Lilly.

"We've been friends for over six years, and I love you dearly. I only want to see you happy, but you're miserable. You have been since your arrival. What's going on in that head of yours?"

Jacob stared at the sea, the full moon reflecting off the waves. "Lilly would love it here. The natural beauty would be so inspiring to her."

"Now we're getting somewhere. Who's Lilly?"

Jacob snapped from his thoughts, unaware he had spoken the words aloud. "Lilly, she's…" He closed his eyes, taking a deep breath. "…she's a friend of mine."

"A friend? No, she's far more than a friend." Miriam studied Jacob's face, his pain evident.

He leaned forward, resting his face in his hands. "Lilly is superb and amazing, but she hates me, and I don't blame her. I hate myself for how I treated her."

"Let's get a drink and we can talk about it. You can tell Victoria we had to film a few extra takes."

Jacob snorted sarcastically. "You know Victoria—"

"Unfortunately," Miriam interjected.

Jacob gave Miriam a pointed stare before nodding in agreement. "She'd insist on hanging out on the sidelines and basking in her pop star glory."

Miriam scoffed, shaking her head. "I always believed you a man of good taste. What do you see in that woman?"

Jacob shook his head, he didn't have a clue. After meeting Lilly, no woman could compare.

"Well, I'm off to sample some local cuisine; enjoy your night with Victoria." Miriam took a few steps but turned back. "One question burning my brain, if it's this obvious to me you're pining for someone else, wouldn't it be obvious to Victoria?"

"It doesn't matter to Victoria. We aren't really dating. We have a business arrangement." He looked up, catching Miriam's eyes. "She wants to spit shine her reputation after shagging half of Hollywood, while we were dating, I might add. If I don't go along with her little plan, she claims she'll destroy my career and ensure I never get the role in Milieu of Madness. It makes no difference that her dirt is a complete fabrication, the media and public eat up Victoria's lies as gospel." Jacob looked at his friend. "Pathetic, right?"

"She's blackmailing you? That's why you're not with this woman, Lilly?"

Jacob nodded. "Lilly tried to understand. She's not in the business, but she knew how important the role was to me. She was willing to go along with the charade, but Victoria's behavior towards her made that impossible."

"Personally, I'm not surprised by Victoria's behavior at all."

"Are we the only people who see through her facade?"

Miriam shook her head. "Most people can't stand being around Victoria, but for some unknown reason, she wields enormous power in Hollywood, and she has no problem throwing down the gauntlet to get her way. I don't think anyone actually respects her. They fear her. I don't even know if her power is real or imagined. But her behavior will catch up to her one day when there's no one left to believe her lies."

Jacob's phone beeped. It was a video message from Janie and when he pressed play, he realized it was shot at the karaoke pub in London. Onstage, Lilly sang a song about unrequited love, her deep bluesy voice tinged with emotion. When the clip ended, Jacob dropped his head, muttering, "Fuck my life."

"Was that Lilly? The woman singing?" Miriam asked, sighing when Jacob nodded. "I'm no psychiatrist, but looking at you and listening to her, it's obvious you're both nursing broken hearts."

"I haven't known her that long." Jacob realized the statement was a futile attempt to convince his heart that what he and Lilly experienced wasn't real.

"What does that matter? I've known people who fall in love the moment their eyes meet. They might not recognize it as love until later, but there's something about that other person that just…" Miriam struggled to find the right term.

"Seems to fit, like they were put on this earth for you? They understand every facet of you, without you having to say a word. And when you touch them, it's like coming home for the first time in your life—your bodies fit together as if they were created just for you."

Miriam raised her eyebrows, nodding and offering a short laugh. "I take it you wouldn't know anything about that kind of love, would you Jacob?" Miriam grinned. "You've got some serious decisions to make. You can stay with Victoria and be miserable or kick her ass to the curb, which she deserves, and risk her wrath to fight for the woman who sings to your soul."

"No, I don't. Lilly wouldn't even consider a reconciliation. Not after what I did to her with Victoria."

Miriam wrapped her arm around Jacob's shoulder. "Shouldn't you let Lilly decide that for herself? But, if she isn't worth fighting for, forget about her. A woman like Lilly will find someone to adore her, mark my words." She kissed Jacob on the cheek and left.

Jacob's phone rang, and he answered without looking. He expected to hear Victoria on the other line, questioning his whereabouts. "I'm leaving in a minute."

"Okay big brother, should I have dinner waiting?" Janie chuckled.

"Janie!" Jacob's voice lightened. "I thought you were someone else."

Janie cleared her throat. "You're still with Victoria. You must be a glutton for punishment, and now I feel stupid for sending that video—"

"No." Jacob cut her off. "Thank you for sending it. How is Lilly?"

Janie paused, and Jacob wondered if he wanted to hear the answer. Miriam's words resonated in his mind, someone like Lilly '*will find someone to adore her.*' Had one of her admirers already stepped up to fill the spot in his absence?

"She's fine."

Jacob huffed. "I'm glad."

"She's not fine Jacob. Not everyone is like you and can jump from person to person without a backward glance."

"You know my situation with Victoria, you know it isn't real."

"Yes, I'm aware of your situation, but I can't understand that level of intimacy with someone you despise. I'm not certain why you believe Victoria would follow through on her threats or that it would even matter to your life in the long run."

"Miriam said the same thing."

Janie laughed dryly. "I've no idea who Miriam is, but she's obviously brilliant."

Jacob chuckled. "That she is. Are you still at the pub?"

"Yes. Hang on Jacob—" Janie started speaking to another woman, and when Jacob realized it was Lilly, his breath caught. "I've got to fly, tons of love."

"You too, tell Lilly—tell her hello."

"Will do. I'm working to set her up. Lilly's too precious a commodity for the open market." Janie hung up, and Jacob stared at his phone, his heart racing at his sister's statement.

What the fuck? My own sister is trying to set Lilly up with another man?

A new emotion welled up inside of Jacob; a wave of fury towards Victoria for the destruction she wreaked upon his life, his heart, and his future with Lilly.

Albert would announce his casting decision within the month, but Jacob couldn't hold out that long. Drawing in a ragged breath, he realized he no longer gave a rat's ass about the consequences; he needed to be free from Victoria's yoke.

Jacob stormed toward his hotel, determined to end this chaos once and for all.

When he walked into his suite, Victoria lay sprawled across the bed, reading the riot act to her assistant about the lack of irises in the bouquets littering the room. Jacob leaned against the wall, glaring holes into her visage until she realized his presence. She hung up the phone and ran to him, throwing her arms around his neck.

"Did you miss me, baby?" Victoria crooned. "You're my handsome movie star again without that awful beard and shaggy hair."

Jacob removed her hands and led her to the sofa, pushing her down against the cushions. Victoria started to rise, but he snapped at her to sit down and stay put.

"Well, aren't you grumpy? Perhaps you need a cocktail and some personal attention?" She cooed in her syrupy voice.

"I'm not grumpy. I told you not to come here, but you did anyway."

"I thought you'd be happy to see me," Victoria pouted, her lower lip protruding.

He glowered at her. "You thought wrong."

Victoria's face registered genuine surprise.

"I've been pondering our arrangement the last few weeks, and I've reached a realization. I can't stand being around you, in any form. You're vile and loathsome and conniving. I'm done with this charade between you and me, I'm done pretending."

Victoria's lower lip quivered. "You don't mean that. You're just tired."

"Stop, for the love of God, stop pretending. I am tired, I'm exhausted from all this. But I also mean every word."

Victoria's eyes narrowed, anger flashing across her face. "Is this about that stupid fucking nurse?"

"God help you if you say one more word about Lilly."

"Is it?" Victoria's voice shrieked as she paced the floor of the suite.

Jacob lost his temper, his voice ricocheting off the walls. "Your behavior ended my chances with Lilly, but I'm done whoring myself for your public relations whims."

"You'd give up your opportunity for *her?*"

"I'd give up everything for another chance with Lilly."

Victoria brought her face close to Jacob, but Jacob refused to be shaken by her threats. She might threaten hell, but as far as he was concerned, he was already there. "Here I thought you were done slumming."

"Victoria—" Jacob warned, his fists clenching. He didn't know how long he could stand there and listen to this woman insult Lilly.

A slow, vile smile spread across her lips. "I guess that role isn't important to you after all. What a pity. I spoke with Albert yesterday, and he said you were the perfect fit. But I guess that doesn't matter to you anymore."

Jacob shook his head. "The role means everything to my acting career, but if it means spending one more minute with you and your games, I'll pass." He picked up his cell phone, punching in a phone number.

"Who are you calling?"

"Albert. I figure I'll beat you to the punch and remove myself from contention."

Victoria snatched the phone from his hands, tossing it across the room. "Don't be an idiot."

Jacob shot his ex an icy gaze. He wouldn't allow her to get under his skin again. "I'm hardly an idiot. I'm simply following this illogical chaos to its most logical end."

"You'll regret this."

"I regret every second I've spent with you, but I don't regret leaving you one iota."

"You will pay for this, Jacob. I will ruin you."

His anguish took over as he paced the floor, running his fingers over his scalp. "You've already ruined me! I love Lilly! I'm in fucking love with this woman, and you destroyed it for your own amusement."

"I did it because I love you."

"You never loved me…and I never loved you."

For a split second, Jacob saw a flash of genuine emotion cross Victoria's face; a pain at the realization that he didn't love her like she hoped, but it quickly faded.

"Fuck you, Jacob." Victoria grabbed her phone, screaming at her assistant to get her on the next flight to the States. She walked to the door, her hand on the doorknob. "You haven't seen the last of me, Jacob. Remember, I always get what I want."

Jacob smiled as the door closed, the feeling of freedom settling over his being. He poured himself a glass of whiskey and swigged it down, relishing the burn. He was free, he was finally free.

He dialed Janie to share the good news.

"Hello?"

He almost dropped his phone. It was Lilly's voice on the other end of the line.

"Hello?" Lilly repeated.

"Lilly? God, I missed hearing your voice." He stammered, his stomach in knots.

There was a pregnant pause on the other end. "Jacob?"

Jacob swallowed against the emotion rising in his chest. God, he missed this woman so damn much. "Yeah. How are you?"

Another pause, this was not moving as smoothly as Jacob hoped. "Janie's in the bathroom. She's expecting a call from Audrey, so she asked that I answer her phone."

Jacob fumbled, searching for the right words. "I'm glad you picked up. I watched your video. You have no idea how beautiful you are, Lilly."

He heard the confusion in Lilly's voice. "What video? Oh, Janie's back, take care."

Janie laughed as she came on the line. "That sounded awkward."

"She doesn't want to talk to me, does she?" Jacob asked, hanging his head.

"I wouldn't go that far. Lilly, are you opposed to speaking with my brother?" Janie spoke to someone out of earshot before returning to the call. "She has no problem speaking to you. She said you called my phone, so you obviously wanted to speak to me."

"Jeez Janie, way to be discreet."

"I have a knack for it. What do you want?"

Jacob smiled, still shocked by the bluntness of his recent actions. "I got off the phone with you, returned to my suite and ordered Victoria out of my life."

He could feel his sister staring at the phone, her mouth agape. After what seemed an eternity, she whispered, "Are you serious?"

"As a heart attack."

"Bad choice of terms."

Jacob winced. "Sorry, Little Bit, but yes, your words stuck with me. I've had enough."

"What about the film role?"

"I couldn't care less."

"How do you feel?"

"Fucking fabulous!" Jacob whooped, sending his sister into a fit of giggles.

Lilly

J anie's scream of excitement startled Lilly, but her friend was on a roll, chattering like a hyper chickadee. It was apparently fantastic news on the other end of that phone line, but Lilly wasn't able to partake in her friend's excitement. She shook her head and walked outside the pub.

Spring had arrived in London, and it was a gorgeous starlit evening. She thought back to her brief conversation with Jacob. She hadn't spoken to him in weeks, but he was never far from her thoughts. He sounded genuinely happy to hear her voice, but then again, it could just be his British manners.

But Lilly didn't have time to ponder matters as Janie bounded out the door, her face beaming as she caught Lilly in a fierce embrace.

"Goodness girl, did you win the lottery?" Lilly asked.

"He dumped her ass, kicked her to the curb," Janie exclaimed. "Ding dong the witch is dead!"

"I'm assuming you mean Jacob?"

Janie nodded. "Don't you know what this means?"

Lilly shook her head, keeping her voice calm despite the hammering of her heart. "I have no clue. What does it mean for that film role?"

"Jacob doesn't care. Victoria threw every threat in the book at him, but he insisted she leave. He said it feels amazing to be rid of that woman."

"Good for him, standing up to Victoria and her threats." Lilly plastered on a fake smile, but her heart still hurt.

Janie sent her a side-eye grin. "He also told said something about you. Are you interested?"

Lilly closed her eyes, taking a fortifying breath. "I don't think so."

"Why aren't you happier? Nothing is standing between you two now."

Lilly shot her friend a surprised look. "I have nothing to do with the situation. If I did, Jacob would have chosen me over Victoria weeks ago. But he didn't, he chose his career, and he chose her. There's no future for Jacob and me. But if he's happy about his decision, then I'm thrilled for him."

"Silly girl, you have everything to do with the situation. You're the reason he made the decision. You won't even consider a reconciliation?"

"There's nothing to consider. I handed Jacob my heart, and he trampled it. Apparently, he didn't want it." Lilly stared at her empty glass, knowing if she looked at her friend the anguish would show. "This means one of two things, either I go home, or I buy another drink."

Janie squeezed Lilly's arm as if sensing the pain in her heart. "Easiest choice ever—more alcohol!"

Lilly nodded. "And so it is, the lady speaks."

Back inside the pub, Janie pulled Lilly to the bar. "We're celebrating, make us something fabulous."

The bartender smiled and winked at Janie, his eyes moving to Lilly and roving her form. "What would you ladies like?"

"Anything their heart desires." Lilly turned to see Enrique standing there, his shirt clinging to his physique like a second skin.

"Ricky!" Janie exclaimed, throwing herself at the surgeon. "How are you, lifesaver of mine?"

Enrique chuckled, handing the bartender his credit card. "Not as good as you, apparently. You look amazing, Janie."

"All because of you and Lilly."

Enrique's eyes held Lilly captive, a small smile playing on his lips. "Lilly is a miracle in many ways."

Lilly embraced him, wrapping her arms around his waist. His chest was muscled yet deceptively comfortable. Maybe it was the whiskey, or perhaps a niggling of loneliness, but he felt good, and it felt even better when his arms encircled her and held her close. "It's good to see you. How was your vacation?"

"Sun, sand and tons of bikinis."

"Did Emma go with you?"

Enrique glowered at the question. "No, I was alone. Just me and the beach."

Lilly chuckled. "Can't beat that."

"Yes, I could."

Her eyebrows raised inquisitively. "How so?"

His lips hovered near her ear, his breath tickling her neck. "If a certain someone was enjoying the sun and sand with me. Perhaps next time, you might join me." A fellow surgeon broke into their moment, wanting to speak to Enrique about some surgical advances. He offered a rueful smile and stepped back. "Excuse me, duty calls. Have a wonderful night, ladies. Lilly, it's always lovely seeing you."

Lilly stared at his retreating form, her jaw slack from his statement. Janie elbowed her in the ribs, giggling. "A damn fine specimen of the male form. Hell, he even makes me randy."

"What a proclamation. Should Audrey be worried?" Lilly joked. "He is extremely good looking."

"That's like saying the Pope is an average Catholic. Lilly, he's bloody perfect, and he's hot for you."

"He likely shagged ten women on vacation; one for each day he was in Ibiza. He has quite the reputation."

"I don't doubt it. He's single, Lilly. And drop dead gorgeous. He doesn't seem like a womanizer, though."

Lilly shook her head. "Those aren't the rumors."

Janie's eyes sparkled. "Do tell, this sounds juicy."

"The rumors are that he's the most amazing lover; the things he can do with his hands...and mouth..."

"You're blushing. You like him!"

Lilly hid her smile behind her hand. "I highly respect him. He's my colleague and friend, nothing beyond that."

"Perhaps you should reconsider your stance on Dr. Torres. You could have some mighty fun times with that handsome Spaniard." Janie chewed her lip. "Besides, it would make my brother insane with jealousy."

"Weren't you just convincing me to reconcile with Jacob?"

Janie nodded, sipping her cocktail. "Most definitely, but the bastard should have to work for it, and jealousy is an amazing motivator. I say you shag the sexy surgeon."

Lilly scoffed in amazement, gazing over at the doctor. "No, for so many reasons. One, I would never use Enrique to make anyone jealous and two, Jacob wouldn't give a shit, anyway."

"You sure about that?" Janie handed Lilly her phone. There were ten text messages from Jacob, all ranting about Lilly dating other men.

Lilly read the messages, shooting Janie a confused stare. "What the hell is he talking about? What other men?"

Janie snickered. "I might have mentioned setting you up with someone, and he's been blowing up my phone ever since."

"You'll get yourself in trouble." Lilly tried to ignore her racing heart, but Jacob's messages seemed desperate. *It's another act, don't fall for it—or him—again.*

Janie shrugged, clinking Lilly's glass with her own. "I can handle my brother. The question is, can he handle the woman he loves moving on without him?"

A few evenings later, Lilly gathered for the official opening of the new shelter wing. The local news feed was on hand, but the reporter seemed disappointed Jacob that was not present for the ribbon cutting.

Lilly and the shelter volunteers rescued ten dogs from last-minute euthanasia at the pound, transporting them to their new home. Lilly cried and clapped as the pups ran about, exploring their domain.

The good news didn't end there, the fundraiser brought in sufficient monies to make additional repairs, and one anonymous donor sent a whopping seventy-five thousand pounds, enough to fund another shelter. Lilly nearly fainted when she saw the cashier's check.

Sabina hugged her friend. "I'm so proud of you! And here," she showed Lilly her phone, "I shot a video of the ribbon cutting and pups running in. I'm sending it to you now."

Lilly smiled, returning her attention to the small crowd, thanking each person for their support. As everyone dispersed, Lilly headed into the new wing, petting some dogs before they ran off to play. Her phone chimed, and she replayed the video Sabina recorded, attempting in vain not to notice one man's gaping absence. She forwarded the video to 'Pups Princes,' the group of volunteers who helped construct the kennels, then headed home.

An hour later, she walked out of her shower and noticed several missed texts and a voicemail. The texts were all congratulatory from the group, but she didn't recognize the voicemail number.

Assuming it was a wrong number, she listened, the towel wrapped tight around her body.

Lilly almost dropped the phone when Jacob's voice came on the line. "You're amazing. The new wing looks wonderful, and those dogs wouldn't be alive if it weren't for you. I realize it was a group text, and you probably didn't mean to include me, but I had to call. I figured if I got your voicemail then at least I could hear that Yankee accent again. I'll call again in a little while, and if you don't pick up, I'll take the hint. But I hope you answer. I miss you, Lilly. I miss everything about you." His voice stammered at the end, and Lilly sat there, her entire body trembling.

She pressed play again, falling into his sexy voice that could turn her on from thousands of kilometers away. After listening to his message five times, Lilly tossed the phone aside. She was a pathetically hopeless romantic.

Donning her yoga gear, she decided a cool-down flow would clear her mind and calm her nerves. *You never belonged with those people. Get your head out of the clouds and back down to reality.*

She was in the middle of her yoga routine when a video call came through. She started, never assuming Jacob would try to video conference with her and feeling unprepared in every way to see him face to face.

Lilly inhaled deeply, debating if she should ignore the call. He had said that if she didn't answer, he would take the hint. Wasn't that what she wanted?

Answer the damn call, you know you want to speak with him. Lilly's hammering heart overruled her mind as her shaking hand accepted the call.

He looked entirely different from when he left, his hair cropped and his face clean-shaven. Lilly could almost convince herself the man she knew no longer existed until he spoke.

"Hi, am I interrupting you?" If Lilly didn't know better, Jacob was a bundle of nerves as well, trying to appear relaxed.

Well, ditto for me, sir. Lilly shook her head, trying not to look at the screen. "I wasn't expecting a video call, hence the fantastic loungewear," she replied, motioning to her yoga outfit.

Jacob chuckled. "You are a yoga instructor, you can probably get away with it as business attire."

Lilly's laugh felt as brittle as her wounded heart. "I'll have to check with my accountant."

"Are you going to look at me?" Jacob's voice was pleading, and Lilly bit her lip before swinging her gaze toward the screen.

"I'm looking at you." Her voice was flat and emotionless, but her heart was beating so fast she feared it would jump out of her chest.

Jacob seemed uncertain about how to proceed. "I look totally different, right?" He motioned to his face and hair. "You probably hate it."

Lilly did her best to appear nonchalant, though she knew she was failing miserably at it. She shrugged, shaking her head. "It doesn't matter to me what you look like, that's more your girlfriend's arena."

Jacob sighed, running his hand over his head. "Wow, I deserved that."

Lilly felt awful about her comment, but she couldn't bring her guard down. "I didn't mean it as an insult." She watched him swallow hard. "You don't need me stroking your ego, you have tons of fans to adore you."

"And yet," he said, his hand stroking his chiseled jaw, "your opinion is the only one I give a shit about. And I don't have a girlfriend. Victoria is out of my life—"

His words knocked at the door of her heart, but she couldn't believe them this time. "What do you want, Jacob?" Lilly asked, her words biting.

"I want to talk to you, on the off chance you miss me like I miss you. I'm not sleeping. I can't remember ever sleeping as well as I did those nights I held you."

Lilly buried her face in her hands, fighting back the tears. "I can't do this."

"Lilly, please." His voice was soft but desperate.

She dug deep and looked him dead in the eye. This would hurt like hell, but she needed to say it. "I have no interest in being your runner-up, a consolation prize. Maybe you think I should be grateful you're even bothering to speak to me, but I'm worth more than that."

"You're worth everything, and you were never a runner-up. Do you honestly believe that?"

Lilly's eyes darkened with anger and pain. "Well then, you tell me, what was I to you?" She held up a hand, shaking her head. "Don't bother. It doesn't matter."

Jacob was breathing hard; it was evident this conversation was upsetting him. "It *does* matter, what we had together mattered. It's so complicated—"

"Actually," Lilly hissed, "it's simple. You had a choice, and it wasn't me. What did you expect from this call? Closure? You want to feel better after the way the two of you treated me? I told you when you left that I understood your decision. I didn't like it, but I understood. I wished you happiness, and I wished you love"—she paused, angrily wiping away the tears filling her eyes—"and I don't know what you want from me now, or why you even called me."

Jacob's eyes were glassy with unshed tears as a muscle twitched in his jaw. Her words had gotten the point across. "Lilly, I told you before I left that I'll do anything to make this up to you. Just tell me how to fix this situation because you're breaking my heart."

Lilly took a deep breath, her body shaking with emotion. "I want you to let me go, Jacob."

Her statement rammed into him like a fist, and he looked down, breathing hard. "Lilly, don't say that."

"Let me go, Jacob," Lilly reiterated, her voice a strangled whisper.

He sniffled, running a hand over his buzzed hair and looking anywhere but directly into her eyes. "Is that really what your heart wants?"

Lilly attempted to bite back her tears, but a few escaped and tumbled down her cheeks. "It's what my heart needs."

Jacob looked morose, positively deflated by her words. "I'll let you go then—"

"Okay," Lilly sputtered.

Jacob took a deep breath. "Goodbye, my beautiful angel."

Lilly leaned forward and ended the call, barely hitting the disconnect before she broke down in a sobbing heap. She was still weeping a half hour later, still angry that Jacob tossed her aside for Victoria, but also mad at herself. Lilly promised Jacob when he left that they could attempt being friends, but she had behaved as if he were a leper. She saw the trepidation in his face during the call, he was terrified what she thought of him. But instead of understanding, she treated his feelings with callous disregard. Essentially, she treated him in the same manner he treated her, and two wrongs definitely did not make a right.

This is not you Lilly, you are not cruel. Now get ahold of yourself, you can't hate him because he didn't choose you. If you're going to be his friend, act like one.

Her mind screamed that she was being ridiculous, her heart whispered that she was in love—her heart won. She would rather have Jacob in her life in some capacity than not at all. She ached without him.

She turned on some sad, lilting music and laid in bed, staring at her phone. Finally, she snapped it up and composed a simple text. *'I'm not sleeping either. I'm sorry, I was awful on that call.'*

She sent the message, not expecting a reply, but he responded immediately. *'You want to try again?'*

His reply brought on a fresh set of tears, and she dialed his number.

"I'm glad you called." His voice was thick and muffled. It sounded as if he were crying although Lilly squashed the idea as ridiculous.

"Me too. How have you been?" Lilly asked, realizing she wanted to know the answer.

Their conversation ended a half hour later, with a promise to phone each other that weekend. For the first time since Jacob's departure, Lilly slept.

CHAPTER TWO

Jacob

Miriam pulled Jacob aside the next morning after he finished with hair and makeup. "Something's different."

Jacob shrugged. "Different foundation?"

"Hilarious. No, *you're* different this morning. You spoke to Lilly."

Jacob nodded, shocked Miriam read him with so little effort. "I did, and I sent Victoria packing a few days ago."

Miriam hugged him. "Congratulations on ridding yourself of that parasite. Now, about Ms. Lilly, how was your conversation?"

"The first call was slow, awkward and excruciatingly painful, but the follow up was better."

"Do you still have feelings for her?"

"Without a doubt, but she made it clear she didn't share that sentiment." Jacob sighed when Miriam shot him a perplexed look. "She was cold and distant; made a comment about not being a second-place prize. And she didn't even want to look at me."

Miriam snickered.

"Which part of this situation is amusing?" Jacob responded, brow raised.

"How little you understand about women, my friend. Wipe that appalled look off your face, most men know nothing about women."

Jacob sipped his tea, watching the crew set up a scene. "Well sensei, share your secrets."

"If a woman is over you, you won't see any reaction from her; certainly not anger. And the reason she wouldn't look at you? It's too painful for her at this point. When a woman behaves the way Lilly did, it shows she's hurt, scared, and still in love with you." Miriam patted his shoulder, smirking when Jacob realized the meaning behind her words. "Never thought of that angle, did you?"

"So, what do I do?" Jacob hollered after Miriam as she strolled over to speak with the lighting director, leaving Jacob to wallow in his confusion. "You can't leave me hanging like that. Some sensei you are!"

Jacob accepted Miriam's dinner invitation that evening. Her words from earlier swirled in his mind throughout the day and he needed to pick her brain for more information.

They sat at the open-air restaurant, drinking Ouzo and eating fresh hummus, the salt air creating an intoxicating environment. Jacob only wished Lilly was there to enjoy it with him.

"What a productive day of shooting. I thought that one scene would require at least ten takes, but you nailed it in three. You were on point today, sir." Miriam sipped her drink. "But enough about filming, your mind is focused elsewhere. You want to win Lilly back, right?"

Although Miriam was renowned for her direct manner, her blunt statement took him by surprise. Jacob downed some Ouzo and nodded. "I wonder if reconciliation is possible at this point. You're right, Lilly has a long list of admirers and even my own sister is trying to set her up, probably with the surgeon who saved her life." His fist tightened at the thought of another man's hands on Lilly's body.

"It doesn't matter if Lilly has a mile-long list of admirers. When you love someone, they're the only one you see." Miriam chewed her lip thoughtfully. "But before you try to win back her affections, ask yourself these questions. Is this your ego coming into play or is it your heart? Are you in love with her?"

"I'm completely in love with her. I never realized being in love felt so damn awful."

Miriam chuckled. "It does when it isn't working out. Give me the backstory, I need to know what I'm working with here. And don't spare any details, we women always know when you leave something out."

Taking a deep breath, Jacob described his brief, yet profound journey with Lilly. He recounted the intense highs and devastating lows, and the many times his misguided priorities had hurt her feelings and heart.

Miriam managed one word when he finished. "Shit."

"I messed up," Jacob stared at his drink.

"You did, yes, you did. I give her credit for not telling you to go stuff it. If I were Lilly, I wouldn't be your friend. This woman is far kinder than I would be in her situation."

Jacob glared at his friend. "You're not helping."

"The truth hurts. You're done with Victoria, that debacle is kaput?" Jacob nodded before she continued. "Then your answer is simple, make Lilly fall in love with you again."

Jacob guffawed. "That's your answer? I'm glad I came to you because I never would have thought of that one on my own." Jacob ran his hand over his buzzed hair in frustration. "How am I supposed to make her fall in love with me? I'm thousands of kilometers from her and she's barely speaking to me."

"Looks like you've got your work cut out for you."

"I'm so screwed."

Miriam chuckled, sipping her Ouzo. "Have you ever been in love before?"

"As pathetic as it sounds, never. I stuck to meaningless romps, my heart never got involved. Then I met Lilly and life as I knew it ceased to exist." Jacob slumped in his chair, sighing. "I'm not even sure how I got her to fall in love with me the first time. Dumb luck, I guess."

Miriam gave his arm a reassuring squeeze. "Make her feel like the only person in the world that matters to you, which is simple if you're truly in love. And don't just buy her things, Lilly is obviously not impressed with displays of money. Listen to her and do things for her, from here, that shows you were listening. Do things that make her feel beautiful and desired. Eventually, she'll soften."

"I can do that, I'll give her anything she wants."

Miriam scoffed. "You don't know what she wants, you haven't asked her yet. Jacob, be her friend first. Let her trust you again."

"And what if one of Lilly's admirers snatches her up, what then?"

"Then be her friend, and support her decision, like she supported you and Victoria. I guarantee it'll hurt like hell, but Lilly put on a brave face, and that is what you'll have to do, too."

Jacob slumped in the chair. "Is there any other option?"

"You can walk away and forget her." Miriam saw his expression and smiled. "But if you can't forget her, it's time to fight for her."

Jacob returned to his suite, buzzed from the Ouzo. He looked at the clock and saw it was 11 p.m. With the two-hour time difference, Lilly should be awake.

It was a Friday night though, she might be out with friends, or on a date with the damn surgeon. Jacob was no fool, he knew Enrique wouldn't hesitate to make his move, and Lilly's friends would applaud that match.

He fell onto the bed as memories of their first night flowed back in waves. He remembered the song Lilly played; her belief that it described love in its truest form. What was it she said? When you felt real love for somebody, you would do anything for them, do anything to make them smile. At the time, Jacob found her synopsis quaint, but as he listened to the song's lyrics, he realized she was right.

He sent Lilly a link to the song along with a text message: *'I was thinking of our first night and how you described this song as the pure definition of love. Now I understand. The lyrics echo every emotion in my heart. I hope you're enjoying an evening as wonderful as you are. Goodnight, angel.'* He hit the replay button, sighing.

The phone rang a few minutes later. "Yeah?" Jacob answered, his voice thick with emotion.

"Are you okay?" Lilly's voice was soft and questioning.

Jacob sniffled. "I'm good."

"Are you crying?" Lilly's voice held a degree of concern.

"No." Jacob sniffled again. "I'm not crying, it's allergies."

There was a long pause. "Are you lying?" Her voice held a quiet knowing.

Jacob ignored her last question. "I hope my message didn't interrupt anything."

"Actually, you did. My cat and I were having an in-depth conversation. He was about to disclose the secret of time travel when you texted."

Jacob laughed. Lilly always knew how to lift the mood without prying. "I'm terribly sorry, do you think he'll be able to remember it later?"

"Likely not, it was a one-time deal. So, it appears I shall not live the rest of my life as an Elizabethan queen."

"Definition of tragedy." Her laughter spilled over him like moonlight through the window, the sexiest sound he'd ever heard. "It's Friday night, why are you home?"

Lilly scoffed. "Because I live here, would you rather I leave? Go muck about on the street corner?"

"I figured you'd be out partying with your friends or on some hot date." He mumbled the last part of his statement as if speaking it aloud might breathe it into reality.

Lilly was silent for a moment. "No hot date, sorry."

Jacob's sigh of relief was audible. "Definitely not disappointed by that news."

"What made you think of that song? Did it come on the radio?"

"I was thinking about our first night together."

"What made you think of that?" Her voice trembled as if she didn't want to know the answer.

You flood my every thought, and all I want is to be next to you, Jacob thought, feeling a catch in his chest that had only developed since they parted. "It was the most amazing night even though I was a total ass at the end."

Lilly laughed dryly. "You were trying to protect my chastity so I suppose I can forgive you."

His voice was thick with emotion. "I wish I'd stayed."

Lilly remained quiet for several beats, and Jacob wondered if he'd said too much. He was about to backpedal when Lilly spoke, her voice low and breathy. "You're an incredible lover, it would have been an amazing evening."

Jacob's body responded to her words, and his hand drifted down to grasp his cock, as images of her body moving underneath his spilled into his memory. "*You're* the most amazing lover, Lilly, with the most exquisite body. I'd give anything to have that night back, to have all our times together back."

"Well, if you hadn't interrupted the conversation between my cat and me, you would possess the secret to time travel, and we could relive that evening with a different ending." Lilly changed the subject, lightening the mood, and Jacob was grateful for it. Miriam warned him to take it slow with Lilly, but when they spoke, he felt compelled to vomit every emotion in his heart.

Instead, Jacob laughed, steering the conversation to topics about life in general. The call ended an hour later, with Lilly trying to disguise her yawns. Jacob wished her sweet dreams and fell asleep imagining her naked body wrapped around him.

A text appeared on his phone the following evening, and the sight of it made Jacob's blood pressure skyrocket. He was seething. Granted, the picture was innocent enough—a group of friends posing outside a vineyard—but it was the Spanish surgeon with his arm draped around Lilly that made his blood boil.

His phone rang, and he barked out a greeting.

"Aren't you all sunshine and rainbows today," Janie muttered. "What crawled up your arse and died?"

"Great picture, Janie. So glad you sent it to me."

"It *is* a great picture. We're all looking in the same direction, so it's basically a bloody miracle."

"Not what I meant," Jacob gritted out, pacing the hotel suite.

Janie chuckled. "I know what you meant. You're pissed about Enrique hanging all over Lilly."

"When the hell did this happen? Are they together?"

Silence. Ten seconds of silence—Jacob counted. "They're friends, Jacob. They were friends before you even met Lilly."

Jacob drummed his fingers on the table, taking a swig of whiskey. "He looks more than friendly."

Janie scoffed. "I don't think it's news that he's interested in her. Might I remind you that he's actually a fantastic catch, dear brother."

"Are you encouraging this? Janie, I'm trying to fix things. I don't need

19

my own sister undermining my efforts." Jacob slugged the whiskey, willing his heart rate down.

Janie cleared her throat. "Jakey, it would be wonderful if you and Lilly ended up together, she's already like a sister. But you broke her damn heart. I love you, but I love Lilly too. I won't let you hurt her again."

"It was just a misunderstanding." Christ, his excuse sounded pathetic even to him.

"A misunderstanding? What a load of bollocks. You're lucky Lilly's even speaking to you. The worst thing you can do to a woman is sleep with her and then run off and shag someone else—which is precisely what you did."

"It wasn't like that—"

Janie scoffed, cutting into Jacob's retort. "Really? So, you and Victoria didn't sleep together after you left Roger's house? Don't bother lying either."

His slammed his fist against the wall. Janie knew him too well. "Fuck. Victoria kept threatening…the sex meant nothing."

"It meant something to Lilly. And if you loved Lilly like you claim, it would mean something to you, too."

Her words cut into his heart. She was right, he was a total cad.

"Enrique is really interested in Lilly. She deserves someone to treat her like a queen."

His hand gripped the phone, his knuckles white. "Please don't encourage him, Janie. Let me try to repair the damage I've caused."

Silence again; he hated when his sister took this long to respond. "Fine. I won't encourage them to date, *but* I won't discourage it either. If they find their way into each other's arms, you'll have to learn to live with it."

"What a disaster." Jacob poured more whiskey. At this rate, he'd need several cases sent to his suite.

"If it's any consolation, I think Lilly's still in love with you. Never underestimate the power of a woman's love. Goodnight, big brother."

The line cut off and Jacob downed another shot, the gears of his mind spinning. He'd lost a major battle but not the war. He could turn this situation around if he still held a piece of Lilly's heart.

Lilly

illy glanced at her phone as she sank into her front seat; it was Jacob ringing her back from an earlier conversation. Their first few conversations had been awkward and stilted, but a routine developed over the last several weeks, and a true friendship blossomed. He knew her history, warts and all, and she knew his. There was nothing hidden between them anymore, and Lilly looked forward to their daily chats.

But today, Lilly's mood bordered on frustrated exhaustion with a hint of irritability, and Jacob received that wrath during the earlier call. In fact, thinking back, Lilly realized she hadn't even said goodbye before she clicked off the line.

It wasn't Jacob's fault, not this time, at least. Her workday resembled a poorly scripted horror film—complete with irate managers, a visit from the health advisory board, and a screaming back after she tumbled down the stairs. Thankfully, she landed on her ass instead of her head, but unfortunately for Jacob, he chose that moment to call, and Lilly had been less than accommodating as she sat rubbing her sore tailbone on the cement steps.

Time to apologize for being such a bitch. Lilly laughed as she answered his call. "I'll bet you never heard that many curses strung together in your entire life."

Jacob chuckled in response. "Impressive. I think you even invented a few new ones. Are you headed home?"

"Yes, thank God. Today has been long and awful, but on a high note, I get to do it all again tomorrow." Lilly pulled out of the car park, groaning in anticipation of the hell waiting for her in the office.

"What an optimistic way of looking at things."

"This from the man whose day consists of kissing beautiful starlets and basking on Grecian beaches. The struggle is real, my friend." Lilly giggled but noticed that Jacob remained silent. "Fine, your life is difficult too. Better?"

"I'm not kissing any starlets." His voice was low, firm and brimming with emotion. "I'm not kissing anybody."

How in the world am I supposed to answer that? Should I cheer about his abstinence or console him for it? Lilly just didn't know; their friendship was built upon a powerful, mutual attraction with no demarcated boundaries between friends and lovers...or one-time lovers. "I was only joking."

"I wasn't."

"Are you angry?"

Jacob scoffed. "No, Lilly. I just loathe the fact you think I'm down here cavorting with all these buxom beauties."

"Isn't that one perk of being a movie star?"

Jacob's laugh bordered on sarcasm. "Maybe for some, but my mind is preoccupied with someone; she's all I think about."

Lilly's grip weakened on her phone and it dropped to her lap—his admission rattling her to the core. This was the first time he had mentioned a romantic interest since his arrival in Greece. Their chats centered around safer, platonic topics, even though Lilly's body and heart still ached Jacob. But she hid her feelings behind a friendly banter, hoping to keep her heart a safe distance from the cliff edge.

Jacob often skated around flirtation, but that was his nature, and the fair-haired Apollo had burned Lilly before; she wasn't keen to get too close to the flame only to discover she'd misunderstood his intentions…again. But still there shone that faint glimmer of hope in her heart, the one that believed all his affections were aimed in her direction. She was satisfied with that glimmer, not happy but satisfied, and she wasn't ready to rescind that final piece of Jacob to another woman.

"Lilly!"

She scrambled to retrieve her phone, Jacob's voice echoing out through the receiver. "Sorry, the phone slipped."

"Did my statement shock you that much?"

That's an understatement. "I would say surprised more than shocked. You haven't mentioned any romantic inclinations."

"You haven't asked."

"Because I don't want to know," Lilly muttered under her breath.

"Come on, aren't you curious? Don't you want to hear about this special someone? We never discuss what's happening in our lives romantically." Jacob's pacing increased as he spoke, and Lilly wasn't certain if it was nerves or excitement.

A wave of nausea flooded Lilly. Jacob's generic wording didn't intimate that she was the woman in question, and the idea of discussing his new love interest would be more painful than a root canal without novocaine. "Sadly, I don't have a romantic life at the moment. I suppose I must live vicariously through you." *Or you could just shoot me and put me out of my misery, either way works.*

Jacob's throaty whisper tickled her ear like a caress. "You could have the most amazing romantic life. You're exquisitely beautiful, Lilly. You deserve to have your body and heart worshipped like you goddess you are. But you have to let your guard down and take a chance, trust that your heart won't be broken this time."

Lilly sighed. This was where that line between friends and 'desperately want to be your lover' became gray. Was he referring to himself or someone else as the man who shattered her heart? And who did he have in mind to repair it? "I've never been worshipped before."

"That's not true; you just don't realize it."

Her body flushed in response to his words. Damn him for being able to turn her on with so little effort, and with a high probability his compliment was not sexually intended. *Fat chance there, every word dropping from his lips makes me tingle. Stupid heart.*

"Do you think you might take another chance on love anytime soon, angel?"

"It's easier said than done, but I hope one day to find someone to treat me in the manner you described. It sounds delectable." Lilly paused when Jacob made an involuntary huff. Was he turned on or off by her statement? Better to err on the side of caution. "Enough about me. Tell me about your latest infatuation."

"She's much more than an infatuation, Lilly."

Lilly closed her eyes and groaned. God give her strength. Why couldn't she get over this man and regard him strictly as a friend? How would she hear about this magnificent, mythical creature without vomiting halfway through his romantic narrative? "Fucking wonderful, just my luck," she muttered, realizing too late she spoke the words out loud.

Shit, time for damage control.

Lilly forced a laugh. "You heard that, didn't you?"

"I did." Jacob's voice sounded strained. She hoped she hadn't angered him.

"I'm sorry, it slipped out. Good for you, Jacob. Tell me about her, this magical woman who's captured your fancy. She must be incredible." Lilly pasted on a fake smile to match the fake happiness in her voice; damn, maybe she *could* be an actress.

A pregnant pause only increased Lilly's trepidation. "Maybe another time. It's apparent you don't want to discuss this topic and you've had a rough day. I don't want to saddle you with news that might be unwelcome."

Shoot me now, Lilly thought but mumbled her agreement.

"You're going straight home, right? You sound exhausted."

23

Lilly stretched, her back cramping as she pulled into her driveway. "I just pulled into my driveway and I can't wait to soak this day away in the bath. Wait a second, someone's here."

Lilly got out of her car and hobbled to her front door. A tall redhead waited on the stoop with a large folding table and a backpack. When she spotted Lilly, she thrust out her hand. "I'm Eve, Jacob's masseuse and physical therapist. He told me you took a nasty fall and asked me to check on you after work."

Lilly's face registered her disbelief. "Jacob called you? For me?"

Eve nodded. "I have all sorts of goodies for you. I guarantee you'll feel much better when I'm done."

"I was talking to Jacob, but he didn't mention anything—shit, he's still on the line." Lilly picked up her phone, her voice reedy. "Eve is here?"

"I'm glad she's already arrived."

Lilly couldn't contain her shock. "You arranged her visit?"

"I was concerned when you fell. I wanted her to check you over and help with any pain."

His sweet offer stunned Lilly. "That is the nicest thing anyone's ever done for me. Thank you."

She could hear Jacob's smile in his response. "You're welcome. Now go, enjoy some relaxation."

Lilly hung up the phone and welcomed Eve into the house. Within thirty minutes, she was face down on the table, receiving a fantastic massage. According to Eve, it was vital, since Lilly had more knots than the Scout Association.

"You're special to Jacob. I heard the urgency in his voice when he called me," Eve stated, rubbing Lilly's shoulder.

"We're great friends. He's kind to everyone." Lilly attempted to downplay the comment, sure Jacob was only concerned about any injury after the fall.

"Yes, he's kind, but he's never called me with such an insistent personal request before. He paid for ten hours, in case you needed additional therapy."

Lilly turned and looked up at Eve. "I planned to pay you for your services."

Eve guided Lilly's head back down. "He mentioned that would be your response, and that I was to ignore it. This is his gift to you." She continued to knead Lilly's muscles. "I've never heard him talk about anyone like he does about you, and I've worked with him the better part of a decade. I assumed you were far more than friends."

"What kind of relationship do you think Jacob and I share?"

"From the way he spoke about you, I figured you were his wife."

Lilly remained silent, her mind reeling from Eve's statement. Although she suspected Jacob was merely acting the part of an observant friend, her heart leapt at the notion that there was something more behind his actions. Then she recalled his comment about that special woman in his life and squelched any notion of romance. He was merely a good friend; her best friend, at this point. And that would have to suffice.

How foolish I was to think today would be better than the hell of yesterday. Lilly hoped her work week would improve—but life decided not to cooperate. Her back was better, thanks to Eve's magical hands, but today was a train wreck of epic proportions.

Her patient had just been pronounced dead, and once the arrangements for the body were completed, Lilly sought solace in the locker room.

It wasn't the first time a patient passed on her watch, but this case was particularly heart-wrenching, and her heart had been wrenched enough in recent months.

"Lilly, are you in here?" Sabina poked her head in the door, searching around the room.

"Yeah," Lilly sniffled, wiping her face with her palm. "I'll be out in a few minutes."

Sabina slid down the wall next to where her friend sat crouched on the floor, wrapping an arm around her shoulders. "You did everything you could, Lilly."

"Did I? He seemed stable when he rolled out of the operating theater. Maybe I missed something, maybe if I'd been paying more attention—"

"Stop that nonsense! You couldn't have known, Enrique agrees with me, and he was the surgeon on the case! It was just his time, Lilly. You can't always work a miracle."

The tears started anew, and Lilly let them fall, there was no hope of holding back the onslaught of sorrow in her heart. "My patient was only twenty-five. He hadn't had a life yet. He wasn't supposed to die. It was routine surgery."

Sabina tightened her grip, stroking her shoulder. "Who are we to say how long his life should be?"

"Ladies, I'm coming in." Enrique's low voice carried on the air and within moments he was kneeling in front of Lilly, holding her hands. "Lilly, his heart was so diseased. We did everything to save him."

But Lilly was too busy crying to answer. The case seemed so straightforward. A young man with a hole in his heart; a congenital defect that is a common occurrence and easily repaired. The surgery went off without a hitch and the recovery looked to be equally smooth…until it wasn't.

Lilly fought alongside Enrique and the other doctors for an hour, trying to bring back the young man after he coded, but it was too late. He was gone. The worst part was Lilly had spoken to his parents and fiancée an hour earlier, telling them she hoped to have him off the ventilator within hours—now he lay lifeless in a body bag.

"I told them he would to be fine."

"We all thought he would be fine, Lilly. He likely threw a clot, we couldn't have prepared any better than we did. This is not your fault, it's not my fault—"

"It doesn't matter if it was nobody's fault, what about the family? I told his family he would be fine!" Lilly wailed. "What am I supposed to say to them now?"

Enrique pulled her into a hug. "Ben and I have already spoken with the family—"

"But I told them—*I told them*—that he would be fine. I lied to them."

"Okay, I'm taking Lilly home. She's had enough for today." Enrique got to his feet, pulling Lilly and Sabina up off the floor. "Sabina, let Ben know that Lilly is taking the afternoon off. I'll be back within the hour."

Sabina nodded, smoothing Lilly's hair. "Go home, have a drink and a bath."

Lilly sniffled as she nodded in agreement, although her heart didn't believe a word her friends said. She felt a heavy weight of guilt that this young man would never walk out the doors of the hospital. She wasn't even supposed to be his nurse, but they were short-staffed, and she offered to help.

It seemed cut and dried…shows what I know, Lilly surmised as her inner monologue continued berating her heart.

Sabina handed Lilly her phone, dropped during the chaos of the code and noted the barrage of missed calls and texts from Jacob. "Lilly, Jacob's been calling the front desk too…several times."

Lilly groaned. "Shit, he had just called when the man coded—I hung up and he has no idea what's going on."

"He's aware, I spoke to him. Jacob asked that you call him as soon as possible. He's very concerned about you."

Enrique released a sarcastic snort. "Concerned? That's a laugh. I'm sure he will console himself with a variety of pretty, young distractions. What an ass—"

"Save it, Enrique," Sabina hissed. "She feels bad enough."

Lilly watched Enrique's face contort as if not saying something was physically painful, but he let the matter drop. "Come on Lilly, let's get you home."

"What about my car?"

"Sabina and I will work that out later after I'm done here for the evening."

Enrique led Lilly to his car and she leaned against him, allowing him to support her weight.

After a few minutes of silent driving, save for the soft jazz emanating from the speakers, Lilly spoke. "This is ridiculous. I need to pull it together."

"May I say something you're not going to want to hear?"

"Can't wait," Lilly muttered.

"Have you ever considered that staying in contact with Jacob, after everything he's done, might not be the best idea for your emotional well-being?"

"We're friends," Lilly lied, but Enrique's words resonated. She often wondered the same thing. As much as her heart leapt when she spoke with him, he was no longer within her reach. He was living a glamorous life on location in a foreign locale and the tabloids showcased scads of photos of Jacob gallivanting on the beach with beautiful women.

Lilly never asked about the women, except in sarcastic barbs, and Jacob never admitted outright who was keeping his bed warm. The truth was, she didn't want to know. Her heart wanted to maintain the stance that ignorance was bliss, while her head was convinced her heart was an ignoramus.

"You're not friends, Lilly. Friends don't sleep together...and they certainly don't fuck each other over the way he did."

"You've always hated Jacob—"

"Because of how he treated you. You fawned all over him and he tossed you aside. What, would you rather I applaud his behavior?"

Lilly reached across the car, squeezing Enrique's hand. If only this surgeon commanded her heart the way Jacob did. Stupid, stupid heart. "Perhaps you're right."

"Is he still with that singer?"

"Victoria? No, he claims they broke up several weeks ago."

"And what of the tabloid stories? Any truth to the numerous women he's courting in Greece?"

27

Lilly shot Enrique a narrowed glare. "Since when are you such an avid reader of tabloids?"

Enrique chuckled. "I hate to admit it, but I follow the bastard, waiting to see how long it is before he screws up again."

"You're all heart." A small giggle escaped Lilly's lips and Enrique's face lit up at the sound.

"There, it was all worth it, just to see a smile out of you."

Lilly's smile retreated as the memory of the day seeped back into the moment. She had no right to smile, not after losing that young patient.

Enrique smacked the dashboard. "Lilly, stop beating yourself up."

"I'm not—"

"Bullshit! You beat yourself up about everything, especially things beyond your control. It's maddening."

Lilly chewed the inside of her lip, mulling his words. She did apologize for everything, regardless of her role in the situation. She was raised to be a people pleaser, now she realized she couldn't possibly please all people. "I guess I've always done that—annoying habit, isn't it?"

"No, it's endearing, like pretty much everything else about you." He pulled into her driveway, turning to face her in his seat. "Will you be okay? I need to finish some transcriptions at the hospital. I'll be done in a couple of hours."

Lilly reached over, enveloping him in a soft hug. "I'll be fine. Thank you for taking care of me."

His dark eyes clouded as his gaze focused on something beyond the windshield. "I'd take care of you all the time if you'd let me,"—he forced a smile—"but we both know how stubborn you are."

"Another one of my endearing qualities?" Lilly giggled again and shot Enrique a smile before exiting the vehicle.

An hour later, Lilly was feeling a bit better, although still saddened by the outcome of her patient. Her rational side convinced her emotions there was nothing more she could have done. A bubble bath and a glass of wine didn't hurt matters.

She popped open her laptop and almost immediately the video conference rang—it was Jacob.

Shit, I forgot to call him back.

"Hey there." Lilly felt her chest tighten when his gorgeous face came into view on the screen. "Sorry, it's been a hell of a day."

Jacob offered a small smile, but she noted a twitch in his jaw. "I heard. Are you okay?" His voice sounded strained, as if he were stifling his aggravation.

"Better now. I had a long bubble bath and a glass of wine."

"Let's not forget some personal attention from your favorite surgeon." His tongue clicked against his teeth as his eyes narrowed.

And there it was. "Enrique drove me home. He said I wasn't in any state to drive myself."

"How gallant."

"How do you even know all this? Do you have cameras following me?" Lilly snapped out her retort.

Jacob's chuckle lacked any humor. "I spoke with Sabina when *you* didn't call me back. Since you brought it up, what would I discover if I were having you followed? Anything you care to tell me about you and Dr. Torres?"

What the fuck was his problem? Lilly knew Jacob and Enrique were not enamored with each other, but this biting antagonism was getting ridiculous. Furthermore, Jacob didn't have any reason to dislike Enrique—the surgeon hadn't done anything to hurt Lilly—unlike the fair-haired actor.

"What exactly are you insinuating, Jacob?"

"You tell me. Fill me in on the situation because apparently, I'm in the dark here."

"There is no situation between me and Enrique and the only situation you're in the dark about is what an ass you're being right now." His eyes darkened as that damn jaw twitched again and Lilly's thin line of patience was crossed. "What do you want Jacob?"

That question snapped him out of his anger, his eyes widening in surprise. "I was worried about you, Lilly! You were on the phone with me when that situation happened, and you never called me back. Then Sabina tells me you're hysterically crying and Enrique"—he bit out the name—"is driving you home. Am I intruding on something? Just let me know."

That did it. Lilly was furious. How dare this man act self-righteous after the way he behaved with Victoria? "Are you serious? After the day I've had, are you really grilling me about my relationship with Enrique?"

Apparently, Jacob's anger was bubbling at the surface too because it made a speedy resurgence. "That's exactly what I'm asking."

"It's none of your damn business," Lilly gritted out. "How dare you, Jacob! You have no right to pass judgment on me because of my relationship with my *friends*. Unlike you, I don't fuck my friends!"

"He's not your friend, Lilly. The man is in love with you!"

29

Lilly released a harsh laugh as the tears showed up the millionth time that day. "At least someone is, because God knows you weren't." With that she clicked off the call and snapped her laptop closed, releasing a long, wobbly breath.

She'd had enough of Jacob Edmonton. Sanctimonious bastard.

CHAPTER THREE

Jacob

J acob sighed, rubbing his hand over his eyes. *When did I turn into such an asshole?* He had reverted to his original behavior around Lilly—an utter cad.

He rang Lilly back, but her phone went straight to voicemail, and he didn't dare attempt another video call—his angel was in no mood.

After some pointless pacing and a resigned huff, he dialed Janie, hoping for some words of wisdom, although more likely than not she would simply remind him that he was a moron of the highest order.

"Good evening big brother, how's the film rolling?"

Jacob groaned at the horrible pun. "Don't quit your day job, Janie."

"I don't have much time to chat, I'm headed to the pub…with Ms. Lilly, as a matter of fact."

"I'm sure you'll get an earful tonight, then." His head pounded, but he knew no aspirin would touch this pain.

"You mean about how you jumped all over her after she had a shit day? Would that be the earful to which you're referring?"

"That's the one. I tried ringing her back, but she won't pick up."

"Let her cool down. She's had an awful week and your teenage behavior only concreted the situation."

"Is Enrique going with you?"

Janie remained silent—that was an affirmative.

"Do you guys hang out with him all the damn time?"

"Quite a bit, yes. We've become close friends."

"Fucking wonderful."

"Jacob, she's not enamored with him either at the moment."

Those words perked up his ears. "What did he do?" *Please let it be something devious and vile, anything to make me look like less of a git.*

"He gave her shit for talking to you and you gave her shit for talking to him. Meanwhile, both are you are doing the one thing neither of you want— pushing her away."

Another groan, being compared to that surgeon was physically painful. "Thanks for the pep talk."

"How about thanks for the reality check? Wait a couple hours and call her. A few whiskeys will soothe her nerves."

31

"Take care of her Janie. Please."

"Always do, big brother. Tons of love."

The call clicked off and Jacob stared out at the ocean, feeling like a fool. All he wanted was to tell Lilly how much he adored her but instead he berated her for speaking to another man—as if he had a leg to stand on in that situation. And Lilly never threw Victoria in his face—until tonight.

It was after eleven when Jacob finished for the evening and returned to his suite. Hopefully Lilly was in a happier mood and he could manage *not* to put his foot in his mouth this time.

The sounds of the pub echoed in the background when Lilly answered. "Your sister has assured me that you're *not* going to behave like a jerky treat."

Jacob chuckled, so much for the standard greeting of hello. "I swear I won't behave like a—what did you call me?"

"A jerky treat."

"Are you trying not to curse again?"

Lilly remained silent a few beats. "Yes, but fuck, it isn't going too well. Whiskey and profanity seem to meld like oil and water."

Another chuckle. "You mean oil and vinegar?"

"Whatever, you get my point." She giggled, always a good sign. "What do you want?"

"To apologize. I shouldn't have given you shit about Enrique. I know I don't have any claim to you—"

But Lilly cut off Jacob's admission. "Do you think it's easy for me?"

"What's that?"

"All these pictures of you frolicking with gorgeous women. They're beautiful Ms. Universe types and then there's me. It's pretty apparent which one doesn't belong." Lilly released a sigh along with a dry laugh. "I feel embarrassed."

Jacob's heart sank to his stomach with her words. "I don't know why you would ever feel embarrassed—you're an amazingly beautiful woman—inside and out."

"I don't look like those women."

"What women?" Jacob wracked his brain for what photos she was referring to. "I thought you didn't read tabloids, Lilly."

"I don't, but people are keeping me abreast of the situation—*your* situation—in Greece."

Bloody hell. Jacob braced himself, talk about an uphill battle. "I don't know what pictures you're talking about—"

"It's fine, I don't have a right to say anything. But you don't have a right to say anything either. We're friends, nothing more."

Jacob's heart plummeted—was he dealing with her fear or was she really finished? "Is that all you consider me? Your friend?"

Her silence felt like hours, although he knew it was only a matter of moments. "You know that's not what I consider you...but it doesn't matter... not anymore. You've moved on, now it's my turn."

"Moved on? Lilly—"

"Can we talk another time? Enrique wants me to dance."

Just wonderful. "Sure. Are you free tomorrow?"

"I have work until five and then meetings at the shelter. Tomorrow's full up."

Jacob began feeling the fingers of anxiety creep into his being. "What about the next day?"

"I'm free."

"Not anymore, you're not. It's a date." Jacob knew exactly what he was going to do to get their situation back on track and headed in a forward direction.

However, his train derailed with her final words. "No, it's not, Jacob. Goodnight."

Jacob didn't speak with Lilly the next day, it was the first time in weeks that they hadn't connected. Her comments at the pub bothered the hell out of him, along with the idea that she and Enrique were drawing closer to an intimate relationship. But Lilly was too important to him and he wasn't going down without a fight.

Grabbing his phone, he sent her a reminder text for that evening, *'Don't forget, we have a date at seven o'clock your time. I need you to be at home. Miss you, angel.'*

A few minutes later, a reply beeped in. *'You must think I have the worst memory in history. You told me three times already. I'll "see" you at seven.'*

Jacob counted down the minutes until he could speak to Lilly. He really hoped the night would go off without a hitch because this virtual relationship was getting old—fast.

He connected the video chat and smiled when her face appeared on the screen. Lilly was beyond gorgeous and yet, she had no inkling how she affected him, a situation he planned to remedy by the end of their date. "Good evening beautiful."

Lilly chuckled, looking first at the screen and then at her attire. "I didn't realize we were dressing for the call. You look like a prince and I look like the woman who cleans the prince's toilet."

"You're perfect, just as you are." He heard the doorbell sound in Lilly's cottage and smiled. "You'd better get that."

Lilly's eyes widened. "I'm not expecting anyone."

"I am."

Her eyebrows raised quizzically. "What in the world are you up to? I'll be back in a moment."

A knock sounded at Jacob's door and he opened it to room service with his meal. By the time he signed for it and had it set out on the table, Lilly was back in front of the screen, a wide smile on her face.

"You sent me dinner."

Jacob nodded. "I told you it was a date."

"Now I really feel underdressed."

His eyes burned like gleaming sapphires. "I told you, you're perfect."

Lilly glanced at the trays of food surrounding her. "This food looks unbelievable."

It was quite a spread. He had the hotel chefs replicate the same Mediterranean meal that Lilly was eating. It was the closest thing he could get to a real date, and for now, it would have to do. "This is all typical Grecian cuisine, and I hope you enjoy it. But first, we need a toast and I believe there was a box that arrived with the food."

Lilly nodded, lifting up a small box. "Should I open it now?"

"In a moment." God, he loved her, now he only had to hope she still loved him.

She picked up on his nervousness. "Are you okay?"

Jacob nodded, raising his glass. "Time stops whenever I'm with you, for even it realizes the sanctity of love such as this. It dares not hurry a moment so precious. If ever I'm asked to select one moment from my life to live, again and again, I could not choose, for every moment spent with you is one of utter joy."

Lilly's lips parted in a soft smile, her huge brown eyes glistening. "That was lovely, Jacob. Who wrote that?"

His gaze held hers. "I did."

"I had no idea you were such a talented writer. Is there no end to your abilities? Yet another superpower, I suppose."

She was responding with a lighthearted jest, oblivious to the fact that she was indeed the subject of the passage, but Jacob needed her to understand. "I do lack one superpower."

Her eyebrow lifted. "Really? I don't think you're lacking in anything."

"I lack the ability to stop thinking about you. Open the box, Lilly." Christ, he prayed she responded in kind.

Lilly flushed and bit her lip, his favorite quirk, as she cut the packing tape on the package. She pulled out a padlock, her expression puzzled until the realization of its meaning hit her. "Is this—"

"I'm still taking you to Paris, Lilly. I haven't forgotten. I bought a lock for us, to sneak onto the bridge."

Tears filled her eyes as she gazed at the inscription. "I knew I should have paid attention in French class. I don't know what this says."

"Mon ange, tu me manques."

"What does it mean?"

"My angel, you are missing from me." Jacob felt his chest tighten as he spoke the words aloud. He missed her desperately, every facet of her, and the feelings she awakened in his heart.

She couldn't hold back the tears this time. "I thought...I thought—"

"That everything I said that night was a load of shit?"

Lilly nodded, sending him a rueful smile. "Bingo."

"I meant every word I said that night. I told you that before and it still holds true."

The smile faded from her lips as her expression changed, a mask sliding over her emotions.

"What is it, Lilly?" Jacob's stomach sank at her steely expression.

"If I ask you a question, will you answer me honestly?"

Shit. "Of course." He swallowed against the growing lump in his throat.

Lilly inhaled deeply as if willing herself the strength to continue. "Have you slept with Victoria?"

Fucking hell. Jacob considered lying but what was the point? She would see right through his falsehood with the same ease she saw through every other excuse he created. "Ever?"

She rolled her eyes. "Don't play cute. Just answer the question, Jacob."

He was so screwed. "But you already know the answer, don't you?" His words were flat, deflated, much like his heart was quickly becoming.

"I want to hear it from you."

His throat constricted as his food threatened to reappear. He didn't want to utter the words—not to Lilly. Saying them aloud only further substantiated how wrong he'd been and how poorly he'd behaved. "She pushed me into a corner, threatened my career and yours...it didn't mean anything, Lilly."

When the flush took over her face and the tears filled Lilly's eyes, Jacob felt like a worthless heel. He was witnessing firsthand how his selfishness and misguided ambition had hurt the one person he swore he'd protect.

After several moments of silence, Lilly spoke, her eyes averted. "If she didn't mean anything, why should I believe I did?"

Jacob's heart hit the pavement. "Every touch, every word, every thought I've had about you has been real. You're more real than anything I've ever experienced in my life. If you'll just give me another chance—"

"To what? Break my heart again? I don't want to believe your promises, Jacob. They're too painful. Besides, I'd be an idiot to believe you weren't involved with one—or all—of those women you've been photographed with."

"Lilly, I'm not involved with any of them. I promise. You have to believe me." Jacob's heart raced as his mind scrambled to find a way out of the situation.

"Why?"

"I've never lied to you, Lilly."

"You've never willingly disclosed the full truth either."

The moment was broken by a knock on the door. Who in the world could be interrupting this moment, of all moments? "Shit, don't go anywhere. It's probably housekeeping."

Jacob strode to the door, jerking it open and starting with surprise. "Jackie? What are you doing here?"

Jackie played a minor role in the film and a major role offscreen with any man willing to share her bed. She'd set her sights on Jacob since day one, but he put her firmly in her place. He wanted no part of her escapades, his heart—and body—were not up for grabs. "We're going skinny dipping. Shh, we're not technically allowed but one of the hotel managers is unlocking the west pool area for us. Come on, it'll be fun."

Oh Christ, she was drunk…and loud. "I'm in the middle of an important phone call but have fun. Don't get arrested." He started to close the door, but she stopped it with the heel of her hand.

"Jacob don't be a stick in the mud! You had fun the last time! Come play with me again! I promise I'll make it worth your while."

That did it. Jacob grabbed her arm and steered her further into the hall, closing the door behind him. He could not afford for Lilly to hear the drunk rantings of a girl with a crush. "I'm on the phone, Jackie. I'm not coming with you tonight or any other night. Now go."

He walked back into the room, ignoring the knocks coming from the very persistent Jackie and returned to the computer. Lilly sat kicked back, an all-knowing and very pissed off look on her gorgeous features.

Perhaps if he played it off as nothing, she wouldn't be upset. After all, nothing *had* happened between them. He had gone to dinner with Jackie and some cast members once but left after an hour. That was the extent of his Greek escapades. "Sorry about that, Lilly."

"You're not doing anything with anyone in Greece, huh?"

"No, I'm not! There is nothing going on between Jackie and me—"

"You certainly have a thing for blondes." She pursed her lips, taking a swig of her drink. Jacob noticed she'd swapped her wine for whiskey, not a good sign.

"Wrong again. I have a thing for one very stunning and stubborn brunette—"

Lilly held up a hand. "Save it. I thought I would feel better knowing the truth, but it actually hurts worse now. I'm heading out for the evening, so—"

"But we're not done with our date. Lilly, please, nothing happened with that girl!"

"Pictures in magazines and now she's knocking on your door asking you to skinny-dip. You must think I'm very gullible. Remember before you left, I told you that everyone makes choices?"

The lump in his throat was now the size of a grapefruit and growing rapidly. "Yes."

"You made yours, but I didn't want to believe it. I didn't want to see the truth. I suppose, in your way, you care about me but only on your timeline, and that's not good enough for me."

"I care about you *all* the time."

"Really?" she asked with stifled sincerity.

He bit his cheek, trying to rein in the emotions threatening to spill out. What a disaster. "More than you can possibly imagine."

"Would you like to know what I want from love?" Lilly leaned forward, moving closer to the screen.

"Absolutely. Name it, and it's yours."

"I want a man who adores me. A man who makes me feel beautiful, like I'm the only woman in the world he desires. I want him to be proud to stand by my side. I want him to awaken feelings in me that I never knew existed." She blinked back tears. "Am I foolish romantic? Do you think that man exists?"

"I know he does." His voice was barely a whisper.

"I hope he finds me soon because my heart is tired. Goodnight Jacob, thank you for the food."

Lilly disconnected the call and Jacob slumped back in his seat, mentally and emotionally exhausted.

The last several weeks he had chipped away at the wall she built around her heart, a wall to keep him at bay. He thought he'd made progress but after tonight, he realized he had barely cracked the mortar.

Perhaps he was an emotional moron, incapable of deciphering a woman's needs or following through on them. He certainly made a mess of things with Lilly.

Jacob dialed Miriam and bribed her with Ouzo to join him in the hotel lounge. She strolled in twenty minutes later, clad in sweats and a knowing smirk.

"What did you do this time?"

"I'm an utter fuck-up." Jacob related the evening to Miriam, who shook her head, a mixture of amusement and exasperation on her face.

"You're a smart man but an utter idiot where Lilly is concerned. Granted, Ms. Fancy Pants—or lack thereof—showing up and asking you to cavort naked didn't help matters."

"I thought the dinner date and the lock made my intentions clear, Miriam. It was as if Lilly couldn't even fathom that I was serious about loving her."

Miriam shot him a deep stare, clicking her tongue against her teeth. "Have you apologized for what happened?"

"What happened?" Jacob echoed.

"Yes, fucking Victoria. Have you apologized for that debacle?"

"I told her it didn't mean anything."

"That's not an apology. That's an excuse."

Her words reverberated through his being. She was right. He had never apologized to Lilly for the heart-wrenching treatment she endured...because of him.

Apparently, Miriam wasn't done heaping on the torture. "Let's look at this piece by piece. You wine and dine Lilly, but conveniently forget to tell her about your business arrangement with Victoria, which precedes to blow up in your face about thirty seconds after you consummate your relationship with Lilly. Victoria gives you an ultimatum, and you choose *her* instead of Lilly—"

Jacob raked his hand over his head. "It was the wrong decision."

"No shit. But it's still the one you chose. You were given options and Lilly came out the loser." She held up her hand to stop Jacob before he interrupted. "Then, almost immediately you realized your decision was utter crap and you wanted Lilly back. But it doesn't work like that! You can't muck up in such a manner and then expect to sweep your steaming pile of crap under the rug. The stench remains because you didn't take the time to clean up the mess you made."

"Enough with the analogies, Miriam." Jacob groaned, swigging down his glass of Ouzo. "Is it too late? Is that what you're telling me?"

Miriam released a huff of resignation and patted her friend's hand. "It's never too late to say you're sorry. No matter what else happens, you can't expect Lilly to move forward until you've cleared the path."

"Why am I such a bloody idiot? I had an opportunity to build something real with Lilly. She loved me back. Lilly's not a woman you leave, she's a woman you worship and adore."

"Are you telling me or signing up for the job?"

Jacob straightened, pouring another glass of Ouzo. "I'm winning her back, even if I have to crawl on my hands and knees all the way to London."

Miriam chuckled. "Nice to see the humble side of Jacob Edmonton. I wasn't certain it existed."

"I don't think it did, before her. No one's ever made me strive to be a better man. Only Lilly. She deserves that—and more."

"Now that is something any woman would like to hear. Good luck."

Jacob furrowed his brow.

"You're going to need it."

Lilly

L illy dragged her ass into work the next morning, feeling emotionally and mentally unprepared after the last few days. The death of her patient remained fresh in her mind and the confirmation of Jacob's extracurricular activities was the final nail in the coffin. Although she presumed he was bedding a plethora of gorgeous vixens, the mental image of him cavorting naked with that blonde nymph was more than she could bear.

She had reached a difficult—but necessary—decision. She was cutting all ties with Jacob and moving on with her life. She may have to leave her heart behind as it threatened revolt, but her head knew what was best for the rest of her, sanity included.

With a deep breath she entered the critical care unit. Sabina looked up as she walked in, rushing around the counter to her side.

"How are you feeling, luv?" she asked, pulling her close.

It was amazing how therapeutic an embrace from a genuine friend felt. "Better, thanks."

"Are you headed to your office?"

"I was going to round the units. Did you need something?"

Sabina wrapped an arm around Lilly's shoulder, turning her in the direction of her office. "Let's go in here first."

"O-kay." She spotted Ben out of the corner of her eye, falling into step right behind them, a small smile on his lips. She dug her heels in, halting all forward movement. "What's going on?" she asked, turning to face her friends. "Don't bother making up some lame excuse either. I'm in no mood."

"Grumpy, isn't she?" Ben chortled, ruffling her hair.

Lilly jerked back, her aggravation mounting. "I'm serious."

Sabina guided her to the office door. "We know, which is why we knew this"—she swung open the door—"would make you smile."

Inside were several bouquets of every type of flower imaginable, in all shades of the spectrum. It smelled like an English garden inside her tiny office. "What in the world?" Lilly turned to Ben and Sabina, a smile crossing her face. "You two bought me flowers?"

"I wish we could take credit, but they're not from us," Sabina stated, leading Lilly to a chair in front of a computer.

"Then who—"

Sabina motioned to the screen, and within seconds Jacob appeared. At first Lilly wanted to throw a vase at his face—virtual or no—but something in his expression, his eyes especially, gave her pause.

Without a greeting to Jacob, Lilly looked over her shoulder. "Can you give us a moment please?"

"Actually, I wanted them here, too. I know how much they mean to you."

Wonderful. Apparently, he wanted their dirty laundry aired to everyone. So much for the vestiges of privacy. "What are all these for?" She motioned at the myriad of flowers around the room.

Jacob released a chuckle, looking down as if gathering his courage. "There are seven bouquets."

Lilly raised her brow, her jaw twitching. "I can count."

He took a loud inhale, releasing it slowly. "One for each of the weeks that I owed you an apology."

Her heart—and time—stopped with his words. She hadn't heard him correctly, was he apologizing...to her? "What did you say?"

His blue eyes were bright with emotion as he took another fortuitous breath. "I'm sorry, Lilly."

She wasn't going to cry; she wasn't going to cry—shit. "What are you sorry for?"

"I'm sorry for so many things."

She blinked back tears. "Such as?" She could make it easy on him, the flowers were lovely, but he deserved to squirm a bit.

"I'm sorry I didn't tell you the truth of my arrangement with Victoria. I should have told you everything, from the very beginning, not let you find out secondhand."

Lilly nodded, a bit deflated. Although she was thankful for the apology, she had hoped it would be a bit more personal. "Thank you."

"I'm not done."

She could only manage a nod.

"I'm sorry I ever made you feel like you were less important, because you're the most significant thing that's ever happened to me, Lilly. I'm sorry I broke your heart"—he paused to collect himself, another deep breath—"and I'm sorry I didn't realize how lucky I was to have a woman like you in my life."

Tears broke free and ran down her cheeks, likely smearing her makeup to a point of no return. No matter. This was far more important. "I needed to hear that, Jacob."

He smiled, but there was no joy in it, only sadness and regret. "I'm still not done, angel. I should have apologized immediately for what I did to you after we made love. I took this exceptional moment and destroyed it."

Lilly nodded as the tears continued to fall. His words had unleashed a torrent.

"But mostly, I'm sorry I made the wrong choice—"

"What?" Her heart caught at his words.

"I should have chosen you. I was a coward, Lilly. I'm sorry I wasn't brave enough to love you the way you deserve to be loved." His hand reached out, touching the screen. "I'm sorry for everything, angel."

Sabina touched Lilly on the arm, offering her a tissue. Lilly wiped her face and eyes, releasing a small chuckle. "I probably look like a raccoon."

"You're beautiful, Lilly. So much more beautiful that you'll ever realize. You're likely wondering why I asked Ben and Sabina to stay in the room. They deserve an apology too, because of my choices and decisions, they had to help you pick up the pieces. They love you, Lilly. I know sometimes you feel alone, but you're not. You're so loved."

Sabina and Ben wrapped their arms around Lilly and she choked back a sob. It seemed his words had broken a wall in her heart and the pain poured out from inside.

Jacob raked his hand over his head, a rueful smile on his lips. "I know you have a hard time accepting gifts, so I wanted to do something on your behalf."

Lilly wiped her eyes with the heel of her hand, makeup be damned. "What did you do?"

"I made a donation to a few local shelters, in your name. The monies will buy food and medications for the animals there." His smile widened. "Don't cry, angel."

"Fat chance of that," Lilly snorted. "I'm a mess. That's amazing. Thank you, Jacob."

"One last thing. I know it's hard being so far from your parents' grave. I've paid for someone to bring them flowers every week for the next year."

That did it, the dam busted loose and Lilly laid her head on the desk, weeping.

"Get it out, sweetie. Get it out," Sabina murmured, rubbing her back. "You're a better man than I gave you credit for, Jacob."

"I'm not a good enough man for Lilly, I know that now, but I'm blessed in that she inspires me to strive for more."

Lilly lifted her head, offering Jacob a small smile. "You were always more than enough, Jacob. Thank you for this." She swiveled in her chair. "Can you two give us a few minutes?"

Sabina and Ben exited, and Lilly turned back to the screen, wiping her face which she surmised was red, blotchy and streaked with mascara.

"I'd do anything for you, Lilly. I'm sorry it took me so long. I'm a bit daft in the whole love and relationship department."

Lilly chuckled. "To err is human—"

"To forgive, divine," Jacob finished the Alexander Pope quote, his gaze never wavering. "Will you forgive me, Lilly?"

It's amazing the levity that an apology brings with it. Lilly felt lighter than she had in months. "I forgive you, Jacob. Do you mind if I give these bouquets to the hospice patients? It'll brighten their day."

"I figured you would want to do something along those lines, and that's fine. But Lilly, one day I'm going to give you a gift so dear to me and if you don't want it, I'm not sure what I'll do."

Lilly sat back in her chair, her heart racing. It wasn't an admission of a commitment, but it sure sounded like something along those lines. "I'll always want it," Lilly breathed.

His face lit up with a smile. "I really hope so. I have to go, I'm needed on set, but never forget that you are the most exquisite soul I've ever met. I'm trying to be the man you believe me to be, just give me a chance to prove it to you."

Holy shit, he was asking for a reconciliation, wasn't he? Was she reading too much into it? Could she let her heart take the lead? Screw logic, love wins. "Okay."

His smile widened. "Okay?"

Lilly nodded, returning his smile. "Okay."

"Thank you. God, I wish you were here, Lilly. We're supposed to discover Greece together, remember?"

"I do."

"Maybe you could—" A voice behind him interrupted the moment and he held up his hand in response. "I've got to go, but we'll talk later, okay? Goodbye, angel."

Lilly pressed a kiss to her fingers and then the screen. "Goodbye, Jacob."

Lilly walked into the pub the following evening, just in time to wave at Ben as he wound his way around patrons on his way back to the booth, where

Enrique was already seated.

"TGIF," Ben exclaimed, setting down a tray of drinks.

It had been a rough week, and Lilly welcomed time to unwind with her friends. It also allowed her a distraction from Jacob. Although his ministrations the other day were over the top in the romance department, his proclamations were still vague. He hadn't outright asked about reconciling and the more she thought about things, the more questions arose.

Why hadn't he asked her directly? What was the holdup? Was she reading his intentions wrong, again? She didn't think she could handle looking like a world-class fool for a second time, especially not with the same man.

It didn't help that a new crop of photos with that blonde nitwit had been published. Lilly thought she'd never see the day when she scanned tabloids like a gossip monger—what was this man doing to her?

"To good drinks and great friends. Salud." Enrique held up a glass, snapping Lilly from her reverie.

Lilly took a moment to examine his face, watching how his eyes crinkled when he smiled. Enrique was definitely a catch, although rumors were rampant throughout the hospital that the Spanish surgeon was once again romancing Emma, his golden-haired barrister.

"Cheers," Lilly reiterated, downing the whiskey shot, a bit dribbling past her lips. "So much for grace. That pretty much sums up the week." Embarrassed, she swept her tongue over her lower lip at the exact same time Enrique's thumb brushed the alcohol away.

The result was a highly erotic gesture that left everyone at the table silent and staring. Lilly flushed to the tops of her ears, dabbing at the spot with her napkin. "Thank you."

The surgeon's eyes darkened, and Lilly found it difficult to meet his gaze. Just as suddenly, he called over the bartender and ordered another round. "Would you like another drink, Lilly?"

"Please." She motioned to Enrique's face. "I like the beard."

Enrique leaned back against the booth, his arm slung over the seat, his fingertips brushing Lilly's shoulder. "I wasn't sure about it at first; itched like hell for the first week. I think it grew in well."

"You look very handsome."

Something changed in Enrique's expression at Lilly's statement, but the appearance of his tall, willowy blonde cut their conversation short. Lilly hadn't seen Emma since the night of Janie's surgery, but it was apparent as she snuggled in close to Enrique, that the woman was still smitten with him.

Lilly noted Enrique's stony expression, seemingly in contradiction to the bevy of rumors churning at work. Emma's sudden arrival appeared to be unwelcome.

Emma turned her blue-eyed gaze to Lilly. "Lilly, isn't it?" Her greeting was cordial, but her eyes flashed a warning—stay away from my man.

Lilly nodded, forcing a smile. "Nice to see you again, Emma."

"What are you doing here, Emma? I thought you had meetings tonight." Enrique's voice was strained, his posture stiff as a board.

"I changed my plans. I wanted to see you. It's been a week since we had that dinner—and dessert—at my flat." Emma wrapped her hand around the surgeon's arm, and Lilly saw Enrique's jaw clench.

"Come to the bar with me," Ben demanded, tugging Lilly on the arm.

Lilly excused herself and followed Ben; feeling conflicted as she watched Emma grab Enrique's face and kiss him on the cheek.

"Earth to Lilly." Ben waved another shot in front of her nose. "You look like you could use it."

"Do I look *that* bad?"

Ben laughed. "No, but you could cut the tension with a knife at the table. Best to let Enrique handle that situation. How's life otherwise?"

"It's been a rough week, but you know that already."

"I suppose the tabloids aren't helping matters." Ben sipped his drink, his gaze focused across the bar.

"You mean with his little blonde plaything?" Lilly held her breath, perhaps he knew more about the situation, maybe he'd read a different tabloid.

"Blonde plaything? No, this was about some new relationship—shit—"

There it was, the words Lilly dreaded hearing. She grabbed onto the bar to steady herself, afraid her body might not keep her upright otherwise. "Relationship? What the hell are you talking about?"

"You mean you don't know?"

Lilly's heart lurched. What in the world was Ben babbling on about? "I don't know anything about any relationship. What the fuck are you talking about?"

Ben offered up a sheepish smile. "Bugger. I am so good at putting my foot in it. Lilly, don't—"

Too late. Lilly grabbed out her phone and googled Jacob Edmonton's name. She had to know what new gossip was circulating. Her heart seized when she saw the stories—all seven of them—each from a leading rag mag: photos of Jacob cavorting with a radiant brunette in Greece. The headlines ranging from "Secret Lovers" to "Destination Wedding" all intimated a marriage was imminent for the Hollywood star.

Lilly felt sick. "Oh my God."

"Who knows if they're even true?"

Lilly's eyes widened at her friend. "Seven of them are spouting the same lie? Seven? Seven!" Her voice rose, attracting attention.

"Shh, please try to calm down."

Lilly buried her face in her hands, groaning. "I'm such an idiot. Jacob has been trying to tell me about this amazing woman that he's so in love with, but I kept avoiding the conversation." Lilly downed the rest of the shot, ordering another. "I stupidly thought he was talking about me. All that apologizing and saying he wasn't worthy of me, I thought we were headed for reconciliation. Christ, I'm a moron!"

"It might be a bunch of garbage. Spouted and recirculated lies."

But deep down, Lilly's didn't believe that. S*tupid, silly Lilly. You always knew he would never choose you.* "No, I think there's truth in this story. God, all this time, I'm pining for him and he's falling in love. I'm going to become a nun. I'm done with men."

"You're not Catholic."

"Who cares?"

"Luv, you don't know if this is just a flirtation or an easy lay. His feelings towards you may not have changed in the slightest."

Lilly scoffed. "He fucks me in a bathroom and cavorts with her on a Grecian beach…I can read the writing on the wall."

"He also sent all those flowers not two days ago and apologized—profusely I might add—in front of me and Sabina. Didn't he mention you joining him in Greece?"

"Likely to meet this wonder woman of his," Lilly groaned. "He apologized for not treating me the way I deserved. In hindsight, I see he was actually apologizing for not loving me. The flowers were just padding for my crash landing back to reality." She tortured herself by looking at the pictures again. He was tanned and golden, wearing a genuine smile on his face. "They look good together."

Ben examined the photos. "Eh, he looks bloated."

Lilly smirked. "You're a liar, but I love you for it. I guess it's time to close the book on that romance, if you can even call it a romance. It was bound to happen sooner or later, I just didn't think it would happen *this* soon."

"Find out the whole story before you go picking out china patterns for them."

Lilly nodded, the gears in her mind spinning. She needed the truth, painful as it may be, and the pain would only increase the longer she avoided the dreaded discussion.

"But in my opinion, I still think you should pursue Enrique."

Lilly's eyes widened. "Are you mad? Have you failed to notice the beautiful woman hanging on him?"

"I think you're prettier than Emma."

Lilly scoffed. "Nice try. Not even close."

"Enrique agrees with me. He is not happy she showed up tonight."

Lilly snuck a peek over her shoulder, it appeared Enrique and Emma were embroiled in a heated conversation. "I wonder what they're arguing about."

"Who knows?" Ben shrugged. "My money is on the fact that she wants to date him again and he doesn't want any part of it."

"I thought they were dating." At that moment, Lilly caught the surgeon's eye and spun her barstool in the opposite direction.

"They're not dating, just shagging." Ben's gaze remained fixated across the room.

Lilly sputtered her whiskey. "Will you stop? They're looking right at us." She took another drink and stared at her vague reflection in the bar counter. "Men and their ability to compartmentalize sex. It makes it so much easier. I can't fault his taste, although I do wish she was a little less gorgeous, perhaps an unsightly mole or birthmark somewhere."

Ben laughed, ordering another shot. "Would you expect anything less from Enrique? He's pretty fit himself."

"He certainly is, and the beard definitely ups the ante." Ben began clearing his throat, but Lilly ignored him. "He's certainly easy on the eyes, even if he is taken."

Lilly felt a presence behind her, then lips tickling her ear. "If I'd known how popular the beard would be, I would have grown it a long time ago."

"Kill me now," Lilly muttered. "How much of that did you hear, Dr. Torres?"

Enrique's fingers pushed her hair away from her neck, causing Lilly to tremble. "All of it."

Lilly took a deep breath and turned to face the smirking surgeon. "I stand by my word. You're gorgeous, and I'm sure your girlfriend agrees."

Enrique sobered at her remark, leaning in to place a soft kiss on her ear. "She's not my girlfriend, and I think you know that."

"Fuck buddy, whatever. You know," Lilly directed her comment to both men, the effects of the shots loosening her tongue, "I think I'm done waiting around, pining for true love. I need to get laid."

47

Enrique's jaw dropped as Ben choked on his drink.

"What? You guys can do it. Why can't I?"

Ben hugged his friend. "Because that isn't your style, and that's why we love you. It's the whiskey talking."

"No, it's the hormones talking." Lilly rolled her shoulders, laughing. "Don't look so stricken, Enrique. I wouldn't actually do it."

"I would hope not, a beautiful woman like you needs to be careful." He leaned in to whisper in her ear. "Not that I haven't thought about kissing every inch of your body."

Lilly grabbed onto the edge of the bar to keep from sliding out of her barstool, uncertain which had kicked in—the shot or Enrique's words. "What did you say?"

"You heard me, and don't look so surprised."

Lilly stared into his handsome face, willing her body to feel one iota of the fireworks she felt with Jacob. Hell, a sparkler would be acceptable at this point.

"Yes, what *did* you say, Enrique?" A voice over Lilly's shoulder bit out, and she turned to see Emma glaring holes into Enrique's visage.

"I was speaking to Lilly." His voice was calm, but his eyes blazed at Emma.

"What's the situation between you two? Are you fucking him?" Emma growled.

Lilly's jaw dropped. "What? No! We work together."

"That's a load of bollocks, you two are sleeping together."

"We are—" Lilly began, but Enrique didn't give her a chance to finish.

He grabbed Emma's arm, his jaw twitching. "That's enough, do you hear me? If you can't handle me speaking to Lilly, then you need to leave."

Emma looked at the ground, a flush covering her cheeks. "I'm sorry, I just got upset when I saw you two together." She swung her gaze to Lilly. "I apologize."

Well that was the least sincere apology I've ever received, Lilly thought to herself but nodded in reply, watching Enrique escort Emma back to the booth, leaving Lilly mortified and alone with her highly amused best friend.

"I saw that one coming."

"Nothing's going on between us, I hate to disappoint her. I'm too busy nursing a shattered heart, compliments of Jacob fucking Edmonton."

Apparently, Ben was far more interested in recent events than discussing Jacob for the umpteenth time. "What did Enrique whisper to you?"

"Nothing." Lilly knew she was bright red and hung her head with embarrassment.

Ben leaned in, lifting her chin. "Did he offer his services?"

"Unfortunately, no."

"Would you like me to speak with him about renegotiations?"

"Not a word," Lilly countered, grabbing his collar, but Ben's laughter only increased. "I think I'm done for the evening. Any longer and I'm sure to either wind up in a fist fight or embarrass myself to a point where I'll never show my face in public again."

"Don't leave, come on, hang out with me. Don't make me pull the 'I'm so sad because my boyfriend dumped me' card." Ben's eyes widened, and he forced a sad face, his lower lip pooching out.

Lilly cracked up, he always knew how to turn her mood around. "Only if you maintain that face for the entire evening."

The next couple of hours passed with laughter and conversation. Emma was pleasant, although Lilly didn't know if it was forced by Enrique's hand or genuine. Not that it mattered. Emma was obviously besotted with Enrique, but Lilly knew he didn't return her affections. Still, she kept his bed warm, and that idea made Lilly cringe. She wished casual sex was an option for her, but she simply wasn't built that way.

Lilly felt Enrique's gaze on her several times from across the table, his dark eyes speaking what his mouth wouldn't, but Lilly couldn't allow herself to reciprocate. His social situation was too similar to Jacob's, countless, adoring women lined up to suck his cock and jump his bones. Lilly would stand as much of a chance with Enrique as she had with Jacob.

"Folks, it's been a blast, but my bed is calling me," Ben stated, standing and grabbing his coat.

Lilly's head shot up at his sudden departure, realizing it was time for her to leave to avoid being the proverbial third wheel. "It is getting late. Emma, Enrique, have a wonderful evening."

She was unlocking her car when she felt a hand on her arm. "Enrique?"

"You forgot this." He handed her a scarf.

Lilly felt a slight disappointment as she gazed up at his handsome features, had she missed out on a great opportunity? "It's not mine but thank you regardless."

His dark gaze held hers, his eyes flaring with desire. "I know it isn't, but I wanted to speak with you."

"Okay." Lilly waited a few seconds, but Enrique remained silent, except for his dark stare that screamed volumes. "How are things with you and Emma? She seems absolutely over the moon for you—"

"I don't want to talk about Emma," Enrique whispered, his hands cupping her face as his lips captured hers.

This kiss was not like the last, and Lilly realized rumors of his prowess were not exaggerated. His tongue twirled around hers as he pushed her against the car, his body holding her captive. His hands became more presumptuous, moving down her body to wrap around her hips.

The blast of a car horn made them jump apart; an uncertain look in his eyes that Lilly knew matched her own. He looked rattled, running his hand over his beard.

"I'm sorry," Lilly began, pursing her swollen lips.

His eyes darkened with purpose. "What in hell are you sorry about? I'm not sorry, I only want to kiss you again."

"We can't. You're dating Emma."

"I'm not dating her, Lilly!"

"You're sleeping with her, that's enough. I won't be that person."

The words pierced Enrique's armor, and he banged the roof of the car before giving her a peck on the cheek. "God damn it. Goodnight Lilly."

Lilly drove home, immediately pouring herself a glass of whiskey and drawing a bath. Sobriety was not an option at the moment.

"Why does it have to be so difficult?" she yelled aloud.

Her phone rang, and she grabbed it without looking. "Hello, luv."

"Janie! How are you?"

"Better than you. What's up? I just got your message."

"I wanted to know if you were up for a cocktail with the gang, but we made it an early night."

"What's going on, Lilly?" Janie could see right through her false calm.

"Enrique had a date. That gorgeous barrister I told you about."

"Do you like him? He's always liked you."

Lilly groaned. "I'm in love with your brother, but that's a lost cause. I saw photos of him with some gorgeous brunette down in Greece. Apparently, *she's* the woman he's so crazy about."

Janie was silent for a few moments. "Woman in Greece?"

"If the headlines are to be believed, they'll marry soon. And I stupidly thought Jacob had feelings for me. Fuck my life." Lilly face planted onto her bed, wishing she could stay there forever.

"You and my brother need to have a serious conversation."

"Why? So I can listen to him wax poetic about his perfect woman? The photos were painful enough."

Janie sighed. "I'll have a chat with Jacob—"

"Don't, please. Just leave it alone. I built up our reconciliation strictly in my own mind, he never directly stated anything resembling that idea. But that's not the only highlight of tonight."

"I hear a juicy snippet heading my way," Janie chortled.

"I was walking to my car and Enrique came after me…to return a scarf that wasn't mine. He claimed he needed to speak to me."

"What happened?"

"He kissed me instead."

"Holy shit!"

Lilly chuckled at her friend's boisterous surprise. "I know, shocked the hell out of me too."

"I thought he had a date?"

"He claimed Emma wasn't his girlfriend. I told him I couldn't walk that path regardless."

Janie huffed, obviously shocked. "Is he a good kisser?"

"Janie!"

"Is he?" Janie pressed.

"Yes, but all I thought about was Jacob—how he tasted and felt and—"

"That's my brother, too much information."

"Sorry. I just miss him." Lilly choked up. "But I know I have to move on." She took a deep breath and steeled herself to the truth. "I'm okay, I'm done pining for Jacob. Time to find someone who loves me back. My bath is calling me, talk soon."

As Lilly sunk into the warm waters, the tears flowed, releasing her confusion and pent-up frustration.

CHAPTER FOUR

Jacob

'What in the hell have you done now?'

Jacob stared at the single line text message from his sister. How diabolical to be so vague. He leaned back in his seat, admiring the view of the moon and sent off an equally obscure reply.

'Care to elaborate?'

'How many times do you plan on hurting Lilly?'

Jacob dialed his baby sister, enough of this texting nonsense. "What in the hell do you mean?"

"I thought you were in love with Lilly. Why bother begging me not to encourage Lilly to date when you're cavorting with some bimbo in Greece?" Janie seethed at her brother.

Jacob's mind reeled at his sister's accusation. "What bimbo?"

"The tabloids have pictures of you with some woman and they claim you're getting married; and it's not just one tabloid, it's all of them. So, what the hell is going on?"

Jacob pulled up the internet and searched his name. He normally never bothered because the array of bullshit about him was mind-boggling. His eyes widened when he saw all the headlines about his new love, and then he laughed.

"I'm glad you find the situation amusing. Lilly doesn't share your sentiment."

Jacob sobered at Janie's words. "It's amusing because I am not involved with that woman, except in a professional capacity. She's my director, Miriam, who is, in fact, encouraging my reconciliation with Lilly. People likely overheard me discussing how I plan to marry Lilly if she'll have me."

"Oh, well that makes this situation even worse."

Jacob's stomach flipped. "I would think it would make it better since it isn't true."

"But you're still in love with Lilly?"

"Is that a serious question? Why are you asking?" No reply. "Janie, why?"

"I don't want you to get angry—"

"I'm pretty much already there, so spill it."

"Enrique kissed Lilly tonight."

A wave of nausea overcame Jacob. "You saw them?"

"No, Lilly told me."

Jacob chucked his mobile across the suite, releasing a torrent of obscenities. He knew he should never have listened to Janie and Miriam about taking things slow, now Lilly was in the arms of another man.

He heard his sister yelling his name through the phone and snatched it to his ear. "Why are you telling me this?"

"Because she told me she's in love with you, but she doesn't think you reciprocate those feelings. Time to step up before it's too late. She's ready to give up."

"Did she kiss him back?"

"Don't ask me, talk to Lilly about it."

Any plans of retiring early went out the window with Janie's call. Instead, Jacob sat drinking alcohol like milk, half in the bag after several glasses of Ouzo. He knew he'd regret his actions in the morning, but at the moment, he couldn't care less.

He didn't want to call Lilly, the mental image of her lips against that surgeon's made him want to punch holes in the wall. Eventually, the need for answers became too great, and he dialed her number.

"Hey." Lilly's voice was flat, emotionless.

The copious amount of alcohol Jacob consumed eradicated his filter, so he plowed right into the discussion. "You kissed Enrique. Was it everything you hoped it would be?"

"Wow, good news travels fast."

"I would think it would be great news for you." He sounded like an asshole extraordinaire, but no matter.

"And you would be wrong." Lilly paused for a response before she continued. "Is that why you called? To congratulate me?"

"I called to find out the truth."

"The truth? What do you care about the truth?"

Jacob's hands twitched as his internal boiler rose. "I know better than to believe lies published in tabloids!"

"You were the one who said they print the truth the majority of the time!" Her tone now matched his, this was bound to be a hell of a row.

"Not *this* time, Lilly."

Lilly scoffed in disdain. "What does it matter anyway? You look so happy in those pictures, I can see you're in love. Good for you. I'm trying really hard to be happy for you."

His anger drained as if someone pulled the stopper from a sink. "Lilly, you don't understand—"

53

She sniffled into the phone, she was crying. "You're right. I don't understand anything. I think it's best if we just move on from each other."

And like that, his world fell out. "You don't want to be friends anymore?" Jacob breathed.

"I do, but I don't know if I can. I'm really emotional after tonight. Can we talk tomorrow?"

Jacob didn't want the call to end. The defeat in her voice tormented him, but he realized their emotions were too raw to make any progress. "Promise me that we'll talk tomorrow? I have so much to tell you, so much I want to share with you."

"Can't wait." Another sniffle, each one chipping away at his heart. "Until tomorrow."

Jacob hung up the phone, wishing he could jump on a plane and fly straight into her arms. His sister was right, he had to pull out all the stops and make Lilly his, forever.

The next day Jacob's head felt like a sledgehammer and anvil were dueling, but he was the only loser. He downed a bottle of water and some aspirin before stepping into a scalding shower.

An hour later, an egg white omelet and another bottle of water had Jacob feeling almost human. Now it was time to call Lilly and make things right again.

"Good morning beautiful."

Lilly was still in bed, grumpy and grumbling from the moment the video chat connected. Her hair hung in a messy braid and she didn't have a drop of makeup on. Jacob thought she was the most beautiful woman he'd ever seen.

"What's good about it?" Lilly muttered, making Jacob chuckle. "And stop talking so loud."

"Hung over?"

"I'm beyond reprieve. When we agreed to speak today, I figured it might be after nine in the morning."

Jacob opened another bottle of water and took a swig. "I didn't want to wait. It was bad enough we went to bed angry."

"Are you angry at me?" Her voice sounded small and unsure.

Jacob paused, unsure how to reply without further damaging her feelings. "I'm not angry at you, I could never be angry with you. It just took me by surprise that you and Enrique—"

"Me and Enrique what?" Her brows furrowed, a look of disdained confusion crossing her features.

Jacob couldn't spit out the words, just the thought of speaking them aloud made him want to hurl. "I hated hearing about it."

Lilly averted her gaze, staring past the screen. "It was just a kiss, nothing else happened."

Just a kiss? He readied himself with a sarcastic retort but talked himself down; arguing wasn't going to solve anything except drive a larger wedge between them. "I hate the idea that he touched you, you're mi—" he stopped himself from finishing the statement, literally biting his tongue in the process.

He couldn't force Lilly's hand. Miriam was right, he had to woo her, had to show her why he was the better choice. *I'm buggered if that's the case.* "Can we forget about our argument last night? You're too important me. I don't want to spend what little time I have with you fighting."

A small giggle made his smile widen. "Sure, it wasn't exactly a night to remember. Friends again?"

Friends. He hated that word in regard to Lilly, but he knew she was scared and uncertain, and that he was to blame. "You are so much more than my friend. You're my light in the darkness, and you have no idea the depth of my feelings for you."

"Or mine for you."

Their gazes held, her words warming his heart. Christ, he wished she were there next to him. The things he would do to her, love her until she forgot her own name and certainly forgot about any surgeon pursuing her affections. "Go relax, beautiful girl and take it easy today. I miss you."

Jacob didn't rest on his laurels, despite his thumping head. He had to put his into action, and he knew just the person to help.

"Do you have any idea what time it is in England? Where's the fire?" Janie groaned into the receiver.

"I'm head over heels in love with Lilly."

Another groan. His sister was definitely *not* a morning person. "Tell me something I don't know."

"Who's that?" Audrey's muffled voice inquired in the background.

"It's Jacob. He's in love with Lilly."

"No shit. What's he going to do about it?"

Jacob cut into their conversation, realizing they might continue on for hours otherwise. "It's more than just love, Janie."

"Hold on, you're going on speaker phone for this confession."

Wonderful. Jacob hoped Audrey would find a shred of understanding in lieu of her usual scathing humor.

"You were saying?" Janie prompted, and he could hear the smirk in her voice.

He hated family sometimes, cheeky bastards. "I'm in love with Lilly. I can't stop thinking about her and I know she's the only woman for me. I want to marry her, Janie—and Audrey—and spend the rest of my life making her glad she chose me. I want a beautiful home together filled with scads of children—"

"Scads?" Audrey scoffed. "Don't know how Lilly will feel about birthing scads of children."

"Shush," Janie hissed. "Go ahead, Jacob."

"Scads or a few, as many as she'll give me. Or none, if that's her preference. I just need her, I need Lilly, and I have to pray she still needs me. I have a plan, but I'm so damn far away and I don't want to wait. Will you help me?"

He heard Janie and Audrey exchange a chuckle. "Jakey, with a proclamation like that, how could we say no?"

Lilly

anie held up two bags when Lilly opened the door the following Saturday, pushing herself and Elizabeth into the cottage, her face bubbling with excitement. "These are for you. Go put them on!"

Lilly examined the bags, all from high-end luxury stores along Bond Street, and shot Janie a questioning look. "What is all this? And who did you rob to pay for it all?"

"Never mind that, now go, we don't want to be late!"

"Don't want to be late!" Elizabeth echoed, giggling as Lilly scooped the five-year-old into a hug.

"I'll hurry, but only because Elizabeth insisted. Make yourselves at home." Elizabeth was playing with the cats and Janie was pouring tea by the time Lilly reached her bedroom door. She marveled at their friendship. It was as if she had known Janie her entire life and not a mere few months.

Lilly gasped when she dumped out the contents of the bags. Inside was a stunning burgundy Gucci dress, Louboutin heels, a fascinator from Philip Treacy and matching jewelry set from Cartier. "Holy shit! This is ten-thousand pounds worth of merchandise. Janie, get in here!"

Janie poked her head in the door. "You're not dressed."

"Seriously, did you steal this?" Lilly hissed, holding up the dress. "Is it rented? I'm way too clumsy for anything rented."

"The merchandise is paid in full, thank you very much. And no, I didn't buy it, but I followed strict instructions on what to purchase." She helped Lilly into the dress, her hands resting on her friend's shoulders.

The dress fit as if tailored to Lilly's frame, the elegant fabric hugging her curves. "I've never worn anything this expensive. Who bought this, Janie?"

Janie pretended to examine the bracelet. "Lilly, you know exactly who bought it. It's all part of Jacob's grand plan."

Lilly's heart fluttered. "What plan is that?"

"Remember your conversation about springtime in London? You told him you adored the flowers and the festivities, and Jacob said he wished he was here so he could take you to his favorite spots?" Lilly nodded, dumbfounded as Janie continued. "I'm his stand-in, along with Elizabeth, and we are taking you on a spring tour of London. Jacob planned the entire day, and if you don't hurry, we'll be late."

The ladies meandered through Eltham Palace and Gardens for the rest of the morning. Jacob rented the grounds for the day, granting them unlimited access, complete with a bottle of wine uncorked upon their arrival that cost more than Lilly's weekly salary. As they strolled to the courtyard, Lilly spotted a catered lunch and a cocktail trio playing instrumental music.

A server led them to a table, giving Elizabeth a bowl of cherries and the women a refill of their wine. The host brought over a monitor with a direct feed, and within moments Jacob appeared on the screen, standing against the backdrop of a Grecian seaport.

Lilly's breath caught at the sight of him. He looked every inch a movie star—tanned, toned, his hair lightened by the sun, and incredibly gorgeous.

He broke into a huge smile, gasping when he saw Lilly. "My God, you're exquisite."

Lilly blushed, running her hands along the material. "Hard not to be in clothing fit for royalty. It's lovely, I've never worn anything like this."

"It suits you." His gaze roamed over her body and Lilly felt her blush intensify. It felt like he was undressing her with his eyes—a poor substitute for the man's hands on her body—but she'd take it.

"I hope I don't spill anything on it so you can return it." Lilly meant it as a joke, but Jacob's brow furrowed.

"It's a gift, you're keeping it." He looked from Lilly to Janie. "Where's the necklace?"

"At home, I always wear this and I didn't want to take it off." Lilly pulled up the evil eye pendant, and he rewarded her with a radiant smile.

"I'm glad."

"This is beyond words. What in the world did I do to deserve this treatment?" Lilly beamed at the screen.

Jacob's voice was thick with emotion, his intense gaze daring her to look anywhere but at him. "The world is sunnier with you in my life, I'd walk through hell to protect you, and I'd do anything to make you smile."

And just like that, the butterflies swarmed around her heart, and Lilly welcomed their return. "You remembered what I said about love."

"I was listening more than you can possibly know, angel." He paused for a second. "En sa beauté gît ma mort et ma vie."

Lilly didn't speak French, but his words sent chills up her spine as if he'd revealed the most beautiful secret. She smiled shyly, biting her lip. "I don't know what that means."

"Yes, you do. Your heart understands every word." His eyes were deep blue pools, emanating emotion.

Lilly lost herself in his azure depths, and was startled when Janie cleared her throat, releasing a chuckle. "There are other people here too, big brother, in case you'd like to say hello."

Jacob smiled and greeted his sister and niece before explaining the agenda for the afternoon. "I've arranged a catered lunch with some of my favorite London foods, gluten-free of course, and some specially selected music. It's uncanny how the lyrics resonate with me now."

He addressed all of them, but his gaze never left Lilly's face as the musicians began playing.

Tears sprang to Lilly's eyes, and she smiled, her hand covering her mouth. It was her song—*their* song now, it seemed—and she fought back her overwhelming emotions. Turning back to the screen, she whispered, "Thank you."

"Anything for you, angel."

The song ended a few minutes later, and Lilly wiped her tears. Elizabeth hugged her, saying "Don't cry Lilly. The day is too beautiful to cry."

Lilly smiled radiantly, pulling the little girl onto her lap. "You're right, but these are happy tears, no sadness today."

Then Elizabeth asked a question with the seriousness only a five-year-old could possess. "You're happy because you love my uncle, don't you?"

Lilly felt herself blushing and looked at the screen, hoping Jacob hadn't caught his niece's question. But Jacob's eyes twinkled, he'd heard every word, and now he awaited her response.

She contemplated how to answer the question but realized that truth was always the best course. Taking a deep breath, Lilly replied, "I do love your uncle, Elizabeth, I love him very much."

Jacob looked elated at her statement, but despite his smile, he didn't respond to her declaration; a fact Lilly tried to ignore.

Jacob signed off a few minutes later, sending wishes of a beautiful afternoon for his three favorite girls.

Lilly stepped out of the limousine later that afternoon, slipping out from underneath Elizabeth, who had fallen asleep at her side. Once inside, she ran a bath, looking once more at the beautiful outfit Jacob had selected for the afternoon.

After soaking and ruminating for the better part of an hour, she sent Jacob a text; her favorite Rumi quote. *'The minute I heard my first love story, I started looking for you, not knowing how blind that was. Lovers don't finally meet somewhere. They're in each other all along.'*

Perhaps Jacob wasn't in love with her, and her romantic fantasies were

59

just that—fantasies—but they shared an exquisite bond nonetheless and she loved that man with every fiber of her being.

She wanted to be everything to him—friend, lover, wife, mother—and she was almost ready to confront him about his affections. *Almost.* Perhaps tonight, she could finally clear the air and know if his home was by her side or if his bed was warmed by that woman in Greece. For right now, she was content sharing some love with the man she adored.

CHAPTER FIVE

Jacob

It was after ten when filming wrapped for the night, but Jacob wasn't complaining; it was worth it for the twenty minutes he spent virtually with Lilly. Her declaration of love kept a smile on his lips the rest of the day, and he struggled to appear angry when necessary for his character's role. For once, acting any way other than thrilled was a true challenge.

Miriam asked him to join her for a late dinner, and they met at their local pavilion. A bottle of Ouzo sat on the table, awaiting his arrival.

Handing him a glass, Miriam inquired, "Did Lilly enjoy the garden tour of London?" She insisted that Jacob keep her abreast of each new development, and Jacob often wondered where the line between director and psychiatrist overlapped.

"It was wonderful. One moment, I need to charge my phone. The battery keeps dying." He plugged it in and waited for it to reboot, sipping his Ouzo. "She's so beautiful, Miriam."

"What's the long-term plan here, or have you gotten that far yet?"

Jacob chewed the inside of his lip. He had spouted off on more than one Ouzo-filled night how he planned to marry Lilly immediately, but he knew Miriam doubted his seriousness. "Same plan as before."

Miriam's brows raised, an amused smile on her mouth. "I wasn't certain if that was your heart or the Ouzo speaking. I'm glad it's the first one."

"Oh, I was drunk—on more than one occasion—but I was also completely in earnest. I'm going to marry her, Miriam. I just pray she says yes. I hope she still loves me."

"It seems fairly obvious she cares deeply about you. Are you waiting until you return to London—" Her question was interrupted by a chime on Jacob's phone, indicating he had a text message.

"What's the matter?" Miriam asked, looking at Jacob's awestruck face. She leaned over his shoulder, reading the text from Lilly and giving him a slight punch on the shoulder. "I told you, make her feel like the only woman in the world, and she'll fall in love with you again."

Jacob smiled as he reread the text. "Will you excuse me? I need to call Lilly." He hurried to the dock railing and dialed Lilly's number via video conference, his heart hammering.

"Good evening, sir," Lilly answered.

"Am I interrupting something?" Jacob asked, surprised by the activity in the background.

"We're going out in a little while. There's a Beltane celebration, and we want to check it out."

"Beltane, the pagan holiday of sex?" Just the idea of Lilly participating in anything remotely related to sex—and not involving him—made him slightly ill.

Lilly giggled, the husky sound washing over him. "That's one aspect of the holiday. Beltane is about sensuality, love, fertility and the welcoming of summer, but sex is also encouraged."

Jacob's stomach flipped. "Do you plan on partaking?" He wasn't sure how he would respond if she answered in the affirmative.

Lilly smirked. "To which part would you be referring?"

He reined in his aggravation, swallowing hard. "You know damn well which *part* I'm referring to, Lilly."

Another chuckle, this woman was enjoying his torture. "You're ridiculous." A knock sounded at her door, and Lilly excused herself to answer it. She returned a few moments later, and Jacob heard voices in the background. "Everyone's arrived, but they're going to have a drink first."

"Should I let you go? I didn't realize you had big plans tonight."

"I wouldn't have had big plans if I'd known about the garden this afternoon, but several people already committed to attending. They want to take my mind off these guys at work. There were these family members who were a bit boorish towards me the other day."

"Why didn't you say anything?"

Lilly looked sheepish. "I know how you worry about your friends, and I didn't want you to worry. Besides, they were removed from the premises."

"You're not just one of my friends," Jacob gritted out. "What did they say to you?"

"I suppose it started out innocently enough. They flirted—or attempted to flirt—with me, but when I rebuked their advances, they became angry. Far angrier than normal, in my opinion."

She wasn't telling him the full story and Jacob needed full disclosure. "Lilly, what *exactly* did these men say to you?"

Lilly cleared her throat, obviously uncomfortable with the direction of their conversation. "It was really only one of the men. His buddy seemed to be there as moral support for the asshole. They followed me to the car park."

"They followed you?" This was getting worse by the second.

"Thankfully the security guard was rounding when I entered with them on my tail. He heard their comments and had them removed."

"I'm going to ask one more time, Lilly. What did they say to you?"

Lilly looked away from the screen. "Jacob, please—"

"Tell me, angel. Tell me what these assholes said to you." Jacob's hand was white knuckled around railing, as if his body knew if he let go his anger would boil over.

"Choice comments about screwing me in different positions for when—not if—when they took their opportunity." Her voice was a mumbled whisper, her laugh bitter.

Jacob's blood pounded in his ears. "I want their names."

"This is why I didn't tell you. Hospital security handled it, and it's over. Okay?"

But it wasn't okay. The fact that men were harassing the love of his life was really fucking far from okay. Jacob was about to respond when Enrique wandered on frame, handing Lilly a glass of wine and kissing her on both cheeks.

Jacob bristled, noting that the kisses lingered longer than necessary. He also knew it was an intentional move when the doctor shot a snarky smile at the screen. "Mr. Edmonton, how is Greece? A long way from London."

"It certainly is."

Enrique draped his arm around Lilly's shoulder, his eyes daring the actor to say something. "Also, a long way from Lilly. You must miss her terribly. I'm so lucky to spend so much time with her."

Is it really illegal to hire an assassin, especially when the bloke was asking for it with his behavior? The thought ran through Jacob's mind as he muttered a reply, watching the surgeon move off frame. "How much time exactly do you two spend together?"

Lilly's eyes widened at the pointed question. "We work together, so we see each other almost every day."

"You seem to spend ample time together outside of the hospital, as well."

Lilly chose to ignore his last statement, scooping up the laptop. "I need to change, so you're coming into the bedroom with me." She flashed him a mischievous smile before laying the laptop on her bed and tossing a scarf over the camera. "Now we can chat while still maintaining my modesty."

"Screw your modesty," Jacob grumbled under his breath, his mind running a million miles a minute. "What's wrong with what you're wearing?" Now he sounded like her father, questioning her wardrobe choices.

"You want me to wear sweats to a party? Wouldn't that be sexy."

"I'd prefer you wear a potato sack, personally." *Fan-bloody-tastic, she's going to a sex festival with a doctor who wants nothing more than to shag her every which way since Sunday.*

"That would certainly be memorable, and not in a good way."

"Is something going on with you and Dr. Torres?" Jacob's attempt to sound nonchalant failed miserably.

"What a silly question, Jacob."

"That's not a no." Jacob shook his head in aggravation and willed the scarf to slip off the laptop. Lo and behold, the material slid, and he had a front-row seat for Lilly's unintentional striptease. She slipped off her bra, her full breasts bouncing as she headed to the closet, clothed only in a g-string that showcased her fantastic ass.

Jacob felt his cock hardening and wished to God he wasn't on a public pier for this display.

"Shit!" Lilly cried when she realized the scarf had slipped. She clutched her breasts, shooting him a dirty look. "Why didn't you tell me?"

"No way in hell was I was telling you, and I may stage a coup if you put that scarf back." What Jacob really wanted was to climb through the computer screen, throw Lilly on the bed, and lay kisses along her body until she screamed his name.

Lilly smiled at him, clothed only in her panties, her arm still across her breasts. "What's that grin for?"

Jacob smiled wickedly. "Just enjoying the view, and if you recall, I've seen—and kissed—every inch of your body before."

Lilly's cheeks flamed. "How could I forget? At least I knew you were looking…and licking." She hung her head, releasing a chuckle. "I'm so embarrassed."

"You have nothing to be embarrassed about, but it is about a million degrees here now. I'm so thrilled you're going to a sex festival with a man who's dying to have sex with you." The sarcasm dripped off his words.

"What are you talking about?" Lilly asked as she walked off frame.

"Dr. Torres, he's crazy about you." *And I will kill him if he places one finger on your body.*

Lilly came back into frame, a body-conscious dress covering her curves. "I'm certain you have a long line of adoring starlets to keep you company in Greece, should you get lonely. I doubt your bed is cold, Jacob."

Jacob stiffened. Lilly hadn't denied his statement. "Actually, it's near arctic temperatures at this point."

Something flickered in her wide brown eyes, and Jacob groaned inwardly when he recognized the emotion. She doubted him, doubted everything he said to her. "Seriously? Are you saying that to make me feel better?"

"I already told you, my heart is occupied with someone else, and she takes up every waking thought. I've tried to talk to you about it, but you change the subject every single time. It's like you don't want to know, and you still haven't denied anything is happening with Enrique."

Lilly's face paled, growing serious. "Can we change the subject?"

"Lilly!" Jacob released a frustrated huff—her emotional armor instantly in place when he tried to broach the topic of his romantic interest. He'd been so damn obvious about his affections, she had to know it was her, and she didn't want to talk about it…which meant she likely wasn't interested. *Damn it all, I'm too late, but she's too kind to want to hurt my feelings.*

She lay down on the bed, facing the laptop camera. "Let's talk about what an amazing man you are for arranging today and how much I love you for it."

Jacob's aggravation waned at her smile. Lilly's words warmed his heart. He couldn't be angry with her, even if she didn't return his feelings. He loved her that much and seeing her smile was worth every second of pain he'd endure if he was in love alone.

He touched the screen, tracing the outline of her lips. "You are so worth it." His voice grew thick. "I got your text, that quote was exquisite."

Lilly smiled, biting her lip. "It's my favorite Rumi quote. It made me think of you, and I wanted to share it. You're a different man from the one I met. You've become a complete romantic, and I adore seeing this side of you. You're not closed off anymore, Jacob; you're an open book."

God, he wished she was there right now, it was physically painful being this far apart from the woman he loved…the woman he never had the opportunity *to* truly love. "That's what love does to you. I never knew that until now."

A muscle twitched in her jaw, and he knew she was uncomfortable with the path this conversation was treading…again. "Love is the most amazing gift in the world. I want you to enjoy every second with her, you hear me?"

Jacob chuckled. "I wish I could, but she isn't here. I never miss an opportunity to spend time with her on the phone though."

Lilly's brows furrowed, as if she wanted to ask a question, but she opted against it. Instead, she offered up a soft smile that didn't quite reach her eyes. "That's not good enough for a man of your romantic quotient. If she's that special and you adore her that much, then get her down to Greece, don't waste another second."

Sometimes the direct path was the only path. "Then get on a plane,

Lilly." Jacob's eyes burned with desire, his hands trembling as he disclosed everything in those few words.

Lilly's jaw slackened, and a look of shock washed over her face, but her response was interrupted by a knocking on the door. Sabina burst in, saying their taxi had arrived. She looked between her friend and the screen, "Wait, Jacob, what?"

And then, the screen went black as his phone died. "Bloody hell, you've got to be kidding me!" Jacob yelled as he stomped back to Miriam, cursing the entire way.

"What in the world happened? I'm guessing it didn't go well?"

"I hate technology." He recapped the conversation, and Miriam burst out laughing.

"Talk about a pause while the jury considers their decision."

Jacob glared at his friend, glancing at his phone every few seconds. "You don't understand! She's going to a Beltane festival with a man desperate to sleep with her, and I have no idea if something is going on between them. She never really answered my question, nor did she have time to respond to my request for her to come here."

Miriam placed her hand on Jacob's arm. "Relax, the phone will reboot in the next five minutes."

After what seemed an eternity, his phone turned on. Jacob dialed Lilly's number, but it went to voicemail. "Damn, damn, damn." Looking up, Miriam shot him a sympathetic glance. "What if she is dating this surgeon and not telling me?"

"Remember what I told you a month ago? You have to respect her decisions, even if it means she's dating someone else."

"I can't handle that. I almost lost my shit when Enrique kissed her a couple weeks back. I can't stand the thought of him being anywhere *near* her."

"You didn't give her any option with you and Victoria, so I don't think you have much right to say anything."

He hated Miriam in that moment, hated her for being right. Even if Lilly hooked up with the surgeon, he had no right to say a damn thing.

"Let's not dwell on it, Jacob. There's nothing you can do about it now, aside from flying back to England."

"Is that an option?"

"Not if you want to keep your job," Miriam chuckled.

"It was worth a shot."

"I do like this side of Jacob Edmonton. This woman has been good for you."

Jacob disagreed with her words. Lilly wasn't good for him, she was essential for him. He couldn't lose her now, he just couldn't.

The remainder of the dinner passed in idle conversation, but Jacob's mind was in England, at a Beltane festival.

Jacob must have looked at his phone a thousand times by the time his head hit the pillow. He sent her one last text before falling into a fitful sleep.

'I can't wait any longer. We've skated around the subject but it's time we talked, full disclosure. You've changed the subject every time I try to bring up the woman I'm in love with, and I realize now you don't want to hear it, but I need to come clean to you, Lilly. You might be angry with what I have to say, but I can't carry this secret any longer. I need to speak with you, as soon as possible.'

Lilly

The Beltane Festival was an epic success, but Lilly's mind was preoccupied. Between Sabina's interruption and the call dropping, Lilly had no clue if she heard Jacob's words correctly, and her poor battered heart didn't dare hope for a miracle like Jacob's undying adoration.

"Snap out of it," Sabina handed her a drink, her face lit by the bonfires burning around them. "What's with you tonight?"

Lilly sighed, providing her friend with the abridged version of her conversation with Jacob, concluding with Sabina's inopportune disruption.

"My timing is bloody amazing." Sabina offered her friend a look of apology.

"I probably didn't hear him correctly."

Sabina looked her friend square in the face. "I'm sure you did. And stop looking so surprised, after all Jacob's done in the last few months? The flowers, masseuse, the garden afternoon and a boatload of designer duds? He's working hard to impress you."

"Wow, I can't believe I missed it. He wouldn't go to all this trouble unless..." Lilly's heart skipped. *Unless he's in love with me.*

"Be careful there, my darling friend. Let's not forget Jacob's reputation, or that debacle with Victoria before he left. I doubt his bed is cold in Greece."

Lilly groaned, her momentary elation crashing back into reality. "Thanks for that visual. But you're right, I'm being ridiculous, thinking Jacob Edmonton is in love with me. He likely feels guilty about how he treated me, trying to stave off some bad karma by being kind now." She choked out the final statement, covering her angst with a practiced smile.

Sabina hugged her friend. "I do think he has feelings for you, but I find it unlikely he's been celibate these past few months. Single men don't tend to pass up an easy piece of ass, and Jacob Edmonton has unending offers for sexual escapades."

"And to think, I thought you might make me feel better." Lilly used her sarcasm to lighten the mood, but her heart felt like a punching bag as she pictured Jacob banging a different blonde every night. "Every time I intimate that he's bedding starlets, he gets angry. Why would he lie? What's the point?"

"Do you think he'd admit to bedding a bevy of extras? He respects you. He doesn't want to taint your opinion of him." Sabina motioned to Enrique, standing near one of the bonfires, women circling him like sharks. "Now he is the type of man you should be pursuing. He's crazy about you and he's here. Have a little fun with a fine-looking surgeon!"

"That fine-looking surgeon is sleeping with an equally fine-looking blonde barrister. He's not lily white either, Sabina."

"Shows what you know." Sabina swigged her drink, flashing her friend a huge grin.

"What are you talking about?"

"He and Emma are kaput. Apparently, something happened the other night at the pub with a certain lady and he is trying to mend his reputation." Sabina raised her eyebrows at Lilly. "You wouldn't happen to know anything about that, would you?"

"You think he stopped seeing Emma after he kissed me?"

"I know that's what happened. Right after you told him you wouldn't be a girl on his roster. That comment messed with him and he ended it with Emma that night."

Lilly huffed, shocked by Sabina's admission. "Wow. Sabina, why aren't you pursuing Enrique? You speak so highly of him and I noticed that the two of you hang out together all the time—"

"Stop right there," Sabina interjected, sipping her drink.

"Enrique does not have those types of feelings for me."

"How do you know? You've been so busy trying to hook us up that he would never suspect you had any feelings for him beyond friendship."

"We're just friends."

Lilly grinned, wrapping an arm around her friend's shoulder. "And so you'll remain, as long as you keep pushing him into my arms."

"Can we drop this conversation and focus on you and your sexual needs?"

Lilly bit her lip, considering the question. "Only for the time being."

"Deal. So, go get laid. Have some fun. Leave your heart at home."

"Tell that to my heart," Lilly muttered.

"That's what I'm trying to protect."

"You make it sound so simple, like a switch I can turn off or on at my leisure. I can't just fall out of love with someone, Sabina!"

Sabina hugged her friend tightly. "But what if he can never completely fall *in* love with you?"

Tears pricked Lilly's eyelids as her mind and heart engaged in an emotional battle over Jacob. Her heart argued how he had gone out of his way to make her feel special over the last several weeks. He was always available despite his packed schedule and she never got the impression she was encroaching on his time. And sometimes, during their video chats, she would catch him giving her this look, his eyes simultaneously adoring and ravishing her. It was the way he'd always looked at her, since that first kiss in the pub all those months ago, and even the thought made her body tingle.

Her head's arguments were logical and unfortunately, irrefutable. There were his constant references to this dream woman and photos of him strolling on a Grecian beach, looking utterly contented. More importantly, she couldn't forget how he left her naked and crying in a dressing room, as he rushed back to his ex-girlfriend.

It didn't matter what deal Jacob and Victoria had concocted, their behavior was inexcusable, and the idea of him screwing that blonde bitch the same night he screwed her…that was a mental image reel she could live the rest of her life without.

Jacob was a gorgeous, world-renowned celebrity who dated other gorgeous, world-renowned celebrities; he wasn't in the habit of dating nurses. Jacob was a star and stars belonged in the sky. Lilly was a girl with a slingshot and a dream. So why did her heart refuse to accept the truth? Was she just another pitiful woman, her common sense dissolved by unrequited love? She had traveled this road before with her last relationship, and she sure as hell didn't enjoy revisiting this journey. It was more painful this time too, because she loved Jacob with a depth she'd never experienced before. Even after everything he'd put her through, her heart ached for him.

Her friends all pushed her to hook up with Enrique. There was no doubt he was handsome, intelligent, and talented, and with an air of humility that always appealed to Lilly. She knew he held an affection for her, but she felt nothing for him beyond friendship, no matter how much her head tried to convince her otherwise.

Perhaps that was a safer route, a man whom she liked but didn't adore.

Lilly rolled her shoulders and took a deep breath. Time to return to reality and leave the stars in the sky. She strolled over to Enrique, who rewarded her with a dazzling smile.

"You're attracting quite the harem, Dr. Torres. I'm sure they'd all love a personal examination." Lilly smiled at the women, receiving scathing glares in return. "They don't seem pleased with my sudden appearance."

Enrique shrugged as his dark eyes swept over his female admirers. "Let them be angry. Your appearance makes me very happy."

"Where's Emma?"

"Is that your favorite question?" Enrique hung his head, chuckling.

"Perhaps you're right to ask. I ended things with her, I realized I couldn't say I wanted a serious relationship and still be sleeping with my ex in the interim."

"Bit of a deterrent to any would-be girlfriends."

"I don't know if it matters. I think the woman I'm interested in has her eyes set on someone else."

"The right woman will have eyes for no one but you."

Familiar strains of music streamed through the crowd. It was the song that Lilly played for Jacob that first night, how fitting. It seemed to be haunting her at this point.

"Dance with me, Lilly."

Lilly took a deep breath and pasted on a smile, following him to the dance floor. His well-defined arms pulled her close against him. He was beautiful, but for Lilly, it was all wrong.

She attempted to relax into Enrique's embrace, but her thoughts drifted back to Jacob while the lyrics of the song beat into her mind like a voyeur into a private moment.

"You're beautiful, but I'm sure you tire of hearing that constantly." Enrique's whisper brought her back to the present.

"I always appreciate a compliment like that. Are you having a good time?"

"I am now."

Lilly forced a smile. "You're certainly popular. Those women were hanging on your every word."

Enrique regarded her soberly. "They hear I'm a surgeon and see wealth and penthouses instead of long hours and student loans. They don't know me at all."

"I see a miracle worker, who saves lives every day. No one can take that from you."

Enrique pressed his body closer. "I like how you see me. Perhaps you should know how I see you, how I've thought about you since that night we kissed." His voice trailed off, his lips claiming hers.

He caught Lilly off guard with the kiss, and she pulled back, shaking her head. "Enrique, I—"

His smile was rueful. "I had to know for certain."

"Know what?"

"You're in love with that actor."

Lilly opened her mouth to respond but Enrique spoke the truth. There was no point denying her feelings. "It doesn't matter; he's desperately in love with someone else."

Enrique chuckled. "No he isn't; he's in love with you."

"We're great friends, of **course** he loves me."

"He's *in* love with you, friends don't behave in that manner." Lilly began to protest, but Enrique cut her off. "It's obvious with all the gifts and shenanigans he's been planning, no man does those things if he isn't in love. He wouldn't bother, even for a friend he wouldn't go to those lengths. I hate to admit it because he isn't worthy of you, but I'd be lying if I said I didn't recognize the emotion."

Screw dancing, Lilly needed answers. "You think he's in love with me?" she asked, her voice barely a whisper.

"Definitely but let me remind you, the bastard doesn't deserve you."

"The heart wants what the heart wants," Lilly mumbled, recalling the words the woman spoke at the fundraiser.

Enrique stepped back and crossed his arms, sending her a pointed stare. "That may be true, but I don't want to see you hurt again. I get no joy from helping you clean up the mess that man leaves behind. Promise me, you'll stay far away from Jacob Edmonton."

Was he serious? He tells her the love of her life returns the affection in one breath and demands she keep her distance in the next! He must be insane to think she would agree to such an arrangement. "You can't ask me to do that."

"Don't be a fool again, Lilly. That's what he's banking on."

Lilly had to leave; the crowd was oppressive, and Enrique's anger was growing by the second. She needed space—she needed to marinate on the idea that Jacob was in love—with her. Her heart, desperate for validation that Jacob returned her affections, danced for joy; she couldn't believe she was Jacob's choice.

"I'm sorry Enrique, I've got to go." She rushed through the throng of people, running toward the parking lot. She grabbed her phone and turned it on, desperate to spill her feelings to Jacob, but her breath lodged in her throat when she received his text.   Lilly read the message—again and again—her heart sinking further each time, her knees threatening to dump her body to the pavement. Jacob referred to the woman as a third entity and intimated that Lilly would be unhappy with the news. Her phone trembled in her hands as her mind knocked her heart back into line, and her emotional armor once again fell into place.

I'm such a fool. I got that entirely wrong. Jacob doesn't want me. He's scared to tell me the truth, afraid of how I'd react.

Lilly had a choice. She could walk away from their friendship or she could swallow her pride and feign happiness for him. He was a dear friend, going above and beyond to make her smile. He and Janie knew she lacked family and had adopted her into their own. It was nothing more than the glow of friendship she was basking in this entire time, and it would never be anything more.

Somehow, she would have to let her dream of Jacob go, a thought which wrenched her inside and out.

She texted a reply, keeping it short and simple through her tears. *'I'm sorry that you've felt it necessary to keep anything from me. You've been such a dear friend and your happiness is paramount to my own. I'm free tomorrow evening. I'll call at nine your time; I have some news to disclose as well.'*

Lilly called a cab, sent her friends a goodnight text and turned her phone off; her heart had taken enough blows for one night.

The next day at work dragged. It was one endless meeting after another, but Lilly couldn't recall any of the highlights. Her answers were rudimentary, her smile forced, and her mind focused on her upcoming discussion with Jacob.

She trudged down the long hallway towards the car park, feeling a bit like an inmate headed toward their execution.   Voices bounced off the concrete walls, making Lilly shiver. This hallway was reserved for employees and rarely used during the day, but it wasn't impossible for coworkers to be headed to their vehicles at the same moment.

Despite her positive inner pep talk, she picked up her pace, fumbling in her purse for her keys.

The voices grew louder and closer.

"Well, well, well, look who we have here."

The deep male voice made Lilly's blood turn to ice; her initial instinct was correct. These people had no official business being in this hallway, their business was with her.

"It isn't polite to ignore someone when they're speaking to you, peach."

A hand wrapped around Lilly's arm and she jerked it back, looking up at the man. His dark gray eyes leered at her, his breath foul with the stench of alcohol. It was the family member who had been escorted from the premises after subjecting her to a litany of lewd comments.

"What do you want?" Lilly's voice stayed strong, despite the fear flowing through her veins. She glanced at his partner in crime, but he hung back as if uncertain he should partake in this scenario.

The man leaned in closer, his mouth inches from her face. "You know exactly what I want. I told you the other day."

Jesus Christ, the son of a bitch is going to rape me. Lilly looked to the door of the car park. She could sprint for her vehicle but there was no way to outrun him, especially in heels. He stood at least a foot taller; she wasn't fighting her way out of this one either.

The man edged closer, a smirk playing on his thin lips. He was enjoying this game of cat and mouse. "Where do you think you're going?"

Lilly continued to back down the hallway, her heart hammering in her chest. She pressed the button on her mobile, turning the phone on. Now she prayed she had enough time to activate an emergency call. "If you know what's good for you, you'll leave now."

"Come on mate, this dame's not worth it. Let's get the hell out of here." His partner-in-crime looked as spooked as Lilly felt, his moves erratic and on edge.

But his companion kept coming, oblivious to his friend's pleas. "If you know what's good for *you*, you'll shut your mouth and give me what I want."

His words broke Lilly's anger loose. She wasn't about to stand around and let this man rape her, she would go down fighting. She yanked her phone out of her pocket, pressing in the number for the police.

When the man saw the phone, he lunged for her, but Lilly was ready as her heel made contact with his balls.

"You fucking cunt!" he howled, doubling over.

Lilly turned, making a mad dash for her vehicle as the police dispatcher came on the phone. "I'm being attacked! I'm at St. Luke hospital, in the parking deck—"

Her phone was wrenched out of her grip by her attacker. She saw stars as he slapped her across the face. "You'll pay for that stunt." He pulled her hair, jerking her head **backwards**; his fist making contact with her side and taking her breath.

A mixture of fury and fear bubbled up in Lilly. She jammed her heel down on his foot, her fist punching him hard in the throat.

"What the fuck, man? Get off of her!" His friend wrapped his arm around Lilly, pulling her out of the attacker's grip. He said only one word to her. "Run."

The attacker turned on his friend, punching him in the face. Blood spurted from the man's nose, but his injury gave Lilly a moment to dash to safety. She could escape but then she left his friend—and her savior—alone to his wrath.

"Are you crazy? Run!" His friend reiterated, taking another punch to the jaw.

But Lilly wasn't good at listening and even worse at running. She jumped on the man's back, her fists beating him about the head. He shook her off, and she stumbled back, hearing sirens in the distance. He lumbered toward her, blood dripping down his face and into his eyes. That's when Lilly took her shot.

She swung her fist with all her might, connecting with the attacker's nose. He howled again as Lilly stumbled away from him, but she never saw the concrete upright.

She fell backward, grasping at the air for a handhold before everything went dark.

CHAPTER SIX

Jacob

The alarm sounded at 4 a.m., but Jacob hadn't gotten any sleep. He checked his phone again, but there were no new messages, just the one text from Lilly the night before. His mind spiraled at her words. She had news for him. What in the hell did that even mean?

The makeup artist commented on his haggard appearance, assuming it was due to an overload of alcohol and intercourse. He assured her it was strictly an overload of insomnia, rolling around in the hellish depths of his own mind.

He had no idea how Lilly would react to his confession, but after her message, he wondered whether he should tell her anything. What was her news? Had she and Dr. Torres finally connected? The mental image of that man's hands on his woman's ivory flesh nearly drove him to madness.

How would he react when she told him the news that she and the good doctor had consummated their relationship? How would he handle her joy when he wanted to vomit?

They couldn't remain friends, he didn't give a shit what Miriam said. He adored Lilly, but he could not stand by and let some other man claim her body and her heart. Fuck fair, fairness played no role in matters of love.

The entire crew handled Jacob with care that day, Miriam included. She seemed to understand that his dam of emotions was near the breaking point and if it burst, there would be no stopping the deluge.

Jacob escaped the set a little after seven. He had enough time to grab dinner, take a shot—or ten—of whiskey, and return to his suite.

He called Janie, hoping she might provide some information about Lilly's romantic inclinations, but both her home line and mobile went unanswered. *Great, the truth is so awful my own sister is avoiding me.*

Minutes crawled by like hours. The clock read five minutes after nine, so he verified his computer and internet connection were working. Lilly was never late, it was one of her pet peeves. His mind reasoned she might be stuck in traffic. *Calm down man, it's only five minutes.*

Ten minutes later, and another shot of whiskey. Had Lilly said 9 p.m. his time or 9 p.m. her time? He sighed audibly when he read the message. Their chat was indeed at 9 p.m. his time, and now he'd endured fifteen minutes of torture.

Jacob texted Roger to ensure his phone was receiving phone calls and no major catastrophe had occurred in London. Roger's sarcastic reply arrived a moment later. His phone was working, and the earth was still spinning on its axis.

At 9:30 p.m. he texted Lilly and by 9:45 p.m. he was grimacing at mental images of Lilly and Dr. Torres naked and fornicating.

He called her number again a little after 10 p.m., anger surging through his body. He deserved an explanation. He didn't deserve to be tossed aside… like he had tossed her aside. Was this Lilly's sick idea of retribution? He didn't think the woman had a mean bone in her body, but revenge was a dish best served cold. *Don't be ridiculous, Lilly is not capable of that level of cruelty…I hope.*

By 11 p.m., the last vestiges of his sanity were gone as his thoughts bounced between anger and agony. He redialed Janie, and she answered on the third ring.

"Janie! I tried calling earlier, you didn't answer. Did you get my messages?" Jacob forced himself to sound concerned but calm.

Janie sighed, her breathing ragged. "My phone's been off. It's been a rough night."

"Are you alright? Your heart—"

"Is top notch," Janie interjected. "I'm fine."

Jacob heard the exhaustion in his sister's voice but sensed another emotion—squelched anger. "Something's wrong, Janie. What's going on? Have you spoken from Lilly? She was supposed to call me two hours ago, and it's not like her to forget. I was going to come clean about how much I love her, I have to tell her—"

"She's in the hospital."

Jacob perched on the corner of the bed, a sinking feeling in his gut. "Is she working late?"

Janie's huff answered his question. "She was attacked on the way to the car park, they have admitted her for observation."

He must have misunderstood, he couldn't hear over the blood pounding in his ears. "Lilly was—holy shit—is she okay?"

"She hit her head, and the bastard landed a few good punches, but the doctors say she'll be fine. Thankfully they didn't rape"—Janie's voice broke—"they didn't rape her. She claims one of the men pushed her to safety after the lead guy assaulted her. It would have been much worse if he didn't step in."

"Do they know who did it?" His voice shook as he swallowed straight from the whiskey bottle. The woman he loved lay in a hospital bed, and he was thousands of kilometers away.

"Yes." Janie sniffled. "It was these family members that harassed her the other day."

"I'm going to kill them!" Jacob hissed, his insides raging. Blood dripped from his hand, as he stared at the newly created hole in the wall of the suite.

"Jakey, she'll be okay. You were the first person on her mind; the first name she mentioned once she was stabilized."

He couldn't hear anything more, his tightly reined-in emotions demanded release. Jacob mumbled a goodbye before hanging up, his head collapsing into his hands.

He and Miriam had plans for a nightcap after his chat with Lilly, but he was in no mood to converse with anyone. His head throbbed, as did his hand, but it was a small inconvenience compared to the ache in his heart. He needed to be with Lilly, but with filming it was an impossibility. She needed him and he couldn't be there.

Jacob dialed Miriam, he would quit the film and return to London. Lilly was more important that *any* damn role.

His explanation burst from his body in a torrent, not pausing for breath or interruption. "I'm sorry, but I'm returning to London. Lilly needs me."

"Hold on a second, Jacob. You're not going to quit the film, we're almost finished for Christ's sake! How badly was Lilly injured?"

"I don't know. Janie says she'll recover but there will be emotional wounds to deal with after this attack and I won't let her do it alone. *I won't let her, Miriam.* Please understand, this is what I have to do." Jacob hung up the phone and busied himself packing. It was amazing how much crap accumulated after lodging in a hotel for two months.

His mobile rang a few minutes later, it was Miriam again. *I really hope she doesn't give me a hard time about this, I'm on my last nerve.*

"Are you packed?"

"Just about. I wasn't kidding Miriam, I'm off the film. I'm sorry to do this to you but—"

"Will you shut up for *one* moment? What I called to tell you was that my jet will be on the tarmac in the next hour. It will fly you to Gatwick Airport, and you'll be in London by morning."

"Thank you, I appreciate your help. You're a good friend."

"Here's your end of the bargain—"

Jacob's blood boiled, he didn't have time to wheel and deal. "Miriam!"

"We're ahead of schedule, and although I don't normally let people leave the set, I understand extenuating circumstances. You are *not* quitting the movie. I'm rearranging the shooting schedule. You have a week to return to

London, get Lilly stabilized and get you both back on a plane to Santorini."

"You're letting me leave?" He was shocked at his friend's offer.

"Go get her, Jacob. It's about damn time the knight rescued his fair damsel."

Jacob wished Miriam was standing in front of him. He would hug her until her ribs cracked. He stammered out his thanks and hung up, calling downstairs for a taxi to the airport.

A thick fog rolled in off the sea, leaving the plane grounded for the next few hours. Jacob spent the first hour pacing the length of the plane until the flight attendant directed him to the bed, handing him a cup of chamomile and a sleeping tablet.

Jacob needed to check on Lilly one last time before the sleeping pill kicked in. He dialed Lilly's phone, but it went straight to voicemail. Undeterred, he called Janie again.

"You should be sleeping." Janie's voice sounded muffled. "I should be sleeping."

"I'm sorry I woke you, but I tried calling Lilly again, and it went straight to voicemail."

Janie groaned. "She's having another CT scan right now, and her phone was smashed during the attack."

Jacob's face paled. He didn't fully understand the meaning behind all these tests, but additional testing was never a good sign. "Another CT scan?"

"They want to make certain there isn't a slow bleed in the brain they didn't catch the first time."

"A slow bleed in the brain? Janie, you said she was going to be fine!" Jacob bellowed, his breathing ragged.

"It's just a precaution. She had a headache, no big shock there, but Dr. Torres pitched a fit and demanded a follow-up scan."

"I'm sure he's very concerned." Even under the circumstances, Jacob's jaw tightened at the mention of the man's name.

"We're all concerned. That's how friends react when something like this happens. I'll have Lilly call you once things settle down. Now do yourself a favor and try to sleep. I'm sure you have a long day of filming tomorrow."

Jacob considered mentioning his impending arrival but decided against it. Instead, he asked Janie to replace Lilly's cellular phone. Janie agreed once Lilly was stable and the 'bloody stores opened.'

He drifted off into a sleep full of sinister dreams and awoke in a panic to the flight attendant rousing him. They had landed at Gatwick, and a car service was waiting for him on the tarmac.

Jacob ran up to the admitting desk of St. Luke Hospital. He recognized the clerk from when Janie was rushed into surgery months earlier. It appeared the clerk also remembered their previous encounter.

"Mr. Edmonton, I almost didn't recognize you."

"Haircut and a shave."

She nodded, a tight smile on her lips. "I'm sorry to see you back again." Her tone was reserved, and Jacob realized how rudely he behaved the last time.

He glanced at her badge before speaking. "Good morning, Doris. I'm looking for Lilly Staver. She was admitted after an attack here at the hospital."

The woman raised her eyebrows. "The nurse manager?"

Jacob nodded, holding his breath as the clerk checked her computer.

"She's no longer listed as a patient."

Jacob's panic set in. "What does that mean?"

Doris gave his hand a reassuring squeeze. "She was discharged home early this morning. You can find her there. Good luck."

Jacob smiled, leaning over the counter and pecking her on the cheek. "Thank you, Doris. You're a doll."

Doris placed her hand over her cheek, a flush creeping over her face. "Thank you. My goodness, what a story for my daughter. I may never wash this cheek again."

❧ ❧❧❧ ❧

Janie's eyes widened and her mouth dropped open when she opened the door to Lilly's cottage. "Jakey? What are you doing here?"

Jacob hugged Janie and stepped inside. "Where is she?"

Janie beamed at her brother, squeezing him around the waist. "You came all the way from Greece?"

"I love her Janie."

"She loves you too. She always has." Janie nodded toward the bedroom. "She just laid down. I was going to run her a bath. Poor thing needs to sleep but now that she can, she can't. She will be shocked to see you."

Jacob dreaded the answer to his next question. "Is Dr. Torres here?"

"Enrique? Why would he be here?"

Jacob nodded but didn't answer—his sister's response was promising enough. "Go on home, Little Bit. I've got her from here."

Janie smiled. "You be nice to her, big brother."

"I promise."

Janie grabbed him into another hug, kissing him hard on the mouth.

80

"Go, you two have been waiting long enough."

Jacob waved as Janie backed out of the drive before heading for the bathroom. If Lilly needed to relax, a bath was the perfect remedy, maybe some massage thrown in for good measure. Anything to make his beloved feel safe and adored.

He drew Lilly a bath, adding lavender and rose oil to the water. Then he turned on that song—their song—and headed for her bedroom. He was finally back with the woman he loved.

Lilly

L illy heard the song wafting through the cottage, smiling despite her current predicament. The lyrics held such deep meaning for her that it eased her discomfort, and she felt Jacob's warmth despite the distance. Her body ached, but the pain had dulled considerably; no worse than the morning after she, Sabina and Ben finished off a bottle of tequila.

Sleep was not in the cards, however. When Lilly closed her eyes, she saw that man, heard his taunts and the thud of his fists against her body.

But Lilly's worst injury was sadly self-inflicted. With her typical lack of grace, she fell over the concrete upright and hit her head. The police were swarming the car park moments later, and her attacker was hauled off in handcuffs, while they treated his unwitting accomplice and Lilly in Accident and Emergency. News of her attack spread like wildfire, and in less than five minutes her friends huddled into her hospital bay, pecking around like mother hens. She didn't know who called Janie, but her friend arrived in record time and refused to leave her side.

There was another visitor, a stranger who introduced himself as Albert. He was the uncle of the accomplice. His nephew informed him of the attack and Albert understood if Lilly wanted to press charges, he wanted nothing more than to personally box his nephew's ears. But Lilly knew that Albert's nephew was the reason she escaped with such minor injuries and she had no plans to pursue legal action. Albert seemed shocked by Lilly's generosity, telling her if she ever needed anything to reach out and he would move heaven and earth to make it happen. When she read his business card, she realized he was a Hollywood director; and for some reason, his name echoed with familiarity.

But now she was home in her cottage. Although a temporary residence, it had always been a safe haven for her, but this morning it was suffocating. She needed to speak to Jacob, even though she dreaded hearing his admission, the truth needed to be expressed. Her refusal to discuss the woman he loved was causing Jacob pain, and Lilly couldn't bear that idea. She just hoped her heart could bear one more shattering.

Lilly wondered if he knew about the events of last night…God, she missed him.

"Janie?" Lilly murmured, her eyes closed. "Can I borrow your phone? I need to call Jacob, he had something important to tell me. We were supposed to talk last night, but—"

"I believe a conversation of this magnitude needs to be discussed face to face."

Lilly's eyes flew open. Was her mind playing tricks on her? There stood Jacob, tanned and golden, his eyes observing her with sober concern. Lilly's hand flew to her mouth as tears sprang to her eyes. "What are you doing here?" She stood, a bit unsteadily, and Jacob closed the distance between them, pulling her tight against him. He felt amazing, all strength and warmth and here.

Lilly pulled back, gaping at him. "You are real, right? I did bump my head. This isn't a dream?"

Jacob kissed her face as he whispered, "I'm very real." He tipped her chin up to look her in the eyes. "My angel got attacked. Where else would I be?"

His simple statement broke through the last barriers holding back Lilly's emotions, and she buried her head in his chest, sobbing. "I wanted you here so bad," Lilly sniffled between sobs. "I prayed you would come, but I never thought you would actually be here holding me."

After several minutes, her cries subsided, but Jacob continued stroking her hair, whispering words she couldn't decipher. He might be speaking gibberish, but the smooth timbre of his voice and his gentle caresses soothed her spirit.

She gazed up at him, her face red and puffy, and wiped her tears with the heel of her hand. "What are you doing in London?"

"You're joking."

Lilly's brow knitted in confusion. "It's a legitimate question."

"I flew out last night from Santorini. My director, Miriam, was kind enough to lend me her jet."

"I wish I had friends with jets, my friends only have bicycles, not that they'd lend them to me." Jacob chuckled, and Lilly smiled in return, her first real smile since he left for Greece. "Do you have time to visit with me while you're here?"

Jacob shot her a fake scowl. "You're a bit thick-headed for such a brilliant woman. I'm not leaving your side. I sent Janie home to sleep." He stood, bowing in front of her and pressing his lips to her hand. "I am your official nurse for the next seven days, and the first order of business is a bubble bath, followed by a nap. Come with me."

A light, floral scent tickled Lilly's nostrils as she entered the bathroom. She fingered a fluffy towel on the vanity, closing her eyes to the soft jazz playing on the radio.

"How are you feeling? Any dizziness?" Jacob asked, his arm around her, the weight so warm and familiar.

"No, Dr. Edmonton. I'm fine." Lilly shot him a smile, but it faded when she saw tears glistening in his eyes. "What is it, Jacob?"

He traced the bruise on her jaw with the back of his hand, a muscle twitching in his own jaw. "I should have been here to protect you. It's my job to keep you from harm. I'm sorry, Lilly."

Lilly's hands framed his face, offering up a smile. "You're here now. You'll never know what you being here means to me. You're the best surprise." She perched on the edge of the tub, splashing her hand in the bubbly water.

"Let's get you into that water so you can relax." Jacob knelt at her side, his fingers gliding along her ribs as he raised her tank over her head. His gaze hardened when they fell upon the bruises dotting her side, and when his fists clenched, Lilly wondered if he might punch a hole in the wall.

Lilly crossed her arm over her breasts, offering a rueful smile. "Pretty, right? Real beautiful."

Jacob's hand held her chin, lifting her gaze to his. "Stunning, but I will kill the man who hurt you."

"Cops and karma will handle him. I don't want to talk about the attack now."

"What would you like to talk about?" Jacob's hands traced small, soothing circles on her lower back and hip.

"I want to be here, in this moment, with you. I feel safe with you." Lilly couldn't believe her boldness, laying her emotions bare.

"I would die to protect you." Their eyes locked, and Lilly held Jacob's gaze as he inched forward, his lips grazing against hers, trailing feather-light kisses along her jaw. Goosebumps rose up on her arms, but she knew it wasn't from the cold.

Jacob helped her finish undressing, his hand lingering on the bruise marking her upper leg.

"You're taking this nurse role quite seriously." Lilly surprised herself. Her nudity didn't make her feel vulnerable, not with Jacob. His presence had the opposite effect, wrapping her in a secure cocoon.

He helped her into the bath, clipping her long hair out of her face. "You're a very important patient."

Lilly sank into the hot water, a wave of relaxation washing over her body. "This feels amazing." Jacob knelt by the tub, his fingers gripping the rim. Lilly grabbed his bruised hand, drawing it to her for a closer look. "What in the world happened? Were you injured during filming?"

Jacob shook his head. "It's nothing."

"It's not nothing, you're hurt. It looks like you punched something."

He sighed. "I did, the wall and beam in my suite."

Lilly's eyes widened. "Why?"

"You got attacked and I lost my bloody mind." His eyes resonated an emotion she never noticed in their depths before, an unmitigated yearning. Lilly realized in that moment that the attack was as terrifying for Jacob as it was for her. "It seemed like a good idea at the time."

Lilly smiled wistfully, kissing each swollen finger before placing her cheek against his palm. "It seems we both had a rough night."

"It was torture, beautiful girl." Jacob's phone buzzed. "I'll be right back. My manager is inquiring where in the hell I am."

Lilly watched him leave, her heart tight. He owned her body, heart, and soul, now the only question was whether he wanted that obligation. *What do I do if he doesn't?*

She relaxed against the side of the tub, letting the warm bubbles soothe the aches in her muscles. She ran her hand along her side and winced. The bastard had landed a hell of a punch. She sat up, twisting to examine the bruise.

"Are you okay?" Jacob inquired, a concerned look crossing his features as he sat next to the tub.

"Just looking at my temporary tattoos, the artist sucked."

Jacob snickered, sliding a loose tendril behind Lilly's ear. "Only you can joke at a time like this, Lilly. Are you in pain?"

"I'm sore, but the bath is helping immensely." Lilly leaned back, turning her head to examine Jacob's face.

"What?" Jacob inquired as he massaged the fingers on her right hand.

Lilly brought her other hand to his face, tracing his jawline. "You look so different."

Jacob sighed and hung his head. "I'll grow it back after filming wraps."

Lilly forced him to meet her gaze, a smile on her lips. "I said different, not bad. I like you like this. I had no idea how gorgeous you were under all that hair."

Jacob pressed a kiss to her palm, his sexy smirk on full display. "I win then. I always knew how gorgeous you were."

"I'm real beautiful now." Lilly rolled her eyes, but his words warmed every cell of her body.

"I told you before, you're absolutely stunning."

Lilly couldn't resist. She leaned forward and pressed her lips to his. Even a simple peck felt like a homecoming, reawakening the butterflies that laid dormant since their separation. "Thank you for coming here, for taking care of me."

Jacob nuzzled her nose with his own. "I'll always take care of you. Are you ready to dry off, prune princess?"

Lilly nodded, accepting a towel from Jacob. She stood up, but wobbled a bit, grabbing for the wall. "Whoa, it's like a roller coaster ride inside my body."

"Okay, enough of that." Jacob scooped her naked body from the tub, getting his clothes soaked as he held her against him. "If you wanted to be carried, you only needed to ask."

Lilly's eyes widened in mock anger. "I was doing fine on my own."

His mouth brushed her cheek, and she felt him smile against her skin. "Were you now? And here I thought I was your knight riding in to save the day."

Lilly bit her lip, her cheeks flushing. "You'll always be my brave knight."

Jacob carried her into the bedroom, depositing her gently on the bed.

Lilly grimaced when she saw the water stains on his shirt and pants. "I'm sorry, I got you all wet."

"It's water, no big deal." Jacob took the towel and dried her, his hands gentle against her skin. "What do you sleep in?"

Lilly flushed, looking at the ground. "The nude, normally." She snuck a glance at Jacob as he cleared his throat and stood up. She swore the man was blushing. "But I have a t-shirt and leggings in that drawer if you prefer I retain some modesty."

"I'm never going to tell you to cover that beautiful body. Climb in, you need to sleep." Jacob turned the covers down, his watchful gaze wandering the curves of her body.

"Are you catching a cheap thrill?"

Another blush. God, he was magnificent. "Every chance I get."

"Good." Lilly giggled as she crawled under the covers, fluffing up her pillow, her eyes focused on her golden-haired Adonis. "Will you sleep with me?"

Jacob's eyes widened, and he cleared his throat again. "What?" His voice sounded almost pained.

Lilly buried her head in her pillow; what a Freudian slip. "I didn't mean sex."

"Damn. I thought I was going to get lucky," Jacob joked. "I'll have to wait until my clothes dry, but I'll sit right next to you while you sleep."

But Lilly needed to be closer than that, she couldn't sleep otherwise. She sat up, her fingers undoing the buttons of Jacob's wet shirt.

"What are you doing, Lilly?" Jacob breathed, his voice hitching.

"Don't get too excited; I'm helping you out of your wet clothes so you can sleep. This isn't a forced striptease, rather a facet of your nursing duties."

Jacob chuckled, and shucked his wet shirt and pants; sliding into bed next to Lilly. He turned and faced her, their bodies inches apart, their gazes locked on each other. The heat radiated between them, and Lilly felt an almost insatiable need to touch him, to feel his energy.

Lilly bit her lip, attempting to rein in her emotions as she gazed at the beautiful man laying mere inches away. She needed the warmth and adoration she always found in his arms, especially after being attacked. Jacob was her safe space. He made her feel whole. He was the only man with whom she ever felt truly comfortable, sexually and otherwise.

But she sensed a hesitancy from Jacob. He was maintaining some distance physically and emotionally. It was not the time to paw at him, demanding affection. "I kicked him in the balls."

Jacob's eyes widened. "The piece of shit who attacked you?"

Lilly nodded. "I was wearing stilettos, too. The motherfucker deserved every ounce of agony. Then I punched him in the nose, broke the damn thing." She laughed at Jacob's shocked expression.

His fingers stroked her cheek, an expression of amazement on his face. "My beautiful warrior. I'm impressed and a little scared. Remind me to never piss you off."

"You've been warned," Lilly joked as she tried to control her racing heart. It seemed like forever since he'd touched her, and she ached for him.

He pushed a lock of hair from her face. "I'm proud of you, Lilly. You're so brave."

Lilly blinked back tears, but she willed them away. The son-of-a-bitch attacker didn't deserve her sorrow. "Turns out I was a better fighter than he was. I guess I had more to lose."

Jacob's hand traced along her jaw, his breaths fast and choppy. "I promise, no one will ever lay a hand on you again. I left a message with my lawyers. I will ensure that bastard goes to prison and rots."

"He better hope he does, I'd be afraid for him if he ran into you on the street. I've never seen you so angry."

"He hurt you. No one hurts the woman I love and gets away with it."

Lilly's eyes widened, stunned by his admission. "You love me?"

Jacob pressed his lips to her forehead. "Of course, I love you, Lilly. How could you not know that?"

87

Lilly's heart wanted to explode as she heard the words she feared might never be spoken. They washed over her. Jacob loved her, all her worrying was for naught. She was his choice all along, and as far as she was concerned, all was right with the world. "Will you stay?"

A beautiful smile crossed Jacob's face as he nodded, pulling her to his chest. "Wild horses couldn't drag me from your side."

Lilly offered him one last smile before nestling into his arms and letting sleep finally take hold.

CHAPTER SEVEN

Jacob

Lying next to Lilly was killing him. Torture in its purest form. Jacob gazed down at her sleeping figure, curled against his chest, her breasts rising and falling with each breath.

His fingers traced along her back, God he missed the sensation of her body against his. No one felt like Lilly. He ached with the need to strip her naked, kissing her until she shattered in ecstasy; but his carnal urges needed to remain on lockdown. She was too vulnerable.

His libido nearly won out when she pressed her luscious mouth against his. It took every ounce of his restraint to keep the kiss chaste and sweet.

Lilly moaned in her sleep, snuggling tighter against his side, her arm curling around his neck.

"Lilly?" Jacob tightened his grip on her, pressing his lips to her hair. "I promise, no one will ever hurt you again."

Another sleepy moan, a subconscious attempt at a reply.

Jacob smiled. It may not be the optimal circumstances for professing his love but being near Lilly again was the greatest gift. He stroked her hair back, dusting her face with feather-light kisses. "You're going to be my wife, Lilly. I can't live without you. I'll make you so happy, my angel. I'll give you anything your heart desires."

Her wide brown eyes opened, and she gazed up at him, a smile spreading across her face. "I wasn't dreaming. You're really here."

Jacob forced a smile, but his heart hammered like a locomotive. Had she heard him? Should he repeat his confession? *You are a such a chicken shit, Jacob.* "Go back to sleep, angel. You need your rest."

Her slight hand traced along his jaw, a wry smile playing on her lips. "I'm still tired. Isn't that pitiful?"

"No, it's totally understandable." He kissed the tip of her nose. "I love you, Lilly."

She nuzzled his chest and smiled against his skin. "I just need twenty more minutes—"

"Sleep, my darling." Jacob caressed her hair and felt her body relax into slumber. His mind remained cognizant that Lilly hadn't reciprocated his declaration of love. *Stop bloody overanalyzing everything. Give her a couple days to recuperate before you barrage her with all your plans for the future.*

Jacob started awake to a loud, vigorous knocking at the door. Momentarily confused, he glanced at the clock. It was almost noon. Apparently, they both needed the rest.

He hated leaving Lilly's side, but it was obvious whoever was at the door was not going away. Sighing, Jacob slid his arm from under Lilly, pressing a kiss to her forehead. He slipped on his pants and padded to the front door, rubbing the sleep from his eyes.

"Just a moment," Jacob yawned, pulling open the door.

Enrique stood on the threshold, his eyes narrowing when he saw Jacob. "What are you doing here?"

Jacob's jaw tightened at the surgeon's inquisition; he had every damn right to be here. "I could ask you the same question."

Enrique scoffed, running a hand through his dark mane. "Lilly and I are friends, in case you've forgotten. I'm here to check on her." His eyes took note of Jacob, half-dressed and half-asleep. "Lilly needs rest, not fornication. I do hope you've kept your libido in check."

Jacob scrubbed his face with his hands, willing his temper down. "Save your breath, Enrique. We were asleep. Lilly's still sleeping. What kind of man do you think I am?"

A muscle twitched in Enrique's jaw, and Jacob readied himself for battle. "You don't want that answer, Mr. Edmonton. Why are you really here? What are you trying to prove?"

"Excuse me?" This was going downhill fast.

"You heard me, what are your plans with Lilly? She isn't some floozy for you to fuck! She's an amazing, intelligent and beautiful woman—" With each word, Enrique's frustration and volume increased.

Now Jacob was pissed. "My intentions with Lilly are none of your damn business, but I'm in love with that woman."

"Save it."

"I know I fucked up, but I've been doing everything in my power to win back her love."

"How do you even know if she loves you anymore?"

His words hit like bullets. Jacob knew Lilly loved him, she said it that afternoon in the park. He was less certain of whether her love was platonic or intimate in nature. Still, he couldn't let Enrique worm his way under his skin, at least not any more than the bastard already had.

Enrique smirked, shaking his head. "You think every woman is going to fall at your feet? Lilly isn't just any woman. You may have missed your chance, friend."

"Enrique? What are you doing here? I thought you were in surgery today."

Jacob turned and saw Lilly standing a few feet behind him, wearing a fluffy blue robe and a perplexed look on her gorgeous face. Shit, how long had she been standing there? Despite Jacob's aggravation, Lilly had been through hell. She didn't need to witness two adult men squabbling like teenagers.

"Surgery was canceled; I was worried about you and wanted to drop by to see how you're feeling. I didn't realize you had company." He shot Jacob a pointed stare. "Would you give us some privacy?"

"I think that's up to Lilly."

Lilly patted Jacob's arm, giving him a sleepy smile. "Would you make me some tea? I just need a few minutes."

Fucking wonderful. Jacob didn't like the idea of Enrique alone with Lilly even for a few seconds, but he needed to get his possessiveness in check. "Fine."

Jacob walked into the kitchen and put on the kettle, trying to quiet the storm of anger brewing in his body. He knew they were friends, but Enrique wanted Lilly for himself, that was no secret. Even when asked directly, Lilly never responded to Jacob's questions about the nature of her relationship with Enrique. In fact, she was painfully evasive about the topic.

Fuck, what if I'm reading this wrong? What if Lilly only considers me a friend now? What if she and Enrique…I can't even go there, I'll punch another hole in the wall.

As the water boiled, Jacob leaned against the counter, his body twitching with agitation. He wasn't eavesdropping on their conversation, but he wasn't avoiding it either. Judging from Enrique's raised voice, he wanted Jacob to hear every word.

"I see Mr. Wonderful is back," Enrique muttered.

"He arrived early this morning." Lilly's voice was calm under Enrique's inquisition.

"What is he doing here?"

"He was worried about me after the attack. He flew straight here."

Enrique huffed. "Are you sure that's the only reason he's in London?"

"That's what he told me, and I believe him."

"Why would you believe him? He's lied to you in the past—"

"Enough, I won't have you bashing Jacob. You know how I feel about him." Lilly was becoming more and more anxious, and Jacob counted the seconds until he had to demand the surgeon leave the house.

"You're in love with him; dumbest decision you've ever made—"

91

"It's not your business if I'm in love with Jacob or not."

"He doesn't deserve you." Enrique argued. "Remember him running off to sleep with Victoria the same day he slept with you? How about the woman in Greece, or those starlets the tabloids keep mentioning? Do you think it's all lies, Lilly?"

Whatever Lilly said was too low and mumbled for Jacob to hear, and he feared Enrique's accusations were getting a foothold.

"Do you really think a man like Jacob Edmonton knows how to be monogamous? He's going to break your heart again, Lilly. Send him packing now. Protect yourself."

Jacob tried to be patient, but he'd heard enough of Enrique's crap. The surgeon thought he knew Jacob's inner workings and mindset, but he didn't know a damn thing.

He stalked into the living room, enveloping Lilly in his arms. Her eyes were bright with tears, which spiked Jacob's anger to off-the-chart levels. "You need to leave. You're upsetting Lilly."

If looks could kill, the glare Enrique shot at Jacob would be fatal. "I don't recall you being so concerned when you were off fucking other women—"

"Get out," Jacob growled, moving towards the surgeon. He didn't want it to come to blows, but it was beginning to look like there was no other option.

The surgeon yanked open the door, pausing on the threshold. "Lilly, I sincerely hope he's as in love with you, as you are with him. I'd hate for you to be played the fool again. Don't forget, he is an actor. He can play any role and make you believe it."

The door slammed, and Lilly released a strangled sigh. "Fuck."

Jacob wrapped his arms around Lilly. Her body shaking from the confrontation. "I'm so sorry, Lilly. He's a bastard for upsetting you. You've been through enough."

Lilly chewed her lip, pushing Jacob away. "What if he's right?"

Jacob cupped her face, forcing her to meet his gaze. "You know that isn't the case, Lilly!"

"The only thing my heart knows is that it doesn't know anything anymore. It's been wrong too many times, misread the signs. I can't handle another heartbreak." Lilly wiped a tear with the palm of her hand, her face growing splotchy. "I need to take a shower, put on some real clothes."

"I'll come with you—"

Lilly held up her hand. "No, I need time alone. A few minutes to clear my head."

Jacob stopped cold. Enrique's statements, intimating that Jacob was unfaithful and inherently full of shit had hit the bullseye in Lilly's heart. "Please don't listen to what Enrique said. He's in love with you, and he'll say anything to keep us apart."

Lilly paused a few feet from Jacob, an almost unearthly look on her face. "Do you really believe he's in love with me?"

"It's obvious."

"Perhaps he just loves me as a friend and is concerned for my well-being. He doesn't want to see me hurt again."

"There's a big difference between loving someone and being in love." Jacob's heart seized from her flat tone but even more at the defeated look emanating from her eyes. "I will never hurt you, Lilly. Never again."

Lilly sniffled before offering up a somber smile. "Do you promise? Because I'll hold you to it."

He stood in her living room, admiring this gorgeous creature in front of him. She had no idea how exquisite she was, what she did to his body and mind. "On my life."

"Do you love me, Jacob?"

Enough was enough. He couldn't bear to see the uncertainty on her face a moment longer. Jacob closed the gap between them, pulling her into his arms and lifting her chin until their gazes met. "You know I do, Lilly."

Another batch of tears welled in Lilly's eyes. What the hell was going through her gorgeous head? "But do you love me enough? With everyone else clamoring for a piece of you, how will there ever be enough room left in your heart for me?"

On that note, she pushed from his grasp, turned and walked to the bathroom.

Jacob started to follow until he heard the lock click into place on the door. She had shut him out. His heart ached at the idea of her placing another wall between them when he thought he was finally making headway. "Fuck, what a disaster."

Lilly emerged from the bathroom twenty minutes later, looking far more relaxed. She poured herself a cup of tea and settled onto the couch, snuggling against one of her cats.

"Do you feel better?" Jacob maintained a cheerful tone. Lilly had endured enough doom and gloom in the last twenty-four hours.

"Much better. A great shower makes everything right in the world."

"So does great sex," Jacob muttered, realizing a second too late how the statement made him look like a giant git. *So much for not pushing her, Jacob. Good job, she was physically attacked, and you're referring to sex as a cure-all? What is wrong with you?*

Thankfully, his quip earned a smirk from Lilly. "I wouldn't remember. It's been a while."

Thank God. "For me too."

Lilly chewed her lip, focusing her attention on her cat.

"Lilly, what's going on in that pretty head of yours?"

She shook her head. Whatever she was ruminating on would remain a mystery.

Jacob hated this change in energy. Before Enrique showed up, there had been such love between them. Now, there hung distrust and uncertainty. He stared at Lilly, craving her more than oxygen. He practically had to sit on his hands to keep from reaching for her, pulling her body against him and making sure she knew his intentions.

Christ, he missed the taste of her skin, her kisses that made him forget his own name, and the feeling of her tight pussy surrounding his cock. Jacob felt himself getting hard and stood suddenly, clearing his throat. "Bloody hell."

Lilly glanced up, a surprised look crossing her features. "Is something wrong?"

Yes, I crave your body like a drug, and I don't know how much longer I can hold out.

He shook his head, watching her tongue sweep across her lower lip and almost losing his resolve. A low moan escaped his mouth.

Lilly's eyes widened at the unintentional noise. "What are you looking at, Jacob?"

He couldn't lie if he tried. "You."

His goddess smirked, sending him a flirtatious wink. "You like what you see?"

"Angel, you have no idea."

She stretched on the couch, her eyes roving over his body. "Why don't you enlighten me?"

A knock on the door snapped them from their playful banter, causing Lilly to jump. Her brown eyes moved from the door to Jacob, her expression guarded. "Are you expecting someone?"

"Shit, I forgot to tell you. That's the car service."

"Are you leaving?" There is was, in the back of her voice, the fear that he would do precisely what Enrique said.

Jacob needed to lay all his cards on the table, and soon. A second knock sounded at the door, and Lilly's face fell. She looked deflated. "We are going to my house for the week."

Lilly's brow furrowed. "But—"

Jacob moved to the couch, taking the tea from her hands and pulling her against his chest. "No arguments; this isn't up for debate. You and your cats are moving to my house. It's gated, and there are round-the-clock surveillance cameras, not to mention a heated pool and hot tub."

Lilly gazed up at him, snickering. "I knew it was all about the hot tub."

"Damn straight. And you'll understand why when you sink this gorgeous body into it." His fingers trailed down her back and rested on her ass. God, she had an amazing ass. *Get your mind out of the gutter, Jacob.* He landed a light smack on her rear, eliciting a cry of surprise from Lilly. "Let's get you packed."

Lilly winked again before walking into her bedroom. "Be careful, I might enjoy a good spanking."

Jacob closed his eyes, his cock rock-hard from the statement. "And I would enjoy giving it to you," he whispered under his breath.

The limousine pulled into Jacob's driveway an hour later, the cats howling disdain from their respective carriers.

Hannah ran out to greet them, pulling Lilly to her bosom in a protective hug. Although Hannah only met Lilly twice, she had taken his petite goddess under her wing, stepping into a parental role Lilly desperately needed filled. "Sweetheart, how are you feeling?"

Lilly returned the hug and smiled at Jacob's housekeeper. "I'll be right as rain in a few days, Hannah. Thank you for letting me stay here; I'll try not to be too much trouble."

Hannan patted her arm. "Nonsense. You're not capable of being any trouble. I have an Italian dinner all set up—one to rival the best in Tuscany."

Lilly giggled. "Sounds delicious. You keep cooking dinners like that, and you'll never get me out of here."

Jacob wrapped Lilly into a hug, stealing a kiss from her beautiful lips. "Maybe that's the plan."

Another giggle. God, he loved her laugh. She wrapped her arms around his neck, offering up a dazzling smile. "I like your plan."

The love emanating from Lilly's brown eyes nearly undid Jacob. He had to force himself to stay upright and not drop to one knee, begging her to be his wife. Granted, it would be the least romantic proposal in history, in the entryway of his home with Hannah flanking him and two tabby cats yowling, but the temptation almost overtook him…almost.

Lilly deserved an exquisite proposal, and Jacob was hashing out the final details to make the day he asked for her hand one for the record books.

"Let's take your bags upstairs, Lilly and get you settled. Jacob, will you open a bottle of wine for dinner?"

Jacob reluctantly released Lilly, tucking a long strand of hair behind her ear as his lips brushed her cheek. "Go unpack and get comfortable. I want you to think of this house as your home, Lilly."

Lilly nibbled her lower lip before blowing him a kiss. "Thank you for taking such good care of me." She grabbed her bag and hugged Hannah around the waist. "Both of you, you're wonderful."

Hannah sent Jacob a knowing look. "You're wonderful, my dear. Don't you realize men always behave much better when they're in love?"

Lilly

Hannah led Lilly upstairs, leading her to one of the guest bedrooms. "I set you up in here. The light is beautiful on this side of the house, and there's a balcony overlooking the grounds."

Lilly smiled, but her heart sank; she assumed—or rather hoped—she would sleep with Jacob. *What does this mean? Does it mean anything?*

She pushed the swirling questions to the back of her mind, she was likely reading too much into it. Perhaps Hannah maintained old-fashioned values, she and Jacob were unmarried after all. "This is perfect, thank you, Hannah."

"Jacob's room is across the hall, and I'm in the cottage out back if you need anything. The grounds are completely fenced so your cats may explore to their hearts' content."

"They'll love that, I'm certain."

"I'll leave you to get unpacked." She grinned, her gaze warm and soft. "I'm so glad you're here. Jacob isn't the same without you in his life."

Lilly worried her bottom lip, this nervous tick had become far too common in the last twenty-four hours. "I can't believe he flew back here to take care of me."

"Darling girl, don't you realize how important you are to him? He'd do anything for you, all you have to do is ask."

Lilly watched Hannah close the door as she walked out, perching on the edge of the queen-sized bed. The room was certainly opulent and the view spectacular, but her heart's desire slept across the hall. She couldn't decipher the situation between her and Jacob, if there even *was* a situation. His actions seemed so contradictory—he flies to London to care for her and then puts her up in a separate bedroom. What was going through that man's head?

"Men," Lilly muttered with a chuckle as she focused on unpacking.

The meal was every bit the feast Hannah had promised, and Lilly felt like an overinflated beach ball by the time dessert was served.

Hannah's husband regaled them with tall tales from his childhood in Wales and Lilly's sides hurt from laughing by the time the table was cleared.

The only point of contention was Jacob's conduct. He seemed distant and preoccupied throughout the evening, and their separate sleeping arrangements only increased Lilly's anxiety. He was absent for a good portion of the dinner, answering half a dozen phone calls, all of them taken in another room, away from prying ears.

Stop being paranoid, Lilly. He has every right to discuss his business matters in private. Likely he didn't want to appear rude, talking over everyone at the dinner table. Don't forget he put his career on hold to care for you. Don't let Enrique's words get to you. Remember, Jacob promised he would never hurt you again.

Almost immediately after dinner, Jacob escorted her to her room, pausing outside the bedroom door.

Lilly grasped his hands, hoping to settle her anxiety once and for all. It was time to take the reins of this runaway horse. "I was a bit surprised to find I'm across the hall from you. I assume Hannah choose our sleeping arrangements?"

Jacob released an embarrassed chuckle and shook his head. "It was my request. This is the most beautiful room in the house."

His request? What in the world? Lilly's mind reeled at his statement, but she pressed forward. "I thought we would sleep in the same bed. I always feel safe sleeping next to you—"

His lips pressed against her forehead. "I have some calls and work to finish tonight, I didn't want to keep you awake. But if you get scared, I'm right across the hall. Don't hesitate to come to me." His gaze drifted from her eyes to her trembling lips, and Lilly's breath caught as Jacob bent his head, nuzzling his lips against hers. "Goodnight, beautiful."

Lilly entered the bedroom, her emotions a turbulent, conflicting web. Her overly analytical mind was waging war with her naively romantic heart, and she didn't know which side to believe.

Sinking onto the plush mattress, she ran her hand across the satin coverlet as her mind pondered the events of the evening. She needed some insight into the male brain, and she knew just the person to provide the information.

She turned on her new mobile phone, compliments of Jacob and dialed Ben. If anyone understood men, it was him.

"I was going to call you. How are you feeling?"

"Sore, but better. The dizziness is all but gone. I'm not at the cottage. Jacob brought me to his house for the week." Lilly leaned against the headboard, admiring the frescoes decorating the ceiling; only the ultra-rich could afford to put that much effort into something you only saw when in a horizontal position.

"I heard you were moving—I mean relocating—for the week." Ben stumbled over his words, and Lilly shot the phone a surprised look.

"You knew I was here?"

"Good news travels fast."

Something was definitely up. Ben was acting stranger than usual.

"Did I interrupt you? Are you in the middle of some illicit sexual act?" Lilly joked, hoping that was the reason for his behavior.

"God, I wish; I'm watching the telly."

Time to bite the bullet and ask the question burning into her brain. "Can I ask you something?"

"You just did, Lilly."

"Smart ass. I'm confused by the way Jacob's acting. I don't know what he's thinking, or if he's thinking anything all...about me."

Silence, seconds of silence. That didn't bode well for an easy answer to allay her overactive imagination.

"You don't know his intentions? Isn't it obvious? He flew from Greece to take care of you and you're at his house. What do you think his intentions are towards you?"

"I understand all that, but he also set us up in separate bedrooms—"

"Okay, that's odd."

"I thought so too."

"Did you ask him about it?"

"He said he had work to do this evening and didn't want to disturb me."

"Ah, makes sense. Don't read too much into it. Get some sleep, your body needs the rest."

But Lilly picked up an undercurrent in Ben's words. There was something he wasn't telling her. "He's barely touched me. Could our relationship have moved into the friend zone?"

Ben scoffed so hard he choked a little. Evidently, her question had caused his drink to travel the wrong path. "You were attacked less than thirty-six hours ago, he's likely waiting on you to make the first move, doesn't want to appear like a callous pig. You want to jump his bones? Go for it, embrace feminism."

Lilly giggled, only Ben could make such a connection. "I don't think that's what the founders of the feminist movement had in mind."

"Well, they should have. You have the opportunity to shag Jacob Edmonton. I say you're a whole new level of fool if you don't take advantage. Trust me, if you instigate, he'll respond in kind, and you'll be between the sheets with your dream lover in no time. Just stay away from too much kink, you're still healing."

"Oh my God, you're insane. Goodnight." Lilly hung up the phone, marinating on her friend's words. He was right, Jacob had left a damn movie set to be by her side, it was time to thank him for his gesture.

Lilly took a bubble bath, relaxing her body and nerves before slipping on a new pale purple nightgown and robe. Although her temporary body art didn't add to her appeal, Lilly hoped she could persuade Jacob to overlook the bruises and focus his attention elsewhere.

She smoothed on lotion and added a touch of perfume, the same one she wore the night at the karaoke pub, and she couldn't forget his reaction when she leaned close to him.

Lilly heard music and stepped onto the balcony, looking for the source of the sound. The wind held a slight chill, and she tightened the belt of her robe, inhaling the night air fragrant with the myriad of flowers blooming around the property.

She gazed down at the courtyard and saw the flickering of the outdoor fireplace and the source of the music. Jacob was still awake. She paused, hearing his low timbre carried on the breeze. Did he have company?

Don't be ridiculous, Lilly. It's likely Hannah. It's obvious the man wants to be with you, or he wouldn't have flown overnight on a jet from location to be by your side. Stop being silly and go to him.

Lilly padded downstairs, smiling when she caught sight of her cats snoozing on Charlie's bed. The poor dog didn't stand a chance.

She pushed open the French door onto the courtyard, startling Jacob, who almost dropped his phone onto the brick floor.

He held up a finger, his voice harried. "That's great, I'll have to call you back. I can't talk right now." His last statement was whispered as he turned away from her, and Lilly felt a chill rush over her body.

He hung up the phone and turned to face her, a dazzling smile on his face. "You surprised me, I didn't know you were still awake."

Lilly was prepared to make herself scarce, but she noted how his blue eyes raked over her body. "I didn't mean to interrupt. Should I leave?"

Jacob drew her close, grasping her hands and pressing a kiss to her lips. "No, come sit by the fire. You're always welcome by me, Lilly." He picked up his whiskey glass, the flames dancing in his eyes. Damn, but he was perfect. "I'd offer you a drink, but I'm not certain you should partake tonight, with your injuries."

Time to turn on the feminine charm. "I'm feeling much better. Besides, the whiskey will warm me up...unless you know of another way?" Christ, she sucked at being purposely flirtatious.

A muscle twitched in his jaw as he settled back into the seat, his eyes lasered on the curve of her hips. Without a word, he handed her the whiskey glass.

Not the reaction I hoped for at all. Lilly accepted the offering, sipping the whiskey and wondering if it wasn't safer to flee back to the safety of the guest bedroom.

The first notes of 'La Vie en Rose' played through the speakers and Lilly raised the glass in an unofficial toast. "It's fate, us and this song. To Paris."

Jacob offered her a breathtaking smile, setting her glass on the table before pulling her into his arms. "Dance with me."

"Gladly." Lilly nuzzled against him, releasing a contented sigh when his arms tightened around her frame. She stared up at him, resting her chin on his chest as she met his penetrating gaze. "You feel like home."

His fingers wound into her hair, pulling lightly on her scalp. "You are my home, Lilly."

The remainder of the song played as their bodies swayed, their gazes never breaking and their souls connecting on a far deeper level. Lilly no longer heard the music, she was lost in him; lost in the feeling only Jacob could bring out of her. She needed him, and she needed him to know how badly she desired his touch.

Jacob kissed her wrist at the end of the song, a wry smile on his lips. "Thank you, Lilly."

"As I've told you before, I'm hardly the consummate dance partner."

"That's not what I'm talking about. Thank you for giving me another chance. I know I'm not worthy of someone like you in my life, but I'm forever grateful that for some reason, you believe I am." His words seemed to unhinge him, and he released her hand, picking up his glass and settling into the chair closest to the fireplace.

Lilly bit her lip, seeing the hesitancy on his face. Did he truly believe he was unworthy of her affection? Granted, his past actions were hurtful, but he had more than made up for his indiscretions. His presence here now was proof of that fact.

Emboldened, she settled onto his lap, feeling him tense slightly as she leaned against his chest. Her hand traced lightly along his scalp as her lips pressed against his temple. "The fire feels nice."

She heard his breath catch as he turned his head and pressed his lips against her neck. "You feel nice, Lilly."

A flush of warmth flew through Lilly's body at the feel of his lips against her body. She needed Jacob to remind her of everything she loved and make her forget the atrocities of the last couple days. Wrapping her arm around his neck, she smiled when he pulled her closer.

"Jacob?" Lilly asked, placing a finger under his chin.

"Yes, angel?"

She saw the fire burning in his eyes, and the desire there. Now she had to hope it was aimed in her direction. "I want to kiss you."

His breathing increased as his fingers tightened around her body, but he didn't say a word as she moved her lips closer.

"Is it okay?" Lilly needed to know if she was welcome, if he still wanted her touch.

His only reply was a low moan, his eyes half closed.

It was enough of an answer for Lilly as she traced his bottom lip, smiling when his mouth closed around her fingertip. She nuzzled his mouth, her lips brushing against his with the softest caresses.

Jacob let her take the lead, let her direct the movement, and Lilly wanted more. She curled her fingers around his jaw, gazing once more into his blue eyes before capturing him in a fierce kiss.

He didn't hesitate, opening his mouth and letting her tongue tangle with his, a deep groan emanating from his throat as his hands ran through her hair. He swept her into an earth-shattering kiss, laving his tongue against hers and demanding all the passion she possessed.

His hand curved around her neck, as his mouth made love to her, and Lilly fell into a sea of ecstasy. Jacob pulled back, nipping her lower lip and earning a squeal from Lilly. He pressed his forehead against hers, his fingers tracing the planes of her face. "I missed you, Lilly."

Lilly deposited kisses all along his mouth. "I missed you, too."

"Jacob? I wanted to know if you needed anything before I turned in—" Hannah walked onto the courtyard, catching them locked in an embrace.

Jacob smiled at Hannah, his grip on Lilly tightening. "We're fine."

Hannah sent them a knowing smirk. "Sorry for the interruption, far be it from me to stop the wheels of romance."

Lilly blushed, a small giggle escaping her lips.

"Don't wear her out too much, Jacob."

Jacob looked between Hannah and Lilly, that world famous sexy smirk on his lips. "I'll behave."

"Goodnight, you two."

Lilly giggled at Jacob after Hannah left, pressing a kiss to his lips. "You certainly don't have to behave. I'd much prefer you didn't. Do you want to go to bed?"

His expression changed. "I have a few calls to make. Why don't you go upstairs and get some rest? I'll check on you before I turn in."

Lilly's giggle died in her throat. *What in the world? That kiss was exquisite, every nerve ending in my body is tingling from his touch and now he has calls to make?*

Jacob stroked her cheek, pressing his lips to her skin. "Don't read too much into that, Lilly."

Read too much into what? The kiss or his sudden personality change? Lilly forced a smile, pushing herself to a standing position.

Jacob's phone rang on the table, and Lilly instinctively glanced over, her heart sinking into the pit of her stomach. The caller ID photo showed a beautiful brunette, the same woman photographed with Jacob on the beaches of Greece.

Jacob also noted the call, grabbing the phone. "I have to take this call. It's important."

I'll bet it is. Lilly's heart wrenched, but she plastered on a smile and nodded. "Of course, I bid you goodnight, sir."

He smiled but his eyes were unreadable, and Lilly needed to escape before she made a bigger fool of herself. "Goodnight, angel."

Lilly ran back to her temporary bedroom, pulling off her nightgown and yanking the comforter over her head. God, she was an idiot. She threw herself at Jacob and he sent her packing to the guest room so he could speak with another woman. Now she understood why he was so distant and lacking in affection. He had told earlier that there was a distinct difference between loving someone and being in love. Christ, how stupid could one heart be?

Grabbing her phone, she sent Ben a message. *"So much for taking the bull by the horns, turns out his affection is aimed elsewhere. I'll be returning to the cottage tomorrow. He's done his duty as my friend."*

She felt her phone vibrate a moment later but ignored Ben's reply. She wasn't up for rehashing the embarrassing moments of the evening.

CHAPTER EIGHT

Jacob

J acob watched Lilly depart, willing himself to stay where he was and not run after her, wanting nothing more than to spend the rest of the night making love to her. He saw the look of confusion drift across her face. Obviously, she thought he didn't want her physically, but nothing could be further from the truth. Christ, couldn't she *feel* how much he wanted her? But he couldn't cave to his carnal instincts, he desired every facet of Lilly, a reassurance she would belong to him on every level.

He messed up his chance with Lilly the first time, there was no way in hell he would let that happen again.

Even worse was the lie he told about answering Miriam's call. Who broke off kissing a breathtaking woman to answer a damned phone? The hurt in her eyes almost broke his resolve. She had put herself out there and he rebuked her advances, now she was afraid to love him.

"Hi Miriam." Jacob prayed there were no filming emergencies that would curtail his trip.

"How are things going up north? How's Lilly?"

"She's recovering, no permanent damage, thankfully. I brought her to my house for the rest of the week."

"Good. Did I catch you at a bad time? Knowing your addiction to that woman, you've likely been naked in bed the entire time."

Jacob chuckled. Christ, he wished. "Not at all, actually."

Miriam let out a surprised guffaw. "Really? Is she no longer interested?"

Jacob paused before rehashing the last twenty-four hours. It seemed no matter what path he chose with Lilly, he always ended up bungling it, despite best intentions. "I'm taking my time with her, she's been through so much the last couple days. I thought rushing her intimately would be bad form. She did kiss me right before you called, though."

"And you're speaking to me why? The woman you adore kissed you and let you know your affections are welcome and you sent her packing? Are you daft?"

"I don't want her to think I'm only after sex."

Miriam snorted. "You men are something else. She came to you! She obviously is fine with the idea of intimacy if she instigated the act! Stop behaving like a blooming ass, hang up and go make love to her! That's an

104

order."

Normally, Jacob would laugh and do exactly as Miriam intimated, but his mind was troubled. "It's not that simple."

Miriam let out an exasperated sigh. "Yes, Jacob, it is exactly that simple."

He paced the courtyard, his emotions warring. He wanted Lilly, he'd never wanted a woman more, but he needed her to understand this relationship was not purely physical. "I still don't know if something happened with her and that surgeon. He came to Lilly's house and read me the riot act."

"He would, he wants to be with Lilly, but she's with you. You're being dense."

Jacob clutched the phone. "I'm terrified."

"Of what? This is *everything* you've been wanting these last couple months."

Jacob swigged his whiskey. "I'm asking Lilly to marry me. I've set up this grand proposal for tomorrow. She walked in while I was speaking to my lawyer about getting a marriage license. If she'd been five seconds earlier, she would know everything."

"I like this side of you, my friend. Very romantic."

"What if she says no?"

"God, men are impossible," Miriam chuckled. "She won't say no. Get off the damn phone and go to her. I'm hanging up now. Goodnight Jacob."

Jacob downed another glass of whiskey before climbing the stairs to Lilly's bedroom. He hated that she was sleeping in any bed other than his own, but he needed answers before they moved forward. Even if it killed him first.

He pushed the door open and his breath caught as he watched the moonlight spilling across her naked form. She looked like an angel. Her porcelain skin glistened in the low light, her full breasts on display above the silk sheet.

His erection was painful at this point; he craved this woman. Biting his lip and clenching his fists, he crept to her bedside, his heart—and pants—near bursting.

Tears filled his eyes as they passed over her bruised side; his heart breaking at the fear she endured in his absence.

He knelt there, pulling the sheet up her body, his fingers grazing against her nipple. Just the feel of her breast under his hand nearly undid him. He wanted to bury his face in her curves and run his tongue along every inch of her exquisite form.

His lips brushed her hair. "You're my angel, Lilly. Don't ever think I don't want you, my darling, but I need all of you now. If I have my way, you'll be wife within a week."

Lilly shifted, pushing the sheet down again. Christ, this woman was going to kill him. She let out a low moan before her hand clasped around his arm. "I love you, Jacob."

Holy shit, if she heard what I said and that's her response, I'm burying myself inside her and staying there for the next week. He held his breath, looking for any indication that she was awake, but she snuffled her face into the pillow.

Jacob brushed his lips against hers, smiling as he nuzzled her nose. "Tomorrow, my love."

"I could seriously kick your ass," Janie exclaimed as she flounced into the kitchen the following morning, Elizabeth a few steps behind.

Jacob glanced up from his tea, his blue eyes amused. "What did I do now?"

"I went to Lilly's house yesterday and damn near had another heart attack when no one was there. I thought something happened!"

"I wanted her here. My house is safer."

Janie wrapped her arms around her brother's neck, landing a kiss on the top of his head. "Look like a regular squaddie, Jacob, ready for action."

Jacob chuckled. "I know, it's not my favorite look either. Or Lilly's."

"Or Lilly's what?"

His gaze shot up to Lilly, leaning against a counter as she poured herself some tea. She looked so right in his house, *their* house, for all intents and purposes. "My hair, or lack thereof. It's not a good look for me."

Lilly padded to the table, dropping a kiss on Janie's cheek, her eyes avoiding Jacob's gaze. "I don't think it's possible for you to have a bad look, Jacob, but I actually like you better like this."

He was hard again. Every word she spoke went straight to his cock. Janie shot him a knowing look before hiding a smile behind her cup of tea.

"How are you feeling, luv? Elizabeth be careful. Lilly got hurt, she's still quite sore."

"She's fine, Elizabeth is always welcome by me." Lilly scooped up the small blonde, snuggling her on her lap.

Jacob couldn't take his eyes off Lilly with his niece, the desire to have a child with her was growing stronger by the minute.

"Lilly, you need to get married and have a ton of babies. You're a natural mother." Janie shot her brother a look, arching an eyebrow.

Lilly blushed, turning red to the tops of her ears. "Thanks for the compliment but I would need a willing participant first."

Now Janie looked utterly confused, her glance moving between Jacob and Lilly. She recovered quickly, patting her friend's hand. "I guarantee should you desire such a match; you would have no shortage of suitors."

Jacob kept his gaze on Lilly as she bit her lip, an insignificant gesture that drove him wild. "I'm not so sure about that. Besides, I still believe in fairytales and fireworks."

Jacob looked down into his tea, clearing his throat. "And butterflies."

"What?" Janie asked.

"Lilly says she has to feel butterflies when she kisses someone. She says it rarely happens."

Janie grabbed her friend's hand, giving it a squeeze. Meanwhile, Lilly looked like she wanted to crawl under the table. "Butterflies are rare, indeed, Lilly."

"I see butterflies all the time, Mum," Elizabeth interjected, causing the adults to chuckle.

"These are different types of butterflies. Ones you only see when you're all grown up," Lilly stated, tweaking Elizabeth's nose.

"I can't wait to be grown up. I hope I'm beautiful like you, Lilly."

The smile that spread across Lilly's face lit her up brighter than the sun. "Please don't do it too fast; stay young forever. You're far more beautiful than any of us."

"How many times have you seen the rare butterflies?" Elizabeth questioned, snuggling against Lilly.

There was Lilly's adorable blush again. "Umm, well...just once, Elizabeth."

"I've only experienced them once too," Jacob added, smiling at Lilly when her gaze swung to meet his. "The woman I knew I'd spend the rest of my life with. I felt them with her."

Jacob expected a radiant smile from Lilly, but her features clouded, and she looked away. He glanced to his sister for guidance, but she shrugged.

"Enough about rare adult butterflies, what do you say you and I go into the garden with the kitties and look for real butterflies and fairies?" Lilly inquired, earning a shriek of approval from Jacob's niece.

Janie watched her daughter and Lilly leave the room before turning to her brother. "I'm confused. I'm getting such mixed signals from you two. What's going on?"

"I'm taking it slow and she may have misinterpreted it as disinterest on my part."

"Are you mucking up again?" Janie chortled, sipping her tea.

"No, I'm not. I have an entire day planned—complete with music and a catered lunch and a list about a mile long telling Lilly every reason why I love her." He rubbed his palms nervously. "I'm asking her to marry me, Janie—"

Janie released a yelp of excitement and threw her arms around Jacob. "That's bloody fantastic!"

Even discussing his upcoming proposal made him break out in a sweat. Christ, he was nervous. "I don't have a ring because I want to design one for her and it has to be as unique and ethereal as Lilly. Mum gave me Nanny's ring, but I have to get it sized, so it won't be ready today. Do you think I need a ring first? I can go to the jewelers and get one now—"

Janie knelt by her brother, rubbing his arms affectionately. "You're terrified, aren't you?"

"Scared shitless. I haven't been intimate with Lilly because first, I didn't want to push that on her and second, because I don't want her to think it's just about sex. I want everything."

"What's everything?"

"Marriage, children, a lifetime together. I want her every single day for the rest of my life, Janie."

Her blue eyes widened, her jaw slackening. "Who are you? What have you done with my brother? God, this is thrilling! You couldn't have picked a better woman. But how in hell are you holding back? You've been pining for Lilly for months."

"I'm fucking dying, that's how," Jacob snorted, bursting out in laughter with his sister. "I think I can survive another eight hours and that's about it."

"Poor man, the troubles in your life." Janie stood up, peering out the window at Lilly and Elizabeth engaged in a game on the patio. "I really want to be an aunt. Can you get on that please?"

"Your lips to God's ears," Jacob whispered, hoping the plan would go off without a hitch.

However, Mother Nature opted not to cooperate. The clouds broke loose with the rain a half hour later, drenching everything in sight.

Lilly and Elizabeth ran into the house, squealing and soaking wet from the downpour. Jacob thought his future wife never looked more beautiful.

"I was wondering where you all went," Audrey stated, smiling as her daughter ran to her side. "Hey Lilly, how are you feeling, doll?"

Jacob smiled at the adoration emanating from Audrey. She far preferred

Lilly to her brother-in-law any day.

"I'm better, and Elizabeth has given me a magical fairy flower, so no harm can come to me. Best part, no deluge of rain can affect the magic." She motioned to the tiny rose that Elizabeth had tucked behind her ear an hour earlier.

"My child is part fey."

Lilly shivered, her clothes sticking to her like a second skin as water dripped off her hair. "Don't I know it? Excuse me all for a moment, I'm going to grab some towels."

Once Lilly was out of sight, Audrey shot her brother in law a smirk. "Well?"

Jacob shot Audrey a confused stare. "What?"

"Are you engaged? Has your time in Greece smartened you up a bit?"

Jacob grinned. "Unfortunately, I'm still single, but hopefully that will change very soon. I have a call into the consulate."

"Why do you need to speak with the consulate to propose marriage?"

"I don't know the requisites for getting married in England; haven't ever been interested in it before."

"Well, the consulate is known for being ball-busters, even if you are God's gift to straight women."

Jacob scoffed, his sister-in-law never missed a trick. "You don't think I'm charming enough to earn any special favors?"

"I don't think you're charming, period. Now your future wife? She's the cat's pajamas."

"She absolutely is, and I don't deserve her."

"Now you're speaking my language," Audrey quipped.

"If I were you, I'd contact the consulate now, before Lilly gets back," Janie interjected, realizing a moment too late that Lilly was already back.

"Why do you need to contact them before I get back?" Lilly asked, her hand on the doorknob, a wary expression on her face.

Shit, there goes that surprise.

"Janie, let's leave them alone, shall we? These two have some important things to discuss. We'll be in the living room, getting this little sprite dried off," Audrey stated, taking the towel Lilly offered before pulling her wife and daughter out the door.

Jacob's nerves were in overdrive. This was not how he planned this moment to play out. He cleared his throat, wracking his mind for the best explanation.

He needn't have bothered, Lilly was done waiting.

"Why do you need to contact the consulate, Jacob?" Her voice trembled with reined-in emotion.

Jacob met her gaze, his hands trembling. "You need the consulate's permission to get married in England."

His words hit her like a train. She actually fell backwards a step. Her mouth opened but no sound came out, as though she had literally lost the words. Finally, she managed a tortured whisper. "You're getting married?"

Jacob stood up and walked to her, but Lilly waved him off, tears in her eyes. "Lilly—"

"I—I need a few minutes, okay?"

He grabbed her wrists, fuck, this was a disaster. "Please, let me explain. You weren't supposed to hear that. This is not how I wanted to have this conversation."

Lilly bit her lip, her breathing short and huffed. "I know we need to have this conversation, but I need a few minutes first. Please?" She squirmed from his grasp, dashing out the door.

Jacob took off after her, running into Janie and Audrey in the living room.

"What in the world happened? Lilly just ran past us, crying hysterically. What's going on?" Janie asked, concern crossing her face.

Jacob ran his hand over his scalp, so much for planning a fantastic proposal. It was time for damage control. "I think she might think I'm marrying someone else. What a bloody nightmare. I'll speak to you both later. I have to go try to fix this mess, if it's even fixable at this point."

Janie's face blanched with realization. "She thinks you're engaged to the woman in Greece. The one who appeared in those photographs. The tabloids were speculating that you and this woman were seriously involved and planning on getting married soon."

Jacob's heart dropped when he realized which mystery woman Janie was referring to. "You mean Miriam, my director?"

"A tall brunette—"

Jacob nodded his head, his stomach churning. "There's *nothing* going on there. But…oh shit. Miriam called last night, and I sent Lilly to bed so I could take the call. Bugger. What the fuck do I do now?" He sputtered as he poured some whiskey and tossed it back, willing his nerves to settle.

"Well don't just stand there! Get your arse upstairs!" Audrey boomed out.

He downed another shot, his hands shaking. "How did I fuck it up so bad?"

Audrey grabbed his shoulders. "You didn't. It's a misunderstanding. Hey, you know by her reaction that she's definitely in love with you. Go make her yours."

Jacob nodded, forcing a smile. "You think she'll forgive me?"

Audrey shot him a smirk as she, Janie and Elizabeth headed for the front door. "I don't know, how talented is your tongue?"

Lilly

illy sank into the jacuzzi tub, the water almost too warm to be comfortable. *Screw it, what's a little more pain at this point?*

She gathered all her strength just to calm down, and accept the fact that Jacob was getting married, and it wasn't to her. She foolishly believed when he showed up on her doorstep that he loved her. He told her he loved her, but Lilly realized now that he wasn't *in* love with her, his heart belonged to that statuesque beauty in Greece.

Her mind replayed the last day, the truth of the situation now glaringly obvious; separate bedrooms, his polite refusal of her advances, consulate discussions with Janie—she missed each and every sign.

Why didn't Janie warn me? Why didn't Jacob tell me sooner? Why am I such an idiot?

Questions circled in her head, knocking against her battered heart and ego. She claimed to be a good judge of people; what a load of crap.

Time to rein in her emotions and relinquish the idea of a romance with Jacob. It wasn't in the cards. She wouldn't destroy a friendship because he didn't return her erotic inclinations, but it was time to put some real—and permanent—distance between them.

Lilly sucked in a few deep breaths, fighting back the nausea and steeling herself for the inevitable conversation. They would have their discussion and then she would go back to her cottage and prepare for her return to America. She would hold it together, act the part of the good friend and then drown her sorrows in several bottles of whiskey later that day.

After all, she couldn't stay in the tub forever, could she?

"Lilly, I'm coming in." Jacob entered the bathroom, a resolute expression on his gorgeous face. "Are you finished?"

Lilly fluffed up the bubbles to cover herself, but realized it was moot. Why bother? She already felt stripped bare in front of this man. "I suppose, did you need the tub?"

His fingers twitched, his movements agitated. Shit, this was going to be worse than Lilly thought. "No, I need you *out* of the tub. It's time to talk. I'm going to implode if I delay this conversation any longer."

"Okay, I'll dry off and be out in a minute." Lilly glanced around, looking for the closest towel, hanging across the room.

Jacob followed her gaze, pulling the towel off the rack and striding to the tub. His azure gaze pierced hers, making her tremble. "Stand up."

"You don't need to—"

His eyes flashed a warning, he was not messing around. "I want to, now stand up, Lilly."

She could deny this man nothing. She stood, the soapy water clinging to her curves. Jacob's pupils dilated but he didn't say a thing as he pulled out the tub stopper and turned on the shower head. He aimed the warm spray at her skin, his gaze following the rivulets of water as they cascaded down her body.

Lilly's breath caught at the intimate act, but she maintained her cool exterior. Time to test her own acting skills. "Thank you."

Jacob offered his trademark sexy smirk while his hands kept busy toweling her off from top to bottom. The man didn't miss an inch of her body; damn his attention to detail.

Lilly wanted to halt his movements, but her body threatened anarchy if she said one word. All she could manage was a faint moan as tingles danced across her skin.

His breath hitched as his eyes moved all over her. "Lilly, you're—"

"Cold?" *And naked in front of a man who's about to shatter my heart— again?*

"Shit, I'm sorry." Jacob wrapped the towel around her body, scooping her into his arms. "Let's get you warmed up."

Lilly wanted to bawl at the familiar gesture, it was only yesterday he carried her to the bedroom this way. Yesterday, she believed he was in love with her, today she knew the truth. "You smell like whiskey."

"I did a few shots. Needed some liquid courage."

Wonderful, he needs whiskey to have this conversation with me. "Where are you taking me?"

"You are too wound up and need to relax. I'm going to give you a massage."

"I don't want a massage." Liar, liar.

"The topic isn't up for debate." He laid her on the bed, his eyes dark with emotion. Without a word, he poured massage oil into his palm and began kneading her foot.

Lilly tried to pull her foot back, but he held firm. "You don't have to give me a massage."

"It's my pleasure. Touching you is always a pleasure."

Lilly moaned as he hit a sensitive area, forcing a smile. "Part of your VIP nursing treatment?"

113

Jacob laid a kiss on her instep. "Something like that."

Enough stalling, Lilly. "Ready for our now notorious conversation?"

Jacob paused, taking a deep breath. "No time like the present, although I'm shocked you didn't figure it out sooner."

Why drag this out any further, hammer the damn nail in the coffin. "I suppose I was a bit dense. I concocted a different story in my head. But the whole consulate and marriage chat cleared away any doubt. I knew you were in love, I didn't know you'd met the one." *So far, so good. No tears, screams or meltdowns. Just my heart cracking, piece by brittle piece.*

He bit back a grin as his hands curved around her calf. He really didn't need to look so overjoyed. He could fake a tinge of sorrow. "I've fallen inescapably and madly in love."

Lilly's breath caught; this wasn't news. They'd danced around this topic for weeks, but hearing his admission made her heart seize. "I see that. It's written all over your face."

"What about you?"

Lilly scrunched her nose. "What about me?"

"Are you in love?"

"We aren't discussing me, Jacob." *Can't I just crawl into a hole and die instead of answering that question?*

He laid another kiss along the inside of her ankle. "Yes, my darling, we are most definitely discussing you. Conversations are a two-way street. So, are you in love?"

She could lie, but that wasn't Lilly's style. "Inescapably and madly in love."

His eyes held her captive. "Does he know?"

Lilly blinked back tears, focusing her gaze over his shoulder. "Doesn't matter. He doesn't return the affection."

Jacob chuckled, and Lilly's eyes widened. What was so all-fired funny about unrequited love?

"Are you quite sure, Lilly?"

"Pretty damn sure, can we stop talking about my non-existent love life now? Focus on your perfect goddess?" Lilly didn't know how long she could maintain the facade of best buddy. It was physically painful.

Another chuckle, the man was a true sadist. "Sure, I can spend hours talking about her."

Lilly gave him a thumbs up, her smile more of a pained smirk. "Lucky me. Can we forget the massage and focus on our conversation?"

"I can multi-task."

"So, that's a no."

Jacob paused, his hand wrapped around her foot before he smiled, continuing his torment. "My love is the most incredible woman I've ever met. She's kind beyond measure, has the most giving heart, and she loves so completely. I'm a better man knowing her and a far better man loving her." Love emanated through his voice.

"She sounds perfect," Lilly choked out, her body temperature rising as his hands stroked her thigh. If he thought his movements were relaxing her, he was mistaken, every touch stirred a firestorm within her body.

His hands slid further up her legs, and Lilly shot him a wide-eyed warning. "Don't give me that look, Lilly. Relax, you've earned this."

Earned it? I'm a bloody masochist. Lilly huffed but relented, leaning back and closing her eyes. She might as well enjoy the experience of Jacob's hands on her body. His new wife certainly wouldn't allow her to feel them again.

"She has the most gorgeous body, all curves and softness. Her skin is as smooth as silk, and after knowing what she feels like, no other woman compares. She's my heaven."

Lilly groaned, glowering at his adoring expression. "Do me a favor, spare me the gory details about her perfect body and lovemaking skills."

His eyes twinkled, and he smirked. The bastard smirked. "Lilly, *you* asked about this woman. I hadn't mentioned her ability as a lover, although she is by far the best I've ever had. The way she feels when I slide inside her, feel her tighten around me—"

"Okay, that's enough." Lilly propped up on her elbows. This conversation was over. She got the picture.

Her attempt to swing her legs off the bed was thwarted by one sadistic golden-haired Adonis, intent on inflicting the full extent of his torturous arsenal. "We aren't finished." His movements, innocent in the beginning, segued as he cupped her ass, his fingers dancing along her curves.

"I'm good," Lilly choked out, struggling to comprehend his movements, so contradictory to his speech.

He smiled. "You're more than good, Lilly, you're exquisite. But we aren't done, not by a long shot." His hands stroked forward, his fingers sliding across her folds as his thumb brushed against her clit.

Lilly's hips bucked at the motion, and an involuntary gasp escaped her lips. "Jacob—"

"Now, where was I…" Jacob's fingers danced against her mound, his lips now mere inches from her entrance, pressing against her inner thigh.

Where was he? Fondling my ass and telling me about some other woman. Shoot me now. Lilly groaned, her back arching reflexively. "You're killing me."

He nipped her thigh before grabbing the edges of her towel.

Lilly grabbed for the towel, but a pointed look from Jacob stopped her in her tracks.

"Lilly, let me do this. I want to make you feel good."

"But—"

"Does it feel good?" His fingers slid the towel apart, exposing her body to him.

His gaze held hers and Lilly felt something deep in her soul, a voice telling her to lay back and let him finish his ministrations. "Your touch always feels good, but it's a bit chilly." What a bunch of bunk. Christ, his gaze could scorch her to her core.

Jacob didn't believe her fib either. His hands stroked under her breasts; his fingers brushing against her nipples. "Sorry for any chill. You'll be plenty warm in a minute."

The man didn't sound sorry, in fact, he sounded quite pleased with himself.

"Lilly, when you're in love, everything changes. You begin wanting things you never wanted before, needing those things. They become impossible to live without."

Lilly's heart flipped; he'd spoken these words before, the first and only time they made love.

Jacob's fingers traced down her ribcage, grasping her hips and Lilly arched her back as he ran his tongue along her abs. There would be scorch marks from the heat of his touch. "I dream about her every night. I couldn't be with another woman if I tried, not that I ever would."

Lilly forced a smile, his words conflicting with his erotic exploration. "Go you." God, she sounded like an asshole, and maybe she was. She wasn't going to tell him to stop touching her, no way in hell. She needed to commit his caresses to her memory bank; the one man who fired up every cell in her body.

"Do you remember what I told you several weeks ago?" Jacob settled onto the bed next to her, his fingers tracing the lines of her thigh.

Lilly watched his movements. "You'll need to be a bit more specific."

"You could have the most amazing romantic life, be worshipped and adored—"

"I'll get right on that. Hey, keep your hands PG, mister." Lilly swatted his hand off her inner thigh.

Jacob paid her no mind, his hand moving up her thigh and cupping her ass. "For such a brilliant woman, you certainly are thick-headed."

Lilly groaned, covering her face. "I'm trying to be supportive, Jacob. Believe me, I'm trying. But can't you have this explicit, detailed conversation with your perfect goddess?"

His lips pressed against her abdomen, his tongue flitting along her skin as his finger drew out a word. No, words. I. Love. You. Lilly's eyes flew open. He rested his head on her stomach, his watchful gaze on her. "I just did."

She gaped at him, propping herself on her elbows, her eyes as wide as saucers. "Holy shit." *Well, that was romantic, Lilly. One for the record books.*

"I can't believe you didn't know. I thought I'd made it really obvious—" His hands continued sketching designs across her abdomen, but Lilly detected a faint trembling. He was afraid of her reaction.

Lilly felt herself tearing up, she couldn't have heard him correctly. "You're in love with me?"

The smile that lit up his face was all the answer she needed. "Utterly and inescapably."

Lilly didn't know whether to laugh or cry. Her body decided on a bit of both. She pushed him onto his back, straddling him, a wide grin on her face. "You bastard; you damn near gave me a heart attack!"

Jacob's eyes darkened at her naked body on top of him, his hands running along her curves. "I hope you can forgive me. God, you feel good, Lilly."

"Why haven't you touched me?"

"Darling, you'd just been attacked. I didn't want you to feel pressured."

"So, you do want to sleep with me?"

Jacob laughed. "I've had a permanent hard-on for the last two days, can't you tell?"

Jacob rolled her onto her back, bending down to nip her breast. Lilly squealed but then stilled, remembering the photos in Greece and the phone call from the night before. She couldn't let it slide.

"But that woman in the tabloids, she called you last night—"

"Her name is Miriam, she's my director. She's been trying to fix the mess I made with you since I arrived in Greece." Another kiss, this time at the apex of her thighs, his tongue equal parts searing and soothing.

Lilly reached her hand down to stroke his head, feeling the stubble under her fingers; God, her body was on fire for him. "You know I'm in love with you, right?"

Jacob smiled, pressing a kiss against her stomach as he knelt between her legs. "I do now. I didn't before I got back here. I feared you had moved on with someone else."

"There's never been anyone but you. From the first day we met, it's always been you."

Jacob sent her a wicked grin, his hands playing along her folds. "I dream about the night we made love, I replay it over and over in my mind. There's only one thing that was horribly wrong that first time."

You mean your girlfriend showing up? Lilly almost spit out the comment but realized this moment was too fragile, too precious for sarcasm. "What's that?"

He knelt over her, his hands stroking up her sides, pausing to tease her breasts, his tongue flicking over the hard peaks. "Your body needs to be worshipped. It needs days of unabashed adoration." His teeth raked her neck, and Lilly's fingers pressed into his shoulders.

"Three days?"

His hooded eyes met hers, his lips nuzzling her mouth. "That would be a start." He pounced on top of her and grasped her wrists, holding her body to the mattress as his gaze held her heart hostage. "But Lilly, I want it all with you. You're the love of my life, and I want to spend the rest of my days with you. I need to know if you feel the same—"

His words were cut off as Lilly's lips swooped against his, capturing any remaining platitudes with her mouth. The kiss was ravenous as they poured out every emotion of the last few months.

Jacob groaned low in his throat, holding her in the kiss. Her fingers scratched his scalp as she pulled herself tight against him, while his tongue waged a war on her mouth.

"Not fair, you're not naked. I need to feel every inch of you." Lilly breathed against his lips, grinning as Jacob obliged her request, stripping off his clothing. Damn, he was delicious. She could feast on his body for days.

"Better?" Jacob didn't wait for an answer, claiming her mouth again in a hungry embrace.

Lilly pulled back several moments later, a coy smile playing on her mouth. She still had one question that demanded an answer. "Why did you call the consulate, Jacob?"

He smirked, tickling his fingers along her ribs. "I had an entire day planned, but you, my little scallywag, interrupted the conversation—"

Lilly bit her lip to hold back the shit-eating grin threatening to explode onto her face. "I repeat, why did you call the consulate, Jacob?"

He wound his hands in her hair, bringing her lips against his. "Because I'm making you Mrs. Edmonton, if that's okay with you."

Lilly skewed her mouth, contemplating his statement. "Hmmm, let me give it some thought—"

A cry of joy escaped her lips as he nipped her lips. "Don't even play, my darling angel. I've been tied in knots for days."

Lilly smiled up at the love of her life, running her hands over his scalp. "Lilly Edmonton, it has a nice ring to it."

Her words lit up his face, his happiness a reflection of her own. "Is that a yes?"

She giggled, blinking back the tears. "That's a hell yes." Her finger traced the outline of Jacob's lips as she whispered her request. "And as your future wife, I want my three days now."

Jacob's eyes darkened, his hands wrapping around her hips as he pressed his erection against her. "Only three days?"

Lilly's lips nuzzled along his jawline, repeating his earlier statement. "It's a start."

Jacob chuckled deep in his throat while his hands and tongue roamed the length of her body. "God, I missed these curves. You're exquisite."

Lilly's breath came in ragged gasps as his mouth moved between her thighs. "Open your eyes, Lilly." Lilly's eyes flew open, unsure when they had closed, and met his potent gaze. "I love you. I need to taste every inch of you." With that statement, his mouth latched onto her clit, causing her hips to buck off the bed. "Christ, you taste so fucking good."

His fingers slipped inside her, and Lilly whimpered with need. "Jacob, please don't make me wait any longer."

He smiled against her skin before shooting her a devious grin. "I'm enjoying this torture way too much to end early, beautiful girl." His tongue slipped inside her and Lilly's hands clutched his head as her hips rose against him, earning a moan of appreciation from Jacob. His hands banded around her thighs as his mouth made love to her, holding her against him until an orgasm ripped through her body.

Lilly was still panting when Jacob reclaimed her mouth in a searing kiss. His fingers entwined with hers and held her arms against the mattress. His azure eyes locked on her as his lips danced across her mouth. "So beautiful, I'll never get enough of you."

Her legs wound around his waist, securing him in her embrace. "Make me yours. I need to feel you inside me. Show me how much you love me." She nibbled his lower lip, eliciting another groan from Jacob, gasping as he entered her in one smooth thrust.

Jacob's eyes held hers as he buried himself inside her, cries of ecstasy punctuating the air. They were finally together, after all the time and obstacles, they were one.

Their first time was a pure firestorm—intense pleasure and raw rhythm—Lilly's body arching against his release. Jacob remained inside her, and Lilly took that moment to wind her hands around his neck and pull his mouth to hers, sliding her hips against him.

Jacob's smile of longing and desire couldn't be falsely forged. She basked in his adoration. At that moment, Lilly realized she owned Jacob as much as he owned her. They belonged to each other. She seized upon that knowledge, guiding their rhythm.

If their first time was intense, their second coupling was a smoldering fire that heightened with every movement. The energy built until Lilly was sure the bed would catch fire from their heat. This time was for her, and it was apparent Jacob relished watching every cell in her body awaken. Her second orgasm hit more powerfully than the first, and she screamed his name as her nails dug into his back.

Jacob stroked her dark hair away from her face. "I'm so in love with you, Lilly. I've waited forever for you."

Her lips brushed his with the softest of kisses. "Forever won't be long enough to show you how much I love you." Lilly wanted to freeze that moment and the smile that stretched across Jacob's face as she proclaimed her love.

"I'm going to marry you."

Lilly smiled. "You'd better."

Jacob's playful growl sounded in her ear as he teased her folds, nudging her legs apart to receive him. Then he buried himself inside her, both of them so hypersensitive they could barely contain the feeling. It was exquisite. The entire world could fall away, and neither would care.

She arched her hips upwards and moaned. "I can't...I can't..."

Jacob grabbed her wrists and pinned them with one hand above her head, his other hands guiding her hips. He would not let her escape. She would stay there with him in all the rapturous torture. His mouth claimed the spot below her ear, making her squirm further, her feet pushed into the bed as her hips met him thrust for thrust, every cell in her body threatening to implode.

Her body shook as she came, feeling his release a moment later, and the world as they knew it shattered around them.

CHAPTER NINE

Jacob

acob's hand idly stroked Lilly's body as she slept, feeling a contentment he had never known. It was normal to feel satiated after great sex but usually the afterglow soon disappeared, leaving him scrambling for the quickest escape route. Until now.

This was not just great sex, this was mind-blowing. He came harder than ever before in his life, multiple times, and as his fingers played along her hip, he felt stirrings to bury himself deep inside her again. Her curves were exquisite, clothing should be illegal on Lilly's body.

Of course, Jacob would be thrilled just lying next to Lilly's naked form forever, knowing full well that one glance from this woman could bring him to his knees. Not that he'd mind—he already worshipped her.

In the past, Jacob prided himself on maintaining distance; never letting a woman get too close. Even Victoria was merely a passing fancy, but when Lilly walked into his life, she stepped straight into his heart and tore down every wall he ever constructed.

Lilly twitched and mumbled in her sleep. Her subconscious was caught in the throes of a nightmare. Jacob pulled her against his chest, soothing away the monsters stalking her dreams. "Shh…I'm here, you're safe, angel."

Lilly awoke with a start, settling when she realized she was secure in Jacob's arms. She nuzzled his chest with her nose, planting kisses as she went. "I must have had a nightmare. I hope I didn't wake you."

Jacob traced her lips with his finger. "I wasn't asleep."

Lilly's face fell. "I hoped you would sleep like last time."

"I can fall asleep easily right now. I'm choosing to stay awake. I don't want to miss a second of being with you. You're my heroin, I'm addicted for life." He nibbled her shoulder as she giggled.

"We could try chasing the dragon," Lilly murmured, her hand sliding down to caress his shaft.

Jacob groaned in response as she straddled him. She never looked more beautiful; her hair tousled, skin flushed, and lips swollen from kisses. His body ached for her, he needed to stake another claim.

Lilly guided him inside her, sensing his innate need. Jacob's toes curled with the intensity of her movements, grabbing her hips to deepen the motion and eliciting a moan from Lilly as she tossed her head back, riding him with deep strokes. He felt the pressure building and tried to stamp it down. She made him feel like a kid in secondary school, his emotions and hormones raging like an out-of-control freight train.

Lilly rode him harder, her moves slicing through his every thought until everything shattered, and she collapsed on top of him, panting.

She began giggling, and Jacob smirked. "What's so funny?"

"Doctors told me to avoid any activity that raised my heart rate or got me excited. I have failed miserably in listening to any of their orders, and it's all your fault."

"I'm the worst nurse in history."

Lilly chuckled, her head on his chest. "You're the sexiest nurse in history." She met his eyes again, a soft smile playing on her lips. "If this turns out to be an amazing dream, know I've never had a more wonderful time. You were worth the wait."

Jacob pulled her to him, his lips seizing hers, her words echoing his every sentiment. He had to have this woman. He needed her in his life for every moment of every day. "Marry me." He growled, his voice was thick with emotion. "Marry me as soon as possible."

Lilly tried to hide her huge smile, but it only made her smile more. "When exactly are you thinking, Mr. Edmonton?"

"The sooner the better. Tomorrow works for me. I'll call the consulate right now."

She rewarded him with a deep kiss, laying her head on his chest again.

"I do believe we'll see if you remember making this statement later."

"And if I do?" he asked, knowing he would never forget his statement.

Her smile warmed his heart. He was wrapped around her little finger. "Then, we get married, as soon as possible."

Jacob slipped out of the house later that afternoon while Lilly caught up on some much-needed rest. He jumped in his car and headed towards Bond Street. He had an urgent appointment to make with the jeweler.

Checking his phone, he stiffened when he saw ten voicemails from Victoria. Before he had a chance to listen to the first message, his phone rang, and sure as the sky is blue, it was his ex-girlfriend.

He could ignore the call but judging by the stack of voicemail messages, Victoria wasn't taking silence as a hint. "Yeah." His voice was gruff, different from the softened tone he used around Lilly.

"Baby, where the fuck are you?"

"Excuse me?" Jacob breathed, flabbergasted at her random inquisition. It had been weeks since he kicked Victoria out of his suite, and although she barraged him with calls the first several days, it had been radio silence since then. "Where are *you*?"

"In your hotel suite. I left a voicemail that I was flying in yesterday. I'm recording my new video in Santorini."

Jacob scoffed. "In the same town I happen to be filming, total coincidence, I assume?"

Victoria's laugh was coy and practiced. "Of course not, our last visit didn't end on great terms, and I wanted to make amends. And…we need to talk."

"Victoria, we do not need to talk. I broke up with you. I kicked you out of my life—how the hell did you get into my suite?"

"I paid off the bellhop. Do you really think it's hard for me to get into your suite? You underestimate me."

Jacob clenched his fists. "Clearly. You need to leave immediately. Do not make me call security."

"You're not going to call security. There's a huge hole in the wall, the maid asked me if I knew anything about it. I told her you got angry when you saw those photos of me kissing Mark."

"I don't know who Mark is, nor do I care what you were doing together. Please leave my suite."

Victoria was amazingly talented at ignoring requests she didn't like. "So, where are you? No one at the hotel has seen you in days."

"That's none of your damn business."

Victoria's voice turned to ice. "Either you tell me, or I pay a visit to your film set and ask around until someone spills the beans."

"Stay away from the film set." Jacob huffed, realizing if he didn't give her some version of the truth, she would wreak havoc on the set and infuriate Miriam to no end. "I'm in London. I had a personal situation that required my immediate attention."

"A personal situation? This wouldn't have anything to do with that nurse you fucked a couple of months back?"

Jacob bristled but maintained an even tone. "No, nothing to do with her. I don't even remember her name." He felt awful spouting such grandiose lies, but he needed to throw Victoria off the scent, she was a bloodhound.

Victoria sniffed, unconvinced. "Well, I have to head out to shoot my video. I'll call you later. Have fun in London. And remember, we need to have a serious discussion."

Victoria didn't give Jacob a chance to respond as she ended the call. He rubbed his jaw with his hand, uncertain how he would ever see himself clear of Victoria's antics.

Some hardcore music helped Jacob release his pent-up aggression by the time he reached his front door. He heard eighties pop music playing on the radio and smiled, Lilly adored the bouncy cheesiness of that era.

He found her in the kitchen, sipping on chai, the bruise on her shoulder now an ugly shade of purple. But despite any noticeable soreness, she bebopped around the room, oblivious to his presence. Someone covered his eyes, and he turned to see Janie.

He pulled his sister into a huge hug, and Janie beamed at him. "I couldn't wait any longer. I had to make certain everything was patched up between the two of you. Seems you're both still in one piece."

Lilly turned, her face breaking into a radiant smile when she saw Jacob. "I didn't hear you leave earlier. Janie and I were placing bets."

Jacob wrapped his arms around Lilly, kissing her soundly on the mouth. Just being near her made him feel better. "Oh really? What was the bet?"

Janie laughed. "I said you had errands to run and she said you were on a llama hunt in Nepal."

"So obviously, I won," Lilly giggled.

"Obviously." Jacob tipped up her chin and kissed her deeper this time— his tongue stroking against hers while his hands gripped her ass, pulling her close.

Janie cleared her throat. "Anyone care to fill me in?"

Lilly and Jacob exchanged a loving glance before stating in unison, "No."

Janie groaned. "You two are no fun. Hey big brother, can I borrow you for a second?" She glared at Lilly. "You're not supposed to have caffeine."

Lilly nodded as she sipped her latte. "I know, but as a nurse, I also know I'm the worst patient in the world. I'm going to hop in the shower. I'll see you later." Lilly parted with a kiss to Janie.

Jacob watched her walk up the stairs before turning his attention to his sister. "What?"

"Don't what me," Janie replied, jabbing him in the ribs. "Are you engaged?"

"She's going to be Mrs. Edmonton."

Janie squealed, throwing her arms around her brother. "That's bloody fabulous! Congratulations!"

"All my planning out the window, but it doesn't matter. My angel agreed to marry me."

"I'm thrilled for you both, which makes my news such a damn buzzkill. I didn't want to upset Lilly, but Victoria called me five times in the last two days looking for you."

Jacob felt the color drain from his face. "What did you say?"

"I said there was a family situation and you were here in London."

"Did she know Lilly was attacked?"

Janie nodded. "She called when I was at Lilly's bedside. I was so rattled by the attack that it didn't occur to me *not* to tell her that Lilly was in the hospital. Are you okay?"

"She's been blowing up my phone as well, and broke into my hotel suite. I didn't tell her I was in London because of Lilly. I didn't want Victoria to take advantage of the situation."

"And now, you're caught in a web of half-truths. Which is the better place to be?"

Jacob ran his hand over his head. "I don't trust her, Janie. I don't know what Victoria is capable of, and I don't want her ruining anything between me and Lilly. She's a category five cyclone."

Janie shrugged, unimpressed. "She didn't do a thing when you dumped her, right? I'll bet dollars to doughnuts, she's all talk. It's your decision, but Lilly's going to be your wife. She deserves a real relationship. One without any secrets. I got to run, call me later." Janie pecked her brother on the cheek before walking out the door.

As Jacob watched Janie leave, her words echoed in his head. She was right, Lilly deserved an open and honest relationship.

He dialed Victoria's number and when she answered, he didn't give her an opportunity to speak. "I'm in London with Lilly, I've asked her to marry me, and she's accepted. She'll be returning to Santorini with me in a week, as my wife. So I expect you to be gone—permanently. Goodbye Victoria."

He was overwhelmed with a sense of liberation as he hung up on her frantic statements. He had finally come clean about the woman he loved. Setting down his phone, he headed into the bathroom after Lilly; any additional conversation with Victoria the furthest thing from his mind.

Lilly

L illy might be injured, but she wasn't stupid. She noted the barrage of incoming calls from Victoria on Janie's mobile. The phone lit up five times in as many minutes with calls from Jacob's ex. She cringed, thinking that Victoria was still involved in his life.

She wasn't confident how to handle the situation, and hoped, perhaps naïvely, that it was mere coincidence.

Stepping into the shower, Lilly released a moan as the hot water cascaded over her body. She examined her hodgepodge of temporary body art. They were lovely shades of purple and sore to the touch. Thankfully, the swelling was gone from the affected areas, but as she pressed one of the bruises, she cursed in pain.

"Don't do that, silly girl." Jacob slipped into the shower, wrapping his arms around her waist from behind.

"I'm a glutton for punishment." She paused before forging ahead. "I noticed a certain someone was very active on Janie's phone. Anything I should be worried about?"

Jacob took a deep breath, and Lilly wondered how he would attempt to worm his way out of yet another hole. "I just hung with Victoria."

Lilly's eyebrows raised, her lips pursed, and her heart dropped. "I see."

Jacob shot her a look of amusement, gently placing a kiss on the curve of her neck. "No, you don't see. I told her I'm going to marry you and plan to return to Santorini with you as my wife."

Lilly's eyes widened at his admission and she spun around to face him. "What did she say?"

Jacob shrugged, chuckling. "No idea. She started freaking out, and I hung up."

Lilly gaped at Jacob. "I can't believe you told her!"

"Why?" Jacob nipped Lilly's lips as he backed her against the wall of the shower. "You did say that you would marry me immediately. Are you looking to issue a retraction, miss?"

Lilly smiled against Jacob's mouth. "No, I suppose that would be bad for business." She gasped as his hands slid down her stomach and between her thighs, his fingers sliding inside her, his mouth against her neck.

"I'm glad we're in agreement," Jacob murmured, slipping his length deep inside her, his hips pressing her against the wall.

It only took minutes for Lilly to reach orgasm, her cries echoing off the tile. Jacob spilled himself into her moments later.

"I could get used to this VIP nursing treatment," Lilly murmured as they stepped out of the shower.

"You'd better get used to it. I plan on taking full advantage of all marital perks."

Lilly paused, water dripping from her hair. "You're really serious about this marriage idea, aren't you?"

Jacob's eyes widened in surprise. "You're not?"

"I assumed you were joking."

He ran his hand over his buzzcut, unable to hide his disappointment. "Lilly, I don't go around asking women to marry me. I had an entire day planned, remember?" He hung his head. "You don't want to be my wife?"

A smile crossed Lilly's face. A lifetime with Jacob was precisely how she wanted to spend the rest of her days. "Silly man, I want to be your wife more than I want my next breath. I just didn't think *you* were serious."

Relief flooded Jacob's features as he swept her into his arms and carried her to the bedroom. "I'll show you serious."

Lilly grinned, wrapping her arms around his neck. "I like where this is headed."

The sun was setting, but Lilly and Jacob had barely left the bedroom. They made several attempts, but months of pent-up emotions won out, and they kept finding themselves between the sheets.

But now, Lilly's stomach was winning the battle over her emotions, screaming that it hadn't been fed anything but chai in twenty-four hours. She turned to Jacob, who was dozing next to her, and laid a soft kiss on his lips. "Can I borrow your car? I'll be back in less than an hour."

Jacob grumbled and shot her his best attempt at an angry side-eye. "You woke a chronic insomniac from a deep sleep to borrow a car? Damn you, woman." He grabbed his phone and checked the time before pulling Lilly into his arms.

"Was that you snoring? It sounded like a hyena with a bad case of the hiccups." She giggled as he tickled her ribs. "Please, my car is still at the hospital, and I'm starving."

He kissed her forehead and hopped out of bed in all his naked glory.

Lilly licked her lips at the fine sight.

Jacob smirked as he followed her gaze. "See something you like?"

"I see lots of things I like."

"You keep that up and we won't get past the door, you minx." Jacob winked at her, pulling on his pants. "Let's get some dinner, but I'm driving."

Lilly scoffed, her lower lip protruding. She had hoped to slide behind the wheel of that gorgeous Aston Martin.

"Don't give me that look. You hit your head, you can't drive for a few days. What if you crashed my car and messed up my paint job?"

Whack! A pillow hit Jacob in the leg while Lilly glared at him in mock contempt. "Obviously your main concern would be the safety of your paint job!" She grabbed another pillow, but Jacob shot her a warning look.

"I would retaliate, but my aim is better than yours." His blue eyes were playful as his hand hovered over a throw pillow on a nearby chair.

Lilly gasped in fake horror. "You would attack an injured woman? You heathen!" She giggled when the pillow hit her arm, feigning mortal injury and collapsing onto the bed. "The light is fading, goodbye cruel world."

Jacob fell on top of her again, their laughs mingling between kisses. "You missed your calling as a thespian."

"Trust me, one actor in this relationship is enough." She kissed him before pushing him at his chest. "Now let's get some food."

Forty minutes later Jacob led Lilly into an upscale restaurant in Mayfair. The hostess recognized him instantly and escorted them to a private table in the back courtyard.

Lilly noted the faces of the other patrons as the A-list actor meandered through the room. Their whispers grew but Jacob ignored them, his fingers entwined in hers as they walked by.

The courtyard was quaint with fireplaces along each wall and vining flowers climbing the bricks. A small fountain trickled in the center of the courtyard and the whole area glowed with candlelight.

"This place is beautiful."

"Not as beautiful as you." Jacob caressed Lilly's hand, his tongue playing against her fingers. "I've always loved this restaurant, the food is amazing, and the atmosphere harkens back to a more romantic time."

"Your presence is causing quite a stir, sir."

Jacob shook his head. "I doubt it. I come here often."

Lilly nodded, realizing he had likely dined here with countless other women. What must they think seeing him with someone normal?

Jacob picked up on her train of thought and leaned over the table, capturing her lips in a soft kiss. "I've never brought another woman here. Except my Mum, but I figure she's an exception to the rule."

Lilly smiled and returned the kiss as their drinks and appetizers arrived. They spent the next couple hours engaged in laughter, banter and all manner of feasting. Lilly felt immeasurably better by the time they left the restaurant—truth be told, she felt better than ever before in her life.

A small crowd was gathered outside as word of Jacob's presence spread throughout the neighborhood. When they left, he flashed his dazzling smile and began shaking hands with his fans, his other hand firmly clasping Lilly's. A woman raved about his latest film role before her gaze moved to Lilly, inquiring if this was his girlfriend.

Lilly looked away, feeling a flush rush up her cheeks. The whole situation was so foreign to her, and she was embarrassed by such a direct question from a total stranger.

But Jacob pulled Lilly close against him and wrapped his arm around her shoulder, dropping a kiss on her head. "Lilly's not my girlfriend."

Lilly felt tears backing up in her eyes. *Here we go again.*

"She's my fiancée."

Lilly gaped up at him, unable to respond.

The crowd buzzed with tokens of congratulations, although several women looked as if they'd like nothing more than to beat Lilly with a stick. Jacob signed a few last autographs before bidding them goodnight as the valet pulled up with his car.

They had driven a few minutes when Lilly broke the silence. "I can't believe you told people we're engaged."

Jacob shrugged, nonchalant. "Why wouldn't I tell them? I want to scream it from the rooftops." He grabbed Lilly's hand, bringing it to his lips. "There's a certain lack of privacy in my life, and I know that will be an adjustment for you. I hope you're not angry I said something."

"Definitely not angry." Lilly leaned across the seat, ignoring the ache in her shoulder as the belt dug into her bruises. She grazed her teeth against his neck, her kisses moving along his jaw when she heard Jacob catch his breath.

"If you keep that up, I can't guarantee we'll make it home safely, angel."

Lilly's eyes blazed with longing, her inhibitions quieted by the glass of wine with dinner. Her body craved him. Jacob was right, their addiction to each other was stronger than any drug. She unfastened her belt and leaned across him, her hand massaging his erection.

Jacob gasped, but he didn't stay her hand. She was free to continue her erotic exploration, and she was anxious to taste him. She unfastened his pants and continued stroking him, lowering her head to take his shaft in her mouth.

"Lilly." His voice was ragged, his body tense. "What are you doing to me?"

"You know exactly what I'm doing, and I have no intention of stopping." She flattened her tongue along his length, running it up and under his sensitive tip, as his hips bucked against her mouth.

She felt the car pull off to the side of the road, and Jacob's hand wound into her hair as he leaned the seat back, giving her greater access.

Lilly continued her oral assault, her mouth sucking him deeper with each thrust. His hips jerked erratically, and she increased her tempo, a groan escaping his lips as he tightened his grip on her hair.

"Lilly, it's too good. You've got to stop, or I'm—"

Jacob's words only increased her enthusiasm, and he growled with pleasure as he pumped his hips, his cries echoing through the car as he came.

But Lilly wasn't finished. She spent the next minute torturing him, loving the twitches and whimpers emanating from his sated body.

She sat up, a delicious shudder shooting through her when she saw his eyes ablaze with passion. Jacob grabbed her head, pulling her into a blistering kiss, his tongue stroking every inch of her mouth as if he wanted to suck out her very essence.

They were both panting when they parted, their faces flushed with emotion. His eyes raked hungrily over her body before locking onto her face. "Christ, that was amazing."

"I'm glad you enjoyed yourself. I know I sure as hell did."

He laughed, throwing his head back as an audible sigh escaped his lips. "Enjoy might be a bit of an understatement. Holy shit, what you do to me."

Lilly leaned over for one last kiss, smiling against his lips. "Would you like me to stop?"

"Not in a million years."

Jacob

acob was horribly aggravated, but he fought to hide his frustration
from Lilly. There were piles of red tape to navigate before the
consulate would issue a marriage license and it didn't matter if you
were the Pope or the King, rules were rules. He spent the morning making
calls, hoping for a loophole, but there were none to be found. The paperwork
would take a few weeks to be filed, thus ending Jacob's plan of returning to
Santorini a married man.

Lilly's arms slipped around his neck and he kissed them, letting out a
resigned huff.

"I know you're frustrated, but it's only a few weeks, and you're worth
the wait, my darling," she countered.

"I would rent a jet to Vegas, but *certain* medical personnel won't clear
you fly, thanks Dr. Torres."

Lilly perched on Jacob's lap, her fingers tracing his scalp. "Enrique
wants one additional test—"

Jacob grunted. "No, he doesn't want you leaving with me. You can't
even return to Santorini with me. I had all these plans for us—"

Lilly silenced him with a kiss, her tongue tracing his lips. "I promise I'll
fly to Santorini as soon as the test results are finalized. Do you think your plans
will keep for a week? Can you wait for me?"

"I'll wait forever for you." His mouth crashed against hers as he pressed
her body against him, his hands sliding under her shirt to cup her breasts.
"How am I supposed to live a week without this body?"

Jacob caught sight of the clock and groaned, lifting Lilly off his lap. "We
need to get going."

"Where are we going? I thought we were hanging around the house
today."

Jacob grasped Lilly's hands. "I made an appointment with a jeweler on
Bond Street to design your ring."

Lilly smiled, shaking her head. "I don't need a ring."

"You're getting a ring," Jacob insisted, his eyes crinkling. She was the
least materialistic woman he'd ever met. "But before that, we have a doctor's
appointment."

"What in the world for? Haven't I seen enough doctors this week?"

Jacob sighed; he hoped Lilly wouldn't be too angry with his plans. "It's at a renowned fertility clinic."

Lilly's eyes widened, and she stammered when she spoke. "Oh-oh okay. I am over thirty-five, so I don't know how many options I have regarding pregnancy...shit."

Jacob cupped Lilly's face, his thumbs tracing her cheeks. "I wanted us to explore all our options. I'm fine with adopting. Hell, I never considered having children, but then I met you, and I want to have a baby with you. I hope you don't find me presumptuous."

Lilly's smile lit up her face as she stood on tiptoe to kiss him. "You want to have a baby with me?"

"What have you done to my best friend?" A voice echoed behind them, and Jacob turned to see Roger and his wife Sophie in the doorway, both wearing huge smiles. They strolled over, bearing a bottle of scotch and a tremendous bouquet of irises.

"Whatever do you mean, Roger?" Lilly inquired, an innocent smile on her face.

Roger slipped his arm around Lilly, giving her a fierce hug. "You've ruined him for other women. Good for you." Turning to Jacob, he inquired, "Any news from the consulate?"

Jacob rolled his eyes. "None good. We submitted paperwork, but that will take a few weeks; and I have to be back in Santorini on Sunday."

Roger exchanged a giggle with Lilly, muttering about those 'nonsensical damn Brits' before opening the scotch and pouring a small glass for each of them. "Jacob, you're my best mate for fifteen years. I never thought I'd live to see the day when you'd be so happily smitten, and you couldn't have chosen a finer lady. Congratulations to you both."

Shots were downed and the women left to locate a vase for the flowers.

Roger perched on the edge of Jacob's desk, a knowing smile on his lips. "What time do you expect to arrive in Gloucestershire?"

Jacob smiled. Gloucestershire was another surprise for Lilly—a home in the country with acres of lawn for the animals. He had taken her for a drive through the English countryside a couple days earlier and her eyes lit up when they passed the house. She was breathless with excitement, exclaiming how beautiful it must be to live there. The house was for sale, but Lilly joked she would only be able to afford it when she was 100 if she worked 100 hours per week until that time. They spent an hour wandering the gardens of the vacant home, and upon their return to London, Jacob called his realtor to get the details. Funds were transferred the following day, and the sale would close within the month.

He asked the owner if he might rent the manor house for his last three days in England. He wanted to surprise Lilly with a celebration. He was overjoyed the gentleman agreed.

"Around five," Jacob replied, tossing Roger a set of keys to the house. "You and Sophie driving there soon? Mum, Hannah and Janie will be leaving within the hour."

"Grand, I'll have tons of women to order me around," Roger exclaimed, clapping his friend on the shoulder and heading for the door. "I'm thrilled for you, mate. Of course, I always knew she was the one for you."

Jacob let out a guffaw of laughter. "How exactly did you figure it out?"

"Simple. She was the only woman who ever truly saw you, and she loved you anyway."

Jacob and Lilly strolled back to the car after their appointment at the fertility clinic. Although not conclusive, an initial exam showed that anatomically speaking, Lilly should have no issue carrying a child. The doctor provided some prenatal vitamins and mentioned additional options, should they be necessary.

Lilly was unusually somber on the way to the car, and Jacob worried he had pushed too hard in this arena. He wrapped his arm around her shoulders, dropping a kiss on the top of her head. "Penny for your thoughts?"

"I wish I'd met you years ago when this wasn't an issue."

Jacob stopped her, his hands on her shoulders. "It *isn't* an issue. We have so many options, you don't have to carry a child if you don't want to…do you even want a baby? I'm such a wanker for not asking."

"I gave up on the idea of having a child. Now I have my soulmate and a chance for a baby? Does anyone get that lucky in life?"

Jacob pulled her to him, smiling against her mouth. "I got that lucky when I met you."

Lilly groaned and laughed. "God, you are so good at that."

"What?"

"Spouting the most wonderful, heart-bending statements."

He winked before opening her car door. "I told you when we met, I have skills."

Jacob reserved time at the jewelers, hoping to avoid a media circus. His publicist phoned that morning—whispers were swirling about his rumored engagement and Jacob needed to release an official statement to prevent half-truths from making the paper.

His phone had been ringing off the hook. Victoria was relentless, leaving countless voicemails and texts. He deleted the messages without a second glance.

Lilly stiffened as they walked into the high-end jeweler. She was clearly out of her element. Thankfully, the manager—a man named Clive—had humble roots in Liverpool and didn't emanate the pretension of many of the nouveau rich. His charm put Lilly at ease immediately.

He bustled about, setting out all manner of diamonds in every color, shape, and size. "Now lass, all of these are top quality stones, Mr. Edmonton insisted on nothing less. You let me know what you like, and from there we can create a design for you."

Lilly's laugh echoed her nervousness, her eyes seeking Jacob. "They're all lovely, but I'm an environmentalist and I couldn't wear anything that cost someone their life or legacy. I'm sure you understand."

Clive nodded. "I do understand, as does your fiancée. All of these stones are conflict free. He respects your stance on world issues." He took Lilly's hand. "You have such slight hands. You're not the type to want some dripping collection of jewels, are you?"

"I've never had the occasion, but no, I'd be happy giving the money to the animal shelter."

Clive looked at Jacob, who was staring back in a nonverbal plea for silence. "I see you two have similar causes. Mr. Edmonton made a very generous donation to an animal shelter, just a couple months back."

Jacob cleared his throat, his hand rubbing the back of his neck.

Lilly turned to him, a wry smile on her lips. "You were the anonymous donation. I should have realized." She walked over to him, throwing her arms around his neck. "I love you."

Jacob smiled at Clive over Lilly's shoulder. He loved the fact that his donation meant more to his fiancée than the myriad of glittering gems littering the store.

Something in one of the cases caught Lilly's eye; and she wandered over to examine the piece in detail. It was a bracelet of intricately carved golden lilies and roses, interspersed with diamonds, taaffeites and alexandrites. "That's lovely, is this your design?"

Clive nodded, and Jacob perked up at her interest. "You know lass, I could design a ring utilizing that concept of flowers—especially since you're such a nature lover."

"Have you ever done anything like that before?" Lilly questioned.

"You'd be the first, but it would be breathtaking. I could have a large central diamond and then some of the alexandrites and taaffeites around the design. Your thoughts Mr. Edmonton?"

Jacob nodded, grabbing Lilly's hand. "That would be splendid. It suits her perfectly. What do you think, Lilly? Is this the ring for you?"

Lilly's glance shifted between the counters and her hands. It was apparent she was not accustomed to this level of lavish treatment. "I don't want it cost you too much."

Jacob chuckled and cupped her face. "I'm not worried about the cost. Do you like the idea?"

Lilly bit her lip. "It's exquisite."

"Then it's settled." Jacob left to handle the bill, returning a few moments later. "Are you ready? There's still one more surprise."

Lilly

L illy wanted to pinch herself—this had to be a dream, it couldn't be her reality.

"Are you happy, Lilly?" Jacob grasped her hand, offering her a small smile.

"Ecstatic." She pulled him to her, capturing his mouth in a kiss.

"Jacob Edmonton!"

Lilly and Jacob looked up to see a cameraman snapping a few photos before racing down the street. Jacob shook his head, but the smile never left his face.

"I forget this is your normal. I apologize, I need to learn discretion." Lilly watched the diminishing figure of the reporter and scanned the streets, wondering how many more journalists lurked in the shadows.

Jacob wrapped his arms around her, his lips peppering her nape with kisses. "What are you sorry for? Them?" He motioned his head in the direction of the retreating journalist. "Don't ever apologize for showing me affection. You're the woman I love, and I don't care if the world knows it."

Lilly stared into his admiring gaze before hugging him about the waist. In that moment, she believed him.

She slid into the passenger seat, trying to wrap her head around the events of the day. This was a whole new world for her. She simply was not accustomed to someone showering her with gifts. How could she ever keep up?

"Wait, don't drive anywhere yet."

Jacob's brow furrowed.

Lilly reached into her overnight bag, pulling out a burlap wrapped package. "Here."

Jacob shot her a quizzical look as she handed him the package. "What's this?"

Lilly's eyes widened. "I know it's not a custom ring or a designer ensemble, but I found this a couple months ago, and I had to buy it for you. I hope you like it." Her last words were barely a whisper, uncertain of his response.

Jacob smiled and unwrapped the gift, his jaw slackening as he looked at the book. "Holy shit, Lilly! This is a first edition Oscar Wilde...and it's signed!

Where did you find this? I knew there were a few books still circulating, but I never came across this one, not even in an auction house." He turned in his seat, his delight obvious.

"I found it locked in a case at an antique store and I remembered you stating how his works influenced not only your career but your life in general. You quoted him that first night before...."

"You don't love someone for their looks, or their clothes, or for their fancy car, but because they sing a song only you can hear." Jacob quoted Oscar Wilde as he picked up the book again, gently fingering the spine. "This must have cost a fortune."

"The price doesn't matter. It matters if you like it." Lilly didn't bother to mention that it had cost her more than a month's salary, and she had held onto it even through her heartbreak. His beaming smiling now was worth every pound.

Jacob gazed at the book before leaning across to steal a kiss from Lilly. "I love it, and I love you. You are the music of my heart." With another quick kiss, he started the car and headed for the English countryside.

"Where are we gallivanting to for your last few days home?"

Jacob smiled but said nothing, turning the radio to a classic rock station.

Lilly glared at him in mock annoyance. "Oh, we're going to play it that way? I see how it is."

"Sit back and enjoy the scenery."

Lilly reached for his hand, interlacing their fingers. "Thank you, for taking me out of the city. I love London, but I adore the countryside."

They drove at a leisurely pace, stopping for tea and pictures of livestock as they grazed. Jacob joked Lilly must have a picture of every sheep in England.

Lilly perked up when she saw the sign for The Cotswolds, clapping her hands with excitement. "We're spending time in Gloucestershire?"

Jacob nodded and chuckled, his future wife absolutely glowed with happiness. Lilly's eyes widened when that beautiful manor home came into view and Jacob pulled into the circular driveway. "We've arrived."

"I don't understand. Is squatting in a vacant house on your bucket list?"

"I know how much you adore this house, so I rented the property for the next few days."

Lilly beamed at him, before catching sight of Janie in the side yard. "Janie? What are you doing here? What an amazing surprise!" Lilly scooped up Elizabeth who had come running toward the vehicle. "Ben? Sabina?" Her eyes grew wider as friends and family appeared. "What in the world?"

Jacob strolled up behind her, dropping a kiss on the base of her neck.

"It's a celebration."

"Of what?"

Jacob kissed Lilly's lips, his tongue licking the outline of her mouth. "You. I want to celebrate you."

Lilly's eyes grew bright with unshed tears.

"No tears, my angel. Let's go inside and freshen up."

Lilly clasped Jacob's hand, following him into the home. The decor was a mixture of dark antiques and bright paints, exuding class without an ounce of pretension. A breeze streamed through the windows as Jacob led her upstairs to the master suite, the king size bed decorated with rose petals.

Lilly shook her head, smiling. "You did all this?"

"No, I was with you." Lilly playfully punched his chest, as he admitted, "Yes, of course, I orchestrated it."

Lilly's fingers hooked in Jacob's belt loops, pulling him towards the bed. "I think we should put into practice what the good doctor told us earlier; if you have no objections?" Lilly leaned back against the mattress, her seductive smile inviting him to join her, and Jacob wasted no time fulfilling her request.

They joined the guests an hour later, freshly showered and fully sated. The party was in full swing, and everyone applauded as they walked into the main living area. Roger offered them glasses of champagne as Jacob addressed the group.

"Good evening everyone! Thank you for making the somewhat arduous journey to the countryside to celebrate with us." He squeezed Lilly's hand, shooting her a radiant smile. "I think you all know I'm ridiculously and madly in love with this woman, and through some amazing stroke of luck, she has agreed to be my wife."

The guests cheered and Lilly blushed, leaning in to whisper so only Jacob could hear. "I love you."

"Lilly fell in love with this house the moment she laid eyes on it," Jacob continued, "and felt great peace and sanctuary here, surrounded by the rolling hills."

"Which is why I'm so grateful you rented it for our last few days together," Lilly interjected.

Roger chuckled. "You didn't tell her, did you?"

Lilly shot Jacob a questioning look. "Tell me what? I don't think I can handle any more surprises today!"

Jacob set down his champagne and took her hands, his eyes warm on her face. "I didn't rent the house. I bought it, for us."

Lilly feared she might faint dead away. "You what?"

He cupped her face and kissed her. "It's ours."

"This is our house? Oh my God!" She was simultaneously crying and laughing as Jacob knelt in front of her.

"And because I didn't do it properly when I first asked, I thought it only fitting to do it now." He opened a box, a beautiful emerald and diamond ring glistening inside. "It was my grandmother's ring. She prayed I would find a woman who captured my heart, someone exceptional in every way, and I found you." Jacob took the ring from the box, his blue eyes bright. "Lilly, will you do me the honor of becoming my wife?"

Lilly's tears flowed freely as she nodded. "You know I will!" The partygoers went wild as Jacob slipped the ring on her finger, picking her off her feet and swinging her around. "I love you Jacob. I didn't need all this. All I need is you."

"Well, can you get used to me and all this?" Jacob smiled, his lips against hers.

Lilly considered his offer for a second before laughing. "Ah, what the hell."

The festivities continued into the night, as guests mingled, drank and lost their shirts at poker. The sounds of laughter floated above Lilly's head as she snuggled on Jacob's lap. After a couple hours they retreated to the sanctity of the library, allowing her a few moments for the whirlwind of the last week to sink in.

"Are you having a good time?" Jacob inquired as he ran his fingers through her long dark hair.

"It's a fairytale come true. I've got my ballgown...or sundress,"—she kissed his nose—"my castle,"—her lips brushed against each cheek—"and most importantly, my prince." Lilly captured his lips with her own, the kiss slow and coaxing.

Jacob's arms tightened around her back as he pulled her against him, his mouth demanding and possessive. She felt the intensity of his love as his mouth wandered from her lips, dropping kisses along her throat. "Let's go upstairs. I want to make love to you again."

"You want to desert our own party?" Her hand trailed down his abdomen to drop feather-light strokes along his shaft.

Jacob jerked against her hand, his breathing labored as he leaned his head against the back of the chair. "If it means you'll keep touching me, then yes. Let's desert the damn party."

"How did I know I'd find you two hiding in here, squirreled away and doing all manner of naughty things?" Jacob and Lilly jerked their heads up to see Roger leaning against the doorframe, a knowing smirk on his face.

"If you knew we'd be in here, you should have let us be, mate," Jacob replied with a scowl.

"Learn to lock the bloody door, then. Come along, the family is feeling a bit sozzled and are clamoring for dessert. Care to oblige?"

Lilly chuckled as she pushed herself to a standing position, ignoring Jacob's grunt of disapproval. "How can I deny you wonderful people anything?"

"I have no issue with it," Jacob grumbled, wrapping his arm around Lilly and adjusting the waistband of his pants.

Another smirk from Roger. "Your pants a bit tight?"

"Sod off."

"Don't you wish. Come along. There will be plenty of time for baby-making later." He let loose another chuckle when Lilly's face flamed. "It's not exactly a secret, Ms. Staver."

"Soon to be Mrs. Edmonton," Lilly replied, earning a brilliant smile from Jacob.

"Not soon enough." Jacob pressed his lips to her hair before the trio rejoined the party.

Lilly meandered through the crowd, socializing with their friends and family when she noticed Edward off by himself on a bench. She strolled over and took a seat next to him.

"Edward, it's wonderful to see you! We haven't talked since...never mind. Are you having a good time?" Lilly gave him a hug and a kiss on the cheek, but Edward's smile was forced.

"Hell of a party. Jacob certainly pulled out all the stops."

"A glorious celebration of a most glorious engagement," Lilly teased, leaning back and raising her glass.

"How are you in such a good mood, all things considered?"

Lilly's stomach turned at Edward's question. "All things considered? The man I adore asked me to marry him. Why shouldn't be I floating on a cloud? Are you feeling okay?"

Edward stared into his glass as if searching for the right words. "The bastard hasn't told you."

Lilly's brows raised in confusion. "Told me what, exactly?"

"Damn it, I hate doing this to you, you are such a decent person. And who knows, maybe it won't matter in the long run. You two weren't together at the time."

Even though Lilly didn't know what Edward was about to say, she felt a cold chill wash over her body as her heart hammered with foreboding. "What are you trying to say? I've always found honesty is the best policy."

Edward turned, their gazes locking. "Victoria's pregnant."

Lilly struggled to find her breath. It felt like she'd been hit in the face with a ball of ice, but she maintained a calm facade and offered a strained smile. "Really?"

Edward squeezed Lilly's trembling hands. "It's Jacob's baby."

Tears sprang to her eyes as she nodded. "How can she be certain? Didn't she have countless liaisons when she was dating Jacob?"

"She did; but that was before they reconciled."

Now her heart was racing like a runaway train. She couldn't handle anymore deception. "Reconciled?"

"They reconciled right before he left for Greece."

"Right after he fucked me...yes, I remember it well." Edward reached over, squeezing her hand, but Lilly shook him away. She was in no mood to be coddled.

"They weren't together long before Jacob showed her the door. I don't think he ever *wanted* to be with her—"

"No matter. That still doesn't answer my question. She's slept with so many men, how does she know Jacob is the father?"

"She swears she was only with him, nobody else."

Lilly swallowed down the nausea. "Well, that's just...wow."

"I don't think Victoria expects them to reconcile at this point, but she does want him involved in the baby's life." He stood, his movements agitated. "How could Jacob not tell you?"

"Tell her what?" Jacob's voice carried through the darkness as he walked over, his fists clenching as his gaze drifted from Edward's angered face to Lilly's tear-stained one. "What the fuck is going on here?"

Lilly stood, smoothing her dress before taking a deep breath. "It appears your past has caught up with you again."

"Angel, what the hell are you talking about?" Jacob asked, his face twisting with concern as he grabbed Lilly's shoulders.

"There's a bounty of good news today, but I'll let you, Edward and Victoria sort this out. I don't have a dog in this fight." She loosened from Jacob's grip, wiping her face. "If you'll excuse me."

Lilly stumbled towards the house, blinded by tears, the sounds of the party now a mocking sneer at her absurd belief in happiness.

CHAPTER ELEVEN

Jacob

J acob watched Lilly's retreating form before whirling to face Edward. "What the fuck did you say to her?"

Edward looked away, shuffling his feet. "Look, mate, I'm just the messenger, but why didn't you talk to Lilly about Victoria's situation?"

"What situation? I haven't seen Victoria in weeks!" Jacob bellowed.

"About the baby. Victoria said she's been calling you for days and leaving messages."

"What baby?" Jacob shrieked, his mind racing.

Edward looked Jacob in the eye, glaring with disdain. "She's pregnant, about ten weeks, and the baby is yours."

Jacob couldn't breathe, the world he so carefully assembled shattering with Edward's statement. "What?"

"You're a real piece of work, you know that? Didn't you even listen to your messages? Victoria told you the situation. Hell, she even insisted I drive here to inform Lilly. Victoria wanted to save her from any embarrassment when she announced it to the press."

Jacob's laugh was rough as sandpaper. "Right, because she gives a damn about Lilly's feelings. Why should I believe Victoria, anyway? That woman fucks anything with a heartbeat."

"She claims you're the last man she slept with, and according to the timeline, it's your baby. She isn't thrilled about the situation either, but you need to have a conversation…with both women."

Jacob grabbed Edward by the collar, pushing him backward. "You stay the fuck away from Lilly, do you hear me?"

"Whoa!" Janie's voice shouted out as she approached the men. "What's going on here? Jacob, let him go."

Jacob pushed Edward off and turned away, running his hand over his head. "Victoria's lied about everything else. Now she pulls this shit? Unbelievable. She can't let me be happy, can she?"

"Victoria's upset too, and scared. She doesn't want to raise the baby alone." Edward appeared as aggravated as Jacob at this point, his breath coming in huffs.

Janie hung her head when she heard Edward's statement. "That explains Victoria's call from earlier."

Jacob grabbed his sister by the shoulders. "What call? Why didn't you tell me she called?"

"She was upset. I figured it was because of the engagement party. She was desperate to speak to you. She muttered something about you denying your legacy, but I honestly didn't pay her any mind. She's known for her dramatics." She looked at Jacob. "More importantly, where's Lilly?"

Jacob felt tears spring to his eyes. "I don't know. She walked off after hearing the news. You haven't seen her?"

Janie shook her head. "I'll go locate her. You need to find out if Victoria is making up another story to screw with your head. Get all the facts first, and remember, you need a paternity test." Janie walked back towards the house, leaving the men alone.

Edward started to speak, but Jacob held up his hand. "Don't even bother." Jacob pulled out his phone and searched through his deleted messages, wandering off to a quiet area to listen to Victoria's messages.

'*Jacob, I know you don't want to speak to me, but you can't deny our child either. I know this news will wreck your relationship with Lilly, but we created this life, and I can't do this alone. Please, talk to me.*' Victoria's voice lacked its usual practiced tone, replaced by a pleading sincerity.

Jacob stared at the ground, wondering how in the world he was going to deal with this situation. Victoria would never consent to an abortion. Jacob didn't want one regardless. She was far too vain to carry a child and give it up for adoption. No, she would use this baby to further her fame machine.

He wracked his brain to recall what night might fit the pregnancy timeline, but only one occasion stuck out in his mind. It was the same night he and Lilly made love, the same night he chose his career over the woman he adored.

He woke up to Victoria straddling him, riding him into consciousness. With his brain half-asleep, Jacob questioned if the act actually occurred or if it was a dream. He swore he hadn't finished, that once his mind woke to the reality of the situation, he pushed her off—but now he couldn't be certain.

Dejected, he dialed Victoria's number and she answered immediately. "What's going on, Victoria?"

"I was wondering when you might call. I need you to know I didn't plan any of this."

Jacob scoffed. "Why do I doubt that? How do I even know this baby is mine?"

"I haven't been with anyone since you left for Greece. There's no one else."

143

"What about that Mark character you mentioned just the other day?"

"I...I only said that to make you jealous."

"Worked well, didn't it? I'm not in the mood for your games, Victoria."

"I'm not playing a game, Jacob. You have to believe me."

But Jacob had a difficult time believing anything his ex said. "I'll need proof of paternity."

Victoria let out a cold laugh. "I figured you'd say that. I'm more than happy to provide a paternity test."

He sighed, his heart heavy with resignation. If she was this willing to cooperate, she likely wasn't lying. His heart raced like he was high on speed and he struggled to find his bearings. *What the fuck am I going to do?*

Jacob lost track of time watching the stars and moon twinkle in the sky. He saw the guests leave but made no move to offer his goodbyes. He didn't want to see anyone...except his darling Lilly.

His conversation with Victoria was the most civil in their tenuous courtship. She seemed honestly distraught with the situation.

He was desperate to talk to Lilly, but what could he say? He couldn't outright deny Victoria's claims and he couldn't expect her to want anything further with him after this news.

He was startled from his reverie when a hand touched his shoulder, pushing a glass of whiskey under his nose. He looked up into Lilly's eyes, her face sympathetic and sad.

"How are you holding up?" Lilly asked, sitting next to him on the log.

Jacob scoffed. "Fucking great." He took a swig of whiskey before daring to look at her face. "How are you, besides abhorring me obviously."

Lilly looked at the ground, contemplating her words. "I don't hate you."

"You should hate me."

"Why? What happened between you and Victoria was before we were together; and I refuse to look at any baby as a tragedy. I deal with too much death every day to consider a new life as anything other than beautiful." Lilly sipped her wine. "You wanted a child. You got your wish, you know."

Jacob swallowed around the lump in his throat, feeling nauseous. "I want a baby with you."

Lilly shrugged. "Who knows if I could carry a baby? You need to celebrate that you are going to be a Dad. It's a fantastic journey."

Jacob shook his head in disbelief. "Are you high?"

"I wish," Lilly responded, hiding her sorrow behind a practiced smile. "I'm slightly drunk, but only enough to dull the senses. Will you and Victoria be reconciling?"

"No way in hell!" Jacob gritted out, taking a huge swig of whiskey. "No, definitely no. Victoria understands I'm in love with you and I want to marry you. Of course, that's no longer an option."

"When did you decide that?" Lilly's voice was guarded.

Jacob's eyes widened. "Wasn't much of a leap to assume you would want nothing to do with me after this news." He buried his head in his hands.

Lilly cleared her throat. "I can't say the situation is optimal, or that I'm thrilled by the news, but I also know this is just something that happened, and you weren't trying to hurt me." Lilly waved her arms around the property. "I don't think you would have done all this if you didn't love me."

Jacob grabbed Lilly by the shoulders, his eyes boring into hers. "I love you more than I thought it possible to love another person. I've never wanted to marry anyone, and I dream about you being my wife. I know you can't forgive me, but you are the truest love I've ever known."

Lilly placed her slight hand against his cheek. "There's nothing to forgive." She turned back to face the gardens. "It broke my heart when Edward told me, and I had to escape for a bit to consider my position. I asked myself if I could be married to you while another woman was carrying your child, and although I'm not certain how I'll be able to handle it, I'm willing to give it a try…if you still wanted to be with me in that way."

Jacob shook his head, positive he heard her wrong. "Are you saying you'll still marry me?"

Lilly swallowed hard. "I'm saying, I'm not ruling out the possibility. That is, if you still want to marry me—"

"It's the only thing I want in this world," Jacob answered, his voice strained.

"Then we'll see. Let's wait until the shock wears off, and perhaps we can reach an understanding."

Jacob reached over to kiss Lilly, but she backed away. "I'm not there yet."

Jacob nodded. "Whatever time you need. Do you want to return to London?" *Please say no, I don't want to be amongst the throngs of media when this breaks.*

Lilly shook her head. "I'd like to spend the last few days here. Try to enjoy this beautiful place. I feel peace when I'm in the country, and I need peace now."

Jacob brushed a piece of hair behind Lilly's ear. "I'll do whatever you want, whatever makes you comfortable. I just want to be near you. I need you near me now more than ever."

Lilly took his hand in hers. "I'm not going anywhere, except to bed. I'm exhausted. The guests have left. Your news pretty much killed any all-night party plans. We're the only ones awake, us and the dormouse." She pushed herself up to a standing position, pulling him up with her.

They walked toward the house, but Jacob's gaze remained on the ethereal beauty at his side.

"It's wonderful here, isn't it?" Lilly commented, looking around her as if she doubted she would ever see it again.

Jacob wanted to hold her and tell her he only loved her and this child wasn't going to affect that, but she was far too intelligent to blindly fall into his words anymore. He didn't know what this child meant for their future, but he couldn't imagine his world without Lilly. "You're the most wondrous creature I've ever known."

Lilly smiled slightly and nodded. "And why is that?"

"The fact you're even speaking to me right now. You have the biggest heart, Lilly. Your capacity to forgive—"

They reached the bottom of the stairs, and Lilly climbed a step before turning to him. "I told you before, there's nothing to forgive. I've set myself up in a guest room, so I bid you goodnight." She leaned in and gave him a quick kiss on the cheek, pausing as if she wanted to say something else, but thinking better of it, turned and walked up the stairs.

Jacob grabbed another glass of whiskey, there would be no sleep tonight.

Lilly

illy opened her eyes and instinctively reached for Jacob, tears filling her eyes as the memory of the night before flooded her consciousness. Part of her wanted to scream and rail against the unfairness of it all—Jacob finally made his choice and chose her—but Victoria's pregnancy upended her newly minted happiness.

Her mind urged her to run as fast as she could—away from Jacob and Victoria and their baby...*their* baby. Jacob was going to be a father, and she wasn't the mother. How in the world was her heart and mind supposed to rectify this situation?

Dragging herself from the bed, she slipped a robe over her gown—a short, sexy number designed to entice the man who fathered another woman's child—and padded downstairs.

She hoped to sneak into the kitchen, grab something and retreat to the sanctity of her bedroom, but that idea fizzled when she saw Janie and Audrey seated with Jacob around the table.

Their conversation halted mid-sentence when she entered the room, six eyes tracking her every move.

"Good morning, Lilly," Janie offered, getting up to give her a hug.

There's nothing good about it. "Morning." Lilly grabbed a mug, noting the array of foods on the counter and stove. "Someone's been busy."

"I made you breakfast. I wasn't sure what you wanted so I made a bit of everything."

Lilly finally allowed her eyes to meet Jacob's and the pain radiating from his voice was palpable. "I'm not really hungry."

"Please try to eat something, angel." He trembled with emotion as he got up, fixing her a plate of food. "You need your strength. I want you to heal as quickly as possible."

Lilly accepted the plate, averting her eyes. It was too difficult to stare at this beautiful man and know he would never belong completely to her. She sat at the table, only breaking into a smile when Elizabeth scrambled onto her lap, engulfing her in a huge hug.

"Good morning, Elizabeth." Lilly dropped a kiss on the little girl's hair, eating around her as she played with her stuffed animals.

"I can't—" Jacob uttered, turning on his heel and rushing out of the room.

The three women exchanged gazes and Janie jumped up to run after her brother.

"How are you holding up, luv?" Audrey inquired, patting her hand.

"I'm on an emotional rollercoaster from hell, and I want off." The coffee slid down her throat, warming her iced heart from the inside.

"What are you going to do?" Her question was gentle, coaxing.

Lilly wiped away tears as she chewed a bite of melon fifty times, willing her body to let it pass to her stomach. "I don't know. I haven't decided."

Janie came back to the room, her face drawn with worry. "Jacob apologizes for leaving like that. He's so upset."

"We all are," Lilly choked out.

"He said seeing you with Elizabeth only reminds him how desperately he wants you to be the mother of his children."

That statement opened the floodgates as Lilly wiped her face with the heel of her hand. "Well, life had other arrangements. I can't eat anymore."

"You didn't eat anything." Janie regarded Lilly with a sober concern.

"Heartbreak—best damn diet in the world." Lilly stood up, setting Elizabeth on the floor. "I'm meeting Ben and Sabina for lunch. Will you all be here when I get back?"

Janie nodded. "I don't want to leave my brother right now."

Lilly nodded, she didn't want to leave him either, but she may not have a choice. "I'll see you all later."

"So, what's the plan? Are you leaving him or in it for the long haul?" Sabina inquired, flagging the bartender for some shots. It seemed the exact same question was on everybody's mind.

Lilly loved good friends, they didn't tiptoe around disaster, just waded right in, fully clothed. "I haven't decided yet. Am I a fool if I stay with him?"

"You two weren't together when Victoria fell pregnant, right?" Ben asked.

"Fell pregnant. What a term. More like his dick fell into her, Ben," Sabina snorted.

Lilly rolled her eyes. This was turning out to be an experiment in torture. "Pretty much sums it up, but thanks for that visual. Where are those drinks?" She tapped the table with increasing agitation.

"Sorry luv, just keeping it real. But Ben is right, you two weren't speaking when Victoria *fell* pregnant." Sabina shot Ben a side-eye.

Lilly shook her head, grabbing her drink from the server with both hands. The woman likely thought she was a raging alcoholic…not a bad plan. "I don't know if I can handle being his runner-up."

"How are you his runner-up? The man adores you, Lilly. He raced back from Greece to be by your side, he bought you a manor house in Gloucestershire because you liked the gardens, he's begging you to have a child with him—"

"Not going to happen." Lilly wasn't traversing that path, much too complicated to consider at that point.

"What I'm trying to say," Ben grabbed Lilly's hand, giving it a squeeze, "is that you're not his runner-up."

"Personally, I don't think this baby has anything to do with your relationship," Sabina interjected.

"Are you mad?" Lilly hissed, her eyes widening.

"Hear me out. I'm a single mum, and I adore my daughter, but I have more than enough room in my heart for both her *and* the man in my life. It's not an either-or situation."

"With Victoria, it likely will be. I'm sure she won't stand idly by and let me marry the man of her dreams." Lilly rested her head in her hands. "I even purchased bridal magazines, which I swore I'd never do. I got swept away with the idea of marrying my handsome prince—"

Sabina stroked her hair. "What exactly has changed in that scenario? Yes, this situation sucks, but it doesn't have to spell the end for you and Jacob. He's still your handsome, sexy as fuck prince and most importantly, he still wants to marry *you*."

Lilly shook her head, her emotions tangled like a pile of headphone wires. "Can we discuss anything else?"

"You mean how mucked up both of our lives are?" Ben chortled.

"Exactly."

"Speak for yourself. My life is looking up." Sabina's eyes twinkled as she took a sip of whiskey.

"Sabina, what's going on? Did you meet someone?" Lilly grabbed her arm, feeling a burst of excitement. She needed happy news, even if it didn't involve her.

"I did, I did! Totally didn't see it coming. It's really new so I don't want to jinx anything but…I'm happy."

"That's wonderful," Ben exclaimed. "Is it that nurse on the orthopedic floor?"

Sabina did a double-take at her friend. "Walter? He's gay."

149

Ben stroked his chin, nodding thoughtfully. "Really?"

"Yep, all yours, Ben," Sabina chortled.

"Does he work with us?" Lilly inquired, letting the warm burn of the alcohol slide down her throat.

Sabina flushed and looked away. "It's a nice day, you should go back to the house and spend some time with Jacob. Lilly, don't let your fears get in the way of your happily ever after."

"My fears are the only thing keeping me safe right now. But don't change the topic. Who is this guy? He *obviously* works with us."

Sabina shook her head. "I'm not jinxing it. Just know that I'm happy."

Enough said. Lilly embraced her friend. "God I'm glad. You deserve it so damn much."

Ben smiled at his friends. "Congrats, Sabina. Lilly, go to your new home and reclaim your happiness. Figure out the details later."

The bus dropped Lilly just down the street from the manor house. No one had sent Mother Nature the memo that Lilly's heart was shattered. It was a gorgeous day—blue skies with puffy white clouds, flowers blooming everywhere, and the scent of roses carrying on the wind.

She walked down the driveway, deep in thought and started when Jacob called her name.

"Lilly, did you walk?" Jacob had been sitting at the outdoor patio but stood and walked toward her.

She turned, her heart threatening to infarct at the sight of him. She loved him so dearly, but how was she supposed to do this? "Only from the bus stop."

Jacob closed the distance with wide steps, his hands running up and down her arms. "You took the bus? Angel, I would have driven you."

Lilly steeled herself against the feel of his hands on her arms, hands she wanted everywhere on her body. "I needed the time alone." She pulled away and walked to the outdoor table, her breath catching at the bridal magazines she purchased strewn about. "What are you doing?"

Jacob chuckled sheepishly. "I found the magazines in the car and I noticed you dog-eared some of the pages. I was curious."

"You looked through my bridal magazines?"

"Well, women make a huge deal about these twenty-pound magazines. I figured there must be something pretty fantastic inside. Besides, I wanted to see what had caught your fancy." His desire was written all over his face as his long hands fingered the pages. "I did have to wonder about this one."

Lilly glanced at the page and smirked. It showed a model in a gown that looked like something Little Bo Peep would have worn. "I didn't mark that one, I marked the other side." She flipped the page, showing him the gown on the other side.

"I thought you were going for the milkmaid look...if there is such a thing."

"There is, as sad as that may sound."

Jacob's hand traced the picture on the other page, a simple gown that would accentuate her petite hourglass figure. "This dress looks like you. You would look magnificent in it, Lilly."

"It doesn't matter."

Without warning, Jacob reached out and pulled her to him, his fingers tangling in her hair, forcing her chin up and pressing his lips to hers. "It's the only thing that matters. You and the love I have for you are the only things that matter."

Lilly pushed back, her eyes bright and heart smashed. "It's not the only thing anymore. It can't be. You've got a far bigger commitment than me. I need time to myself."

She heard Jacob calling her, beseeching her to turn around, but ignored his pleas. She had to find somewhere to lick her wounds and decide her next steps, and whether those steps would wind back towards Jacob Edmonton or walk away for good.

CHAPTER TWELVE

Jacob

J
acob felt utterly helpless as Lilly raced into the manor house. She
once melted into his arms with a sweetness he'd never known, now
she searched for an escape from them.

"You okay, big brother?"

He turned and forced a smile for Janie, but it didn't reach his eyes. Hell,
it barely reached his mouth. "She's not there yet. I'm scared she's going to run
so far I can't reach her anymore."

"Give her time—"

"Fuck time, Janie. No, I don't want any more time to elapse. I want to
make that amazing woman mine, forever. But it doesn't matter, even if she said
yes, we still don't have a license."

"You could always have a commitment ceremony. It's not legal but it
binds your hearts together. It would show your devotion to her, especially in
light of recent events. It could be beautiful."

"I only have a couple days before I have to return to Santorini."

"It wouldn't need to be fancy. Just a few witnesses and most importantly,
the two of you."

Jacob considered his sister's words. It might work. It would show Lilly
how serious he was to be her husband, and they could still have the big wedding
with Lilly wearing that beautiful dress afterward. This ceremony could be their
secret. "Maybe I should talk to her?"

"It's worth a shot."

Jacob walked inside and headed to Lilly's bedroom. He was a man with
a mission…one that hopefully didn't include too much groveling. He opened
the door to the guestroom and found her lying on the bed, her back to the door.
He crept across the room and slid onto the bed beside her, wrapping an arm
around her waist. "Hi, angel."

Lilly's body tensed at his touch. "Please leave, Jacob."

But he wasn't going to leave, her body was the only home his heart had
ever known. He brushed her long hair from her neck, pressing open-mouth
kisses on her nape. "You're so beautiful, Lilly."

Lilly put her hand on her neck, halting any further caresses. "I can't—"

He pressed his lips to her shoulder, swallowing against the lump in
his throat. The wall she'd erected was practically palpable, he could feel the

barrier between them. "I'll make you a deal. I'll give you all the time you need to plan a wedding and get married."

Lilly turned in his arms, her emotional mask securely in place. "How is that a deal?"

"In return," Jacob murmured as he kissed her forehead, "we have a commitment ceremony."

"A what?" Her face wrinkled in confusion.

"We spiritually and emotionally bind ourselves to each other. You'll be my wife, in every sense of the word—"

"Except legally," Lilly scoffed.

Jacob pressed his fingers to her lips. He wasn't about to let his bossy Yank get the upper hand. "We'll get legally bound as soon as you're ready."

"This is your deal? What's in it for me? Hell, what's in it for you?"

Okay this wasn't going as smoothly as he hoped. "We have the knowledge that we are one, that we are fully committed to each other. I want you to be my wife, Lilly, but I'll gladly take this until I get the marriage contract."

Lilly's fingers picked at an imaginary thread on Jacob's shirt, her eyes averted. "Please don't ask me to do this—"

"Why?"

"Did you just ask me why? Jacob, you knocked up Victoria!"

"It means nothing! It changes nothing!"

"It changes everything," Lilly sputtered, tears streaming down her face. "I'm not interested in any commitment ceremony Jacob; I can't consider something like that now."

Jacob pulled her body against his chest, willing her to open her heart one more time, to let him in, to trust him. "Lilly, I adore you. Please don't let this end us."

Her small hands pushed against him with a force he didn't know she possessed. "You make it sound like I created this scenario, as if you and Victoria are helpless bystanders. Well bullshit! This situation exists *because* of you and Victoria. Don't expect me to make it better for you! Who's going to make it better for me? Who's going to convince my heart that I won't always be your second-place prize?"

He pulled her to him again, using his strength to his advantage. "You are always first with me. You always will be."

"What about children?"

He cupped her face, peppering her mouth with kisses. "What about them? We'll have as many as you want. We can start right now."

"Go, Jacob. Leave me be."

He tried to hold her, his body shaking with fear, the fear of losing the only woman he'd ever loved. "Please Lilly, don't shut me out."

"It's easier than letting you back in." With those words she turned and closed down the conversation. "I don't want to talk anymore. If you love me at all, you'll respect my wishes."

Jacob stared at her back, wanting nothing more than to make love to her until she believed him, but she had made her decision. She needed space and no amount of pushing her was going to speed up the process.

Janie glanced up when he walked into the living room, her hopeful expression sobering. "I take it she wasn't a fan of the idea."

Jacob shook his head. "No, she said she can't fathom something like that now, and that she needs space." He willed back the tears and all-encompassing anger he felt toward Victoria. "I'm losing her, Janie."

Janie hugged her brother fiercely. "Don't give up hope. It's still raw. If she asked for time, give her time."

"I can't live without her."

"You won't have to. Just give her some space. We're heading back to London. You'll be alright?"

Jacob barked out a mirthless laugh. "Define alright." He shook it off and hugged his sister. "I'll be fine Little Bit. Somehow, I'll be fine."

Lilly

illy awoke a bit after 3 a.m., tossing and turning until she realized her heart would not let her sleep. The last two days were surreal, though not entirely unpleasant. Lilly and Jacob spent time together, although as friends instead of passionate lovers and the agony was evident in his face when she kept him at arm's length.

The situation played over in Lilly's mind like a hellacious broken record. How could she reconcile her love for Jacob with the knowledge that he was going to be the father of Victoria's child?

Jacob would return to Greece the next evening, and this was their last full day together. Lilly needed to decide the course of their relationship and she had to stick to her decision. It wasn't fair to leave either of them in limbo.

She adored him. True, the idea of Victoria carrying Jacob's baby cut her like a knife, but conception occurred before she and Jacob were committed. How could she hold that against him?

Janie had phoned several times as well. She was sympathetic to Lilly's perspective but hopeful she might give her brother—and their love—another chance.

Shit or get off the pot, Lilly. Either love him and accept the situation or leave and forget about him. The latter was not an option. She knew how rare a love of their magnitude was, she would never find anything remotely similar in her lifetime.

Taking a deep breath, she wandered over to the dresser and slipped on the engagement ring. Jacob sized it to her finger before the party, another sign of his devotion.

She padded down the hallway to the master suite. Jacob was lying on the bed, his hand over his eyes, but he wasn't sleeping. His eyes flew open when the door creaked and he watched her enter, apprehension rampant in his face.

Lilly crawled into the bed with him, sliding under the covers. "I can't sleep. I thought if you didn't mind—"

Jacob turned to her, adjusting his pillow and cupping her face. "I don't mind." She saw the unshed tears in his eyes, and it softened the hardened edges in her heart.

She leaned in, her lips trembling against his. He didn't move, except to tighten his grip on her cheek. She kissed him again and this time he slid his tongue inside her mouth, groaning her name low in his throat.

His arms wrapped around her as he made love to her mouth, his need evident as he deepened the kiss until Lilly was breathless.

He stripped off her clothes, not a word exchanged between them. There was no need for words, their bodies spoke volumes. He bent his head to suckle her breasts, his tongue swirling around her nipples. His hands wrapped around her hips as his mouth trailed lower, each touch forcing the nightmare of the last two days further into the recesses of her mind.

"You're so exquisite. I could make love to you every day and never be satiated." Jacob breathed deeply against her skin. "You smell like heaven."

Lilly gasped when his lips nuzzled between her thighs, his hands lifting her hips to his mouth. He kissed her as if his life depended on it, his tongue flitting and suckling every inch of her; ignoring her pleas to move back to her mouth and holding her hips against him until she screamed in rapture.

She lay there panting as Jacob continued his oral exploration, drinking deep from her and making her writhe in ecstasy.

After bringing her to another orgasm with his mouth and fingers, he claimed her mouth again. His erection pushed against her, but he made no move to enter her. She needed to determine their next step.

And she did.

"Do you love me enough?" Lilly whispered as she arched her hips, guiding him into her body.

"Until the end of this lifetime, and in every life following, you will always be my choice. I will always choose you. I will always love you."

"I'll hold you to that."

Jacob buried himself to the hilt, deep inside her beloved body. "I don't know how not to love you, Lilly. You're my oxygen." He released a deep sigh as her hips arched against him. "You are my favorite place in the world."

Her tears wet his cheeks as his body moved over her, both melding as they lost themselves in one another's warmth.

They lay together a half hour later, his arms wrapped around her like a vise, holding her body captive against him. Jacob brought her hand to his lips, only then noticing the engagement ring as it sparkled in the moonlight.

He squeezed her tighter, slipping inside her again at her non-verbal commitment to their future.

A warm breeze blew across the meadow as Lilly strolled the gardens later that morning, letting Charlie chase a frisbee to his heart's content. She saw Jacob approach out of the corner of her eye. She had been awake for a few hours, but he needed the rest if he was to resume filming the following day.

"Did you sleep?" she inquired, and he nodded, flashing her a small smile as he grabbed the frisbee from Charlie, flinging it far down the hill.

"I got a call from the fertility clinic."

Lilly's eyebrows raised, surprised. "What did they want?"

"To give us our test results." Jacob wrapped his arms around her, pulling her to him. "Turns out, we are both completely normal."

Lilly snickered, her back pressed against him. "That's debatable."

"True, but physically we are normal." Lilly only nodded, so Jacob continued. "Which means that so long as we engage in lots of sex, we should have no problem conceiving a baby." His lips nuzzled her neck and she felt his smile against her skin. Evidently, for Jacob, this was great news.

Lilly pushed away, turning to face him. "Are we still on that track?"

Jacob crossed his arms, his expression solemn. "I thought we were, don't you want a baby with me?"

Lilly focused on Charlie, tossing the frisbee again. "You're already having a baby."

A muscle jumped in Jacob's jaw, but his voice remained even. "I want a child with you. That's why I made the appointment. I want to share that experience with you. I want to share everything with you."

"You can share it with Victoria." She forced her words to sound light, but it ripped her heart out to consider Jacob's his eternal future with that woman.

Jacob closed his eyes and sank onto the grass, his head in his hands. "Is this our new relationship? Keeping me in your life but at a distance? Staying with me but never actually letting me love you?" His gaze reflected his pain and tugged at her heart. "The doctor wants you to take the vitamins and monitor your temperature so that we could…but, obviously you've made your decision. I guess I don't have a say in it." He turned, walking down the garden path, his dog trotting alongside him.

Lilly watched as he disappeared around the bend and considered her options. She wanted to give him everything, he deserved it. Jacob was a good man, despite some errant mistakes along the way; and he must be serious about having a child with her, or he wouldn't still be pursuing the issue. *But can I live a life perpetually in second place?*

She grabbed her phone and dialed Janie. She needed a woman's advice on this topic before she made any drastic decisions she might regret.

"I was just thinking about you. How are you two doing? Are you coming back to London tonight?"

Lilly smiled at the flood of questions. Janie didn't leave time to over analyze anything. "We're better, I think, and we're headed back in the morning. He returns to Santorini tomorrow night."

"You're still engaged, I hope?"

Lilly laughed dryly. "Unless he's changed his mind."

"Not in a million years. I hate this situation. I hate that it's Victoria who's pregnant because I prayed for my brother to have a child. I wish it were with you."

"Well, I'm older than—"

Janie scoffed. "What a crock. There are women having babies at the age of fifty."

"We went to a fertility doctor in London and had testing done, before the news of Victoria's pregnancy broke."

"What did the doctor say?"

Lilly fingered one of the brilliant rose buds littering the garden, not answering her friend, as she watched Jacob returning, his ever-faithful Charlie at his side.

"Hello! What did the doctor say?" Janie shrieked with impatience.

"Oh, sorry. Um, we're both healthy and physically, there should be no issue with having a baby."

Janie sighed. "Does my idiot brother not want to pursue it now that the unholy bitch is pregnant?"

Lilly cleared her throat. "He desperately wants to pursue it. I'm the one who doesn't think we should move forward. I don't want to feel like I'm second place or worse, that my child is second place."

"You're kidding, right? You will never be second place with my brother. He's going to be a stand-up guy and take responsibility for his child with Victoria but if you were pregnant, God he would dote on you. You have no idea how much he loves you, do you. Granted, there has been some fucked up situations, but it's always been you."

Janie's words warmed her like a blanket from the dryer. Maybe she couldn't see the forest for the trees. Her overly analytical brain served her well at work, but it often hung her up on issues of emotion. "He's walking back now. Thank you for helping me find my center again."

"Have a baby with him, Lilly. Nothing in the world would make him happier."

Jacob sat next to Lilly on one of the many garden benches, and she gazed at him, her face scrunched into a mock scowl.

His eyes widen with apprehension. "What did I do now?"

Lilly chuckled. "Nothing. I'm hungry. Will you take me out to eat?"

They stopped into a local pub for dinner, and Jacob ordered two whiskeys. "Only one please, I'll have water."

Jacob shot her an odd look, placing his hand over hers and giving it a small squeeze. "Are you feeling okay?"

Lilly nodded as she fished a pill bottle out of her bag. She took out a prenatal vitamin and swallowed it before meeting Jacob's questioning gaze. "They recommend not drinking while trying to conceive, so, water."

The smile that spread across Jacob's face was beautiful and contagious. She felt herself flush as she returned the grin.

His hands cupped her face and his lips claimed hers, kissing away all doubts. "Thank you." He rested his forehead against hers, his thumbs caressing her cheeks. "I promise to make you so happy. I will devote my life to you and our children."

They made love several times that night, each time imbued with a gentle longing, a reassurance of their mutual pledge, and lay wrapped in each other's arms until dawn.

The drive back to London the following afternoon was pleasant, but Lilly knew she needed to keep Jacob's mind off his impending departure. It was a futile effort.

"I'll pay for the CT Scan in Santorini. I want you with me, especially after everything that's happened."

Lilly squeezed his hand. "We've been over this, I'll be fine. I've taken care of myself for years. Another week won't kill either of us." She saw his jaw clench. "Besides, you're going to be busy. It'll be better to give you a week to catch up and then you can show me all the beautiful sights on the island."

Jacob grunted in response but left the topic alone for the remainder of the drive.

They spent their final few hours together snuggled in bed as they discussed wedding plans—in between a round or two of lovemaking. Jacob must have told her he loved her a hundred times, whispered how he couldn't wait for her to be his wife and carry their child.

When Lilly gazed into his bright blue eyes and saw the love reflecting back, she believed every word. Their life would be complicated, but their love could survive any obstacle.

Jacob stalled half a dozen times that evening when the car arrived to take him to the airport. "I don't want to leave you, Lilly. It's like I'm walking away and leaving my heart here."

She wrapped her arms around his neck and stood on tiptoe, kissing his lips. "I promise I'll return it to you safely. Are you sure you want me to stay here—"

"Lilly! It's *our* home now. I want you in *our* home." Jacob had insisted Lilly stay at his house and after a bit of resistance, she agreed. After all, it would be their home after the wedding—when they weren't in the English countryside. He paused in his doorway, clutching her as if he would never hold her again.

"Promise me you'll fly down within the week?" Lilly nodded and kissed him again, his kiss deepening as he held her fast to him. He cupped her face and rained kisses on her cheeks, forehead, and chin. "I love you, Mrs. Edmonton."

"I was thinking that when I arrive in Greece, we can have that commitment ceremony—"

Her words were cut off by his mouth against hers, his tongue tangling with hers in the sweetest of wars. He drew back, resting his head against hers. "Thank you, Lilly. I'll plan everything. You plan our wedding. I want to legally marry you as soon as I return to London. Hell, maybe we just get married in Greece, make a baby on the honeymoon. What do you say?"

Her heart raced as she looked at Jacob, and before her mind could intervene, she nodded. "You've got yourself a deal, sir."

"Really? Christ, please tell me you're serious."

"Totally and completely serious. Now go." Lilly grinned at him, giving him one last kiss before shooing him out the door. Closing the door behind her, she smiled at Charlie and her cats. "I'll miss him too, but we'll be together soon."

CHAPTER THIRTEEN

Jacob

acob was on set a few days later, drinking water and avoiding the Grecian sun, when a commotion from the back of the set caught his attention. Scanning the area, he sucked in a breath and hung his head. Victoria was in Santorini and headed straight for him.

Miriam shot him a look that was equal parts questioning and warning. She had dealt with his ex-girlfriend in the past and was apprised of the pregnancy situation.

Jacob grabbed Victoria by the wrist, trying to avoid any photos by local journalists. "What are you doing here?"

"We need to talk, alone. The paparazzi are circling. They suspect something. I thought it best if we discussed specifics and released a joint statement."

Jacob nodded, surprised with Victoria's mature take on the situation. True, she could be playing up a public relations angle, but this calm demeanor suited her—and everyone around her—well. "That's a good idea. I'll be wrapping around seven tonight. Do you want to meet then?"

"Absolutely," Victoria beamed at him, "and although likely not your preference, a discreet location would be favorable considering the topic of discussion. My hotel or yours. Are you still in the same suite?"

"I am. That's fine. I'll see you tonight." Jacob stiffened when her lips grazed his cheek, but he forced a smile, waving her off.

"I smell a rat, and it looks like a pop star," Miriam stated to Jacob without looking up from her script.

"She was well behaved today. Apparently, pregnancy has soothed the savage beast."

Miriam shot Jacob a side-eye. "Or she's plotting something even more elaborate than usual."

"The woman is carrying my child and my fiancée knows the situation. I don't think it can get much more buggered than that. What stunt could she possibly pull at this point?"

"Don't put it past her. Don't put anything past Victoria."

Jacob arrived at his suite that evening and found Victoria laying on the sofa, flipping through Vogue. When he entered, she sat up, looking a trifle guilty at her apparent intrusion.

"I got here early, and my presence caused a bit of a commotion. Management thought it best if I waited inside." She adjusted her sundress, her long legs on full display.

But Victoria's outer beauty no longer appealed to Jacob, she wasn't Lilly. He gave her an absent nod, grabbing some clothes out of the closet. "Are you hungry?"

Victoria giggled. "Starving. I am eating for two, you know."

"Yes, I'm aware." He sat on the chair opposite her. "What type of statement do you want to release? Isn't it a bit early to announce anything? I thought people waited until three or four months…and we haven't completed the paternity test yet."

Victoria looked momentarily stunned by the statement but quickly recovered. "The paternity test. I understand why you're suspicious, and normally, we would wait another month. But our lives are public, and people are already suspecting something. My publicist has been putting out fires for the last several days."

"How would anyone know?"

Victoria blinked away tears. "I was naïve. Someone I believed was a confidante was willing to sell us out for a quick buck. You know him, too. Our dear friend Edward."

Jacob scoffed, his hand rubbing his brow. "Why am I not surprised? The way he acts around Lilly, I almost think he wants her to leave me so he can have a shot."

Victoria's laugh was as fake as her breasts. "Really? How quaint. How is the little woman? Are you two still together?"

"She's wonderful, and yes, we are still engaged."

"I thought you were going to marry her last week and bring her back to Santorini?" Her eyes scanned the suite, looking for signs of Lilly.

"Well the consulate being what it is in Britain made that an impossibility. However, she's set to fly down in the next few days, and I plan to marry her immediately after she lands."

A muscle twitched in Victoria's jaw, but she aimed a well-rehearsed smile in his direction. "How outstanding for you both. I haven't seen any public announcement regarding your engagement. It's going to seem rather odd. Your ex is newly pregnant, and you're suddenly engaged to this nobody—I mean, new person."

Jacob set his jaw and sent Victoria a warning look, but she had a point. Jacob prided himself on maintaining his behavior and reputation. "Simple fix,

I can release news of my engagement today and then in a few weeks—"

"That won't work, remember Edward? If we don't act fast and release the truth, he'll have *his* version in every tabloid. Then your little woman will end up looking like a homewrecker and a hussy." She sent him a sympathetic look. "You wouldn't want that to happen. Think of her reputation, her career, her charity plans…this isn't just about you…or me."

Jacob sighed, she had backed him into yet another corner. "Fine, when is this media field day planned?"

"Thirty minutes. Go get showered."

"I need to call Lilly first—"

"Jacob, there's no time. You can speak to her afterwards. It's not like you're telling the world something she doesn't already know."

A chill ran up Jacob's spine, but he shook it off as he escorted Victoria to the door. "I'll meet you at the press conference."

A crowd of reporters gathered in the hotel conference room, all vying for a prime spot.

Jacob rang Lilly on his way out of the suite, wanting to give her a heads up to the situation but his call went straight to voicemail.

He felt an unease as if something untoward was about to happen, but he surmised it was nerves. Victoria, on the other hand, was glowing. She seemed joyous to attend this press release.

"Good evening everyone," Victoria began, waving graciously at the crowd. "Thank you for gathering here on such short notice. I know we all lead busy lives, so I'll get right to the point. The first announcement is a surprise even to Jacob. He has been offered the lead role in Milieu of Madness!"

The journalists clapped while Jacob sat there, stunned. *What the fuck? Why didn't Albert call me about the role?*

As if on cue, Victoria continued, "Albert was going to speak to Jacob today, but I begged him to let me have the fun of informing him that he's landed the most coveted role in Hollywood!" The applause continued, but Jacob felt as if his world was about to be upended.

Victoria's smile oozed warmth, but Jacob wasn't fooled. "The second announcement is on a much more personal note. Jacob and I are expecting our first child together!" The room erupted into a tizzy, and it was everything Victoria could do to calm them down. "Hold on folks, I'm not done yet. Jacob and I went our separate ways a couple months ago, but with our impending arrival, we decided to get married within the next few weeks. This baby rekindled our love in the best possible manner." Her smiled beamed as her eyes found Jacob. "I'm going to Mrs. Edmonton!"

Just like that, the room fell away, and Jacob thought he might lose consciousness. The noise was dizzying, with cameras flashing and reporters buzzing like a nest of hornets at the news.

He closed his eyes, swallowing back the nausea that threatened to show itself in front of members of the international press. Game, set, match. There was no easy way out of the monstrous lie Victoria fabricated. He didn't give a shit about his reputation, but he knew the media and Victoria's army of fans would have a field day if he contradicted her statement. Lilly would become the harlot and homewrecker, her reputation and safety ripped to shreds.

His mind reeled trying to rectify the situation, but he blanked. He felt Victoria watching him, waiting to see how he would play against her latest hand. She planned this from the beginning, knowing he would walk willingly into her web.

One journalist looked particularly perplexed by the news. "Well, first congratulations on your...news. However, Mr. Edmonton, there have been rumors around London that you are engaged to another woman. I guess there isn't any truth to that story?"

Jacob's head throbbed as he sighed, summoning all his resolve to not overturn the table and smash the room to bits.

If he admitted his love for Lilly, she would be massacred by the press. If he denied any involvement between them, she would be protected from everything except a broken heart. *What kind of choice is this?*

A few more journalists chimed in, demanding to know his business with this other woman. He wanted to scream that she wasn't the "other woman", she was the love of his life, but he remained silent.

Lilly was an innocent soul whose integrity would be forever torn apart if he didn't take steps now to protect her. All her tireless work for the betterment of others would be destroyed in a flash and faith in her actions might never recover. She almost certainly wouldn't get the funding for the sanctuaries she held so dear to her heart, and that would be devastating.

Beyond her charity was the question of her basic safety. If Victoria was this ruthless, he didn't doubt she would hurt Lilly if he didn't play along. The thought of his angel coming to physical harm because of him was beyond comprehension. He couldn't do it, he couldn't put her in danger. He wasn't worth that risk.

Jacob blinked back tears, cleared his throat and told the biggest lie of his life. "There is a woman in London, a dear friend who needed my assistance after a recent injury. However, there is no romantic situation between us." He paused, realizing the press had obtained pictures of him and Lilly kissing while in London. "We dated briefly, but when I learned of Victoria's pregnancy, we decided to part ways as friends. I wish her nothing but the best."

The press release concluded fifteen minutes later, but Jacob didn't move from his seat. He kept his face buried in his hands, unable to comprehend the events of the last hour. There was no coming back from this situation. His future with Lilly was over.

A member of the wait staff asked if he wanted a drink and Jacob ordered a bottle. If he had his druthers, he would get drunk and stay that way indefinitely.

He was halfway through his second glass when the phone rang, and he answered without looking. It no longer mattered who was on the other end of the phone. He was sure of one thing, once the internet caught hold of the story, Lilly would slip forever from his grasp, and that thought made his heart ache with unimaginable pain. "Yep."

Janie's voice seethed with anger. "What the fuck have you done?"

Jacob opened his mouth to speak but realized there was no recourse, no defending his actions so he kept drinking, hoping if he drank enough, he wouldn't have to wake up and deal with this reality.

"If you weren't my brother...I can't even speak to you right now. I hope you're happy. I hope you and that money encrusted bitch are happy now. You two deserve each other. Lilly is way too good for either of you." The line clicked dead, and Jacob laid the phone on the table, the truth of the situation still too clear in his fuzzy thinking.

He stumbled into his suite half a bottle of whiskey later, falling over Victoria's shoes and down the two steps that led into the living room. Victoria sat on the couch, flipping through television stations as he half crawled, half stumbled into one of the chairs.

"You're drunk."

Jacob waved a hand in her direction and began clapping. "And you're the smartest woman I've ever met."

Her eyes narrowed. "Cute."

"And, you deserve the Oscar for best actress. Wait, maybe I deserve the award for best actor because I just convinced the world I actually gave a shit about you."

Victoria walked past him, grabbing his crotch. "Careful what you say, darling, you wouldn't want the press to think you weren't a doting fiancée."

Jacob's anger boiled over. "I *was* a doting fiancée. All I wanted in this stinking world was to marry Lilly. I just wanted to love her, but you made sure that wouldn't happen. You destroyed any chance of happiness I have and for what? Your little control drama? Your need for adoration? You destroyed an angel—my angel—who never did anything to hurt you."

Victoria's eyes narrowed as she bit off a laugh. "I doubt she'll be *your* angel any longer. *You* destroyed her. You could have spoken out, but you chose to play right into my hand. Even now, you could issue a retraction and deny everything we said tonight, but you won't will you? I'll bet you didn't even have the guts to call Lilly." Her face was inches from his. "You got your 'role of a lifetime' honey, you said yourself it was everything you ever wanted. Why aren't you happier?"

Jacob looked at his hands and considered decorating the hotel suite with a few more holes. "I thought it was everything I ever wanted. Now I know that isn't the truth."

Victoria's head cocked to the side with feigned pity. "Oh, so sad; you realize the importance of Lilly's love, but it's not important enough to contact the media, refute my statement and pull out of Milieu of Madness. Face it, friend, you don't give any more of a shit about Lilly than I do. Your main concern was, is and will always be yourself."

Lilly

Ben and Sabina flanked Lilly in her office that afternoon, as soon as the press release hit the airwaves. Due to Victoria and Jacob's immense popularity, it was all any news channel could talk about—a baby of paramount importance. *And to think the day started on such a high note,* Lilly considered as Sabina hugged her for the millionth time.

When they first told her, she scoffed, claiming it was a fabrication. After all, the media had often twisted things in the past. Granted, Jacob never mentioned holding a press release with Victoria, but perhaps he didn't think he needed to disclose information Lilly already knew.

Sabina brought up the video release, her hands shaking as she pressed play. Ben positioned himself behind Lilly, rubbing her shoulders.

Lilly surprised herself when she didn't scream or throw the computer monitor across the room. Instead, she watched Jacob state that he was going to marry Victoria and his dalliance with Lilly—'the unnamed woman in London'—was only a fling and meant nothing long-term.

She didn't say a word as she clenched her jaw, letting her heart process what her mind suspected since she first allowed Jacob into her life. She was a passing fancy, secondary to his career and his ex-girlfriend. It was exactly what had happened with the last man she loved as well. She gave everything she had but, in the end, it didn't matter. She wasn't important enough, pretty enough or valuable enough to come first. It wasn't a surprise, some part of her always knew this truth about Jacob.

"I have to prepare my class for tomorrow."

"Lilly, forget the class," Ben replied, wrapping his arm around her shoulders. "Take the rest of the day off. Hell, take the rest of the month off. That sadistic son-of-a-bitch, I'll kill him if I see him."

Lilly blinked back tears. "Don't you see, Ben? I do that, and they win. I'm not giving them that power. They don't deserve my grief."

Sabina cupped Lilly's face. "Luv, *you* don't deserve your grief."

"Go on, let me get my class organized. I'll be fine." She shooed her friends from her office, watching as they grudgingly departed. Lilly closed the door and waited for the tears to come. She was shocked when her eyes remained dry and she was able to finish the handouts for her class.

She made arrangements to work on the new wing in the shelter that weekend, even surviving when the coordinator mentioned Jacob's engagement and asked her to pass on congratulations to her 'friend'.

She endured the drive home, even when all the stations played sad, sappy songs about unrequited love. Several deep breaths carried her over the threshold of her cottage when the realization hit. Her beloved cats were still at Jacob's house.

Behind enemy lines.

That was the final straw, the last vestiges of strength left her body as she sobbed. She fell to the floor, ignoring the pain from her bruised body as she landed with a soft thud.

Lilly didn't know how long she lay on the floor. She was surprised she hadn't cried enough tears to wash her away like Alice in Wonderland. Her cries gave ways to snuffled sobs and finally to hiccups and huffing breaths. She needed to get her animals back, but she couldn't walk into that house. She couldn't bear to see any reminder of Jacob or the life he so gallantly promised.

Lies, all lies, and yet he made them so believable. She surmised she would willingly drink his poison even after she knew it was toxic, he was that convincing in his tales.

"It doesn't matter anymore, it's done. Now you have to finish collecting things from your end," Lilly whispered to herself, hiccupping through the statement as she grabbed her phone from her purse.

The phone, the same fucking phone he bought her after the accident with the wallpaper photo of the two of them at the manor house. She almost pitched the damn thing across the room. With trembling fingers, she deleted the photograph and dialed Janie.

"Baby girl." Audrey answered Janie's phone, her voice soft and concerned.

"Audrey, I was wondering if you and Janie might help me?"

"Anything you need. You want me to kill him? I know a guy." Audrey's fake mafia accent was atrocious, but Lilly's head was too clouded to process her attempt at humor.

Lilly sniffled loudly and blew her nose, her head pounding from the crying fit. "My cats are still at Jacob's house. I need to get them; their carriers and supplies are there too."

Audrey sighed into the receiver. "We're headed there right now to fetch them. Can we get you some dinner on the way?"

"I'm not hungry, just my cats please."

Audrey agreed, sending her love and telling Lilly they would arrive within the hour. Lilly gazed around the cottage, a flood of homesickness washing over her for the first time since she landed in England. She missed her friends and her homeland, she missed America. Now she needed to work towards getting back there, putting thousands of miles between her and the love she had been foolish enough to believe.

Her phone rang. It was Jacob.

She declined the call, but it rang again. Realizing he wouldn't leave the situation alone, she had two options—speak to him or block his number. There are only so many times you can be played for a fool before you realize it yourself; and Lilly was done playing that role. She changed the settings on the phone so she would never again have to see a call or text from that man.

Then she opened a bottle of wine, poured a glass and let the tears fall again.

Two hours later, Lilly was sufficiently numbed by the wine and surrounded by a roomful of well-intentioned and exceedingly angry friends. Sabina and Ben arrived first with Chinese takeout and wine. Roger and Sophie surprised her with a bottle of whiskey, and a promise to kick his ass. Finally, Janie and Audrey returned with her cats and belongings.

They sat piled in chairs and sofas, drinking and discussing various ways to inflict pain on Jacob and Victoria.

"I don't understand. I know he adores Lilly. He can't stand to be in the same room with Victoria." Roger paced the floor, whiskey in hand. "This is totally unlike him."

"Is it?" Lilly piped up, her first words in the last half hour. "I'd like to believe there was some underlying reason but honestly, Jacob's dumped me more times than I care to recall for that woman. I'm the idiot who keeps forgiving him. Not this time though."

Janie hugged her friend. "I'm going to get to the bottom of this. Roger is right, there has to be an explanation."

"Have you spoken to him?" Roger questioned, and Janie shook her head.

"I called to berate him right after the press release aired, but he didn't say a word—not one word. I hung up, I was too angry to see straight at that point." Janie headed to the kitchen for a refill.

"Well," Sabina piped in, "I will personally kick his ass from here to kingdom come when I see him again; if I see him again. He never even called her after the press release aired, right Lilly?"

Lilly took another swig of wine. Alcohol truly was the nectar of the

Gods. "I blocked his number; he did try calling earlier, but I didn't answer. What is there to say at this point? The words 'I'm sorry' hold very little meaning anymore, particularly from him."

Everyone murmured their agreement, and the conversations swirled around her until the background noise took on a life of its own and Lilly's mind threatened to explode. She grabbed her wine and went onto the back patio, slumping into a chair and staring at the stars, searching for answers.

Lilly heard the door open and turned to see Roger wearing a sympathetic expression. He sat in the other chair and squeezed her hand in reassurance. "Janie and I are flying to Greece. We need answers."

Lilly scoffed. "Please don't trouble yourselves. People get dumped every day. Some in worse ways than this, and they move on with their lives." Her voice cracked at the end, but she sniffled back the tears.

"Look, I get that you hate him. I'm furious with the man, and he's my best mate. I would like nothing better than to beat him black and blue for what they did, but I've known him for fifteen years, and although he is many things, he is never this cruel."

"I beg to differ." Lilly's voice was flat, deflated; much like her heart.

Roger nodded. "You don't know the way he spoke about you. I've never seen a man so in love in my life. Jacob was never like that before you. Love was an extravagance he couldn't afford with his career. You changed all that."

"Apparently not."

"But you did, you did change him. This 180 he pulled in Greece is completely unlike him. Has he dumped women unceremoniously before? Sure, but at least they got a face to face conversation."

Lilly finished off the rest of her wine. "I am special then. I found out he was marrying his pregnant girlfriend along with the rest of the world." Lilly stood, heading toward the door. "I love you for your concern, but please, don't fly to Greece to speak to him on my account. It's not worth it. He made his choice, and mine." With that she re-entered the house and laid down on her bed, oblivious to her friends gathered in the next room.

Perhaps if she could sleep, she would wake up and her time with Jacob would be nothing more than a terrible dream. Lilly could continue her life as it was before. Her life before meeting the man who awakened every cell in her mind and body, who made her feel beautiful, intelligent and beloved…the man who smashed her heart into a billion pieces on international television.

He had left her with only one choice. Lilly needed to find a place where Jacob couldn't hurt her anymore.

A SERIES OF MOMENTS
Unguarded Moments

M.L. BROOME

About the Author

M.L. Broome is a bohemian spirit, but she carries her New York sarcasm with her wherever she travels.

When she isn't communing with nature, she works in animal rescue, and shares her home with several four-footed friends (they regard her as their personal butler and maid).

She rekindles her spirit by the ocean and can lose herself for hours in the lullaby of the waves and the keening of the sea birds.

"You'll climb as high as you dare believe you are capable. The stars are only as far as we imagine them to be, and time is neither friend nor foe. Magic is everywhere."

ALSO FROM M.L. BROOME

"From the Moment We Met," A Series of Moments Book One
"Beautifully Broken Moments," A Series of Moments Book Three

Visit her on the web at ***www.mlbroome.com***
Become a Series Insider to receive updates about upcoming books from M.L. Broome including excerpts, cover reveals, sweepstakes and more.

www.ingramcontent.com/pod-product-compliance
Lightning Source LLC
Chambersburg PA
CBHW021011180626
46814CB00003B/1239